VIOLEN✝DELIGHTS

JESSICA HAWKINS

I was born a princess among criminals. An untouchable among thieves. Heiress to a life others have killed for, and one I'd do anything to escape. I vowed not to leave without Diego, my first love and best friend, but if his ruthless brother has his way, I won't leave at all.

Cristiano de la Rosa is a man as big and bold as his legend. Once upon a time, he was our cartel's best soldier . . . until he became my family's worst enemy. And a man like Cristiano will bend fate to his will to get what he wants—even if it means tearing me from another's arms.

Because in the de la Rosa family, old grudges run deeper than loyalty, and betrayal is a three-letter word: war. But this feud isn't between enemies—it's between brothers. And I'm the prize.

PROLOGUE

On my bedroom balcony, I danced to the upbeat mariachi music coming from the parade in town. Street fireworks popped and crackled to a soundtrack of trumpets and violins, but I couldn't see much beyond the fortress of olive trees surrounding our compound. They'd been planted after my first birthday party, when my father had been shot at in the backyard while holding me. The *sicario* had hit an inflatable bouncy castle instead, trapping kids inside and inciting a mob of screaming parents. That was what my best friend had told me years later, anyway, and Diego would know, since his parents had ordered the hit.

I waved to one of the guards, who tipped his AK-47 to me. I was supposed to be at the Day of the Dead parade now, honoring the deceased. Diego had promised me two slices of sugar skull cake if I went early and got a good spot, but since Papá was out of town with half his security, my mother didn't want me leaving the premises without her. And as important as every man around here acted, she was the neck that turned the head of the Cruz cartel.

I went back inside to see why she was taking so long, twirling through the maze of hallways so the colorful, floral embroidery of my floor-length skirt ran together. Almost an hour ago, my mother had been nearly ready in an off-the-shoulder, white, green, and yellow dress with a red ruffle along the bottom. She'd pulled her hair back with silk, orange marigolds, and I'd stood on a stepstool to clasp her necklace, a starburst with gilded chains heavy enough to sink a small ship.

"We're missing the parade," I called as I skipped down the corridor, my woven leather sandals clicking on the tile. I rounded the corner into my parents' sunny bedroom, tripped, and landed in a puddle.

A pair of combat boots stopped in front of me. I raised my eyes to meet the cold, distant gaze of a man dressed in all black—Cristiano de la Rosa, a high-level member of my father's security team.

"Get out of here," he ordered. "Now."

Cristiano was all brawn, beast, and towering height with opaque eyes to match his hair. Based on the stories Diego had told me, people feared his older brother, but I had no real reason to. Though their parents had been enemies of ours once, Cristiano and Diego had been on our side for eight of the nine years I'd been alive.

Plus, Mamá had always told me—go to Cristiano in an emergency. He would protect me.

But something was off. He didn't like me being here.

In one of his large, powerful hands, he held an army-green duffel bag. In the other, a solid black gun. Then, there was the blood—on his pants, splattered on his shoes and hands.

And on mine. Warm and sticky between my fingers, soaking through my fancy skirt. Not even its metallic smell could mask my mother's signature perfume.

I looked over my shoulder. I hadn't tripped over my own two feet, but hers. Mamá was lying on her back. Sunlight glinted off the large, gold necklace she'd bought for the parade. Her gleaming black hair was coming loose from its bun after she'd spent all that time pinning flowers in it. She shouldn't be on the ground in her expensive new dress—it was already ripped at the neckline. The vibrant design almost hid what seeped through its fabric, pooling on the terra-cotta tile underneath her body.

Blood.

Goose bumps started at my scalp and spread to my fingers and toes. *No.*

Gasping for air, I scrambled to her side. "Mamá."

Her lids eased open as she struggled to focus. "Natalia," she managed.

My chin wobbled as I fought back tears and grasped her still-warm hand. A bruise formed on her cheek.

"*Mija.*" She fought to keep her eyes open, but they went glassy as her gaze shifted over my head. "Please, Cristiano," she begged, her voice strangled. "Please don't . . ." She shuddered with the effort. "My daughter . . ."

"I'm here," I whispered, but she wasn't talking to me.

I looked up at Cristiano. His jaw sharpened as he clenched it and turned his face away. "*Sueña con los angelitos.*"

Dream with little angels. When I turned back, she'd gone still.

"No," I whispered.

Cristiano tossed the bag and gun onto the cloud-like comforter and reached for me. On instinct, I dove under the bed, knowing he'd be too big to follow—and came face to face with *la Monarca Blanca.* I wrapped my hand around the cold, hard metal of my father's two-tone silver-and-gold-plated 9mm. Time slowed as I ran my thumb over the pearl grip where the name was engraved into the side.

White Monarch.

I choked back a sob. This was the kind of emergency I was supposed to go to Cristiano for, but *he* was the one standing over my mother's dead body as she begged him for mercy.

He grabbed my ankles and slid me out from under the bed. I screamed in a way I never had before, ear-splitting, throat-shredding, as I tried to kick him off.

He clamped a hand over my mouth as his other arm circled my body and pinned my arms to my sides. "Natalia, *hush*," he said in his chillingly deep voice as he lifted me off the ground. "Let me handle this."

I wailed against his hand, thrashing and trying to hit him with the gun, but my arms were trapped. I slammed my heels into his thigh and groin.

But Cristiano was the cartel's most lethal soldier for a reason. It wouldn't have mattered who I was—nobody could match his strength, which had to be that of two men. By the age of twenty-three, he had more kills under his belt than most in the cartel.

He'd been raised as a weapon.

His hands had taken the lives of our family's enemies —but never any of our own.

Until now.

Footsteps sounded in the hall, and Diego rushed into the room with his gun drawn. He stopped short and sucked in a breath as he noticed the body. He shut his lids briefly. I tried to call for my best friend, but Cristiano's hand muffled my words.

Diego's eyes flew open and darted over Cristiano and me. He was dressed for the parade in a loose, white button-down and jeans. He scanned the room, his gaze shrewd as he tucked some loose strands of his brown hair behind his ear. "What the hell is this? What happened?"

"I don't know," Cristiano said. "I got here right before you did."

Liar. I inhaled smoke and gunpowder as I squirmed against Cristiano's hand, trying to convey to Diego what I'd seen.

Diego turned his attention on me, his forehead wrinkling as if he was trying to read my mind. *He did this,* I tried to tell him. *Cristiano shot her.*

After a moment, Diego swallowed. "Put Natalia down."

"Holster the gun, and I will," Cristiano answered.

Diego looked at his pistol as if he hadn't realized he'd been holding it. He was no saint, either—he'd done things I wasn't supposed to hear about at my age, according to Papá—but that didn't make Diego anything like his brother. Diego was a lover, not a fighter. He was only sixteen, and he still had a chance to make something of his life. His eyes drifted from the firearm to my mother, then across the room. His expression eased as realization seemed to dawn on him. He turned back to Cristiano.

"After everything they've done for us?" Diego asked and gestured the gun toward my parents' walk-in closet. "This is how you repay them?"

The safe lay open and empty except for scattered paperwork. The White Monarch had been in there, along with cash and my mother's jewels. I tried to nod at the duffel bag but couldn't move my head.

"Careful what you say, Diego," Cristiano said evenly. "You *know* I didn't do this."

"Then who?" Diego asked. "The house is surrounded by security. Who else could get in here? In the safe?"

"It was already open," Cristiano said in an increasingly frustrated voice. "As I said, I walked in right before you."

Diego shoved his fingers through his hair, then spotted the duffel. "What's that?" Diego would never hurt me, but when he raised his gun at us, my heartbeat quickened. He kept the weapon and his eyes on Cristiano as he moved toward the bed. With his free hand, Diego slid the bag across the comforter and glanced inside. "Cash and jewelry from the safe, but not much."

"I know." Cristiano readjusted his grip around my torso. "I found it discarded by the bed."

"Where's the rest of it?"

Cristiano hesitated. "Someone must've been here—"

"Impossible," Diego said, and he was right. My father took no risks when it came to his family's safety. "There are two ways in—through the guards out front or the guards at the tunnels."

Diego took a two-way radio from his back pocket.

"Diego," Cristiano said, warning clear in his voice. "Don't."

He pressed a button and spoke into the device. "*Doña* Bianca has been shot. By Cristiano. I need security in here now."

Cristiano noticeably stiffened behind me. "*Vete a la chingada*," he cursed. "You're going to tell Costa I did this? I'm your blood, Diego."

"And Bianca was just as much my family." The anguish in Diego's eyes conveyed what my mother meant to him. At her urging, my family had taken him in when he was only eight and Cristiano was fifteen. Tears leaked from my eyes and onto Cristiano's hand as I looked anywhere but at her body.

"She was family to *me*, too," Cristiano said through his teeth. He was so angry, his voice broke, and he forgot to keep my mouth covered. "You can't accuse me of hurting her."

"All you do is hurt people," I screamed. "You're a—"

He slapped his hand over my mouth just as the front door slammed downstairs. "*Fuck*," Cristiano said. "Tell them I didn't do this, Diego, or they'll kill me on the spot."

"Release Natalia," Diego begged. "Please. Try to remember who you were before all of this—you wouldn't have hurt an innocent girl."

Cristiano started left then shifted to go right, as if trapped. Finally, he released my mouth but kept me against him like a shield as he one-handedly wrestled the White Monarch from my grip.

He was going to kill Diego next.

Diego.

The boy who'd not only watched me grow up, but had protected me like an older brother. Who'd never treated me like a little girl despite a seven-year age difference. Who brought me stinky marigolds when I was sad and never complained that we could only ride our horses up to and along the fence Papá had built to keep me in, even though *Diego* could go anywhere he wanted.

Diego's eyes widened as Cristiano got the gun from me. It would devastate Diego to kill his own brother, but for Cristiano to shoot Diego, it would mean nothing. Cristiano took lives all the time.

"You're caught, brother," Diego said. His nostrils flared as his anger finally seemed to override his confusion. "Don't make this worse than it is. Put her down and face them."

Boots pounded up the staircase with a chorus of shouting men. Cristiano carried me toward the door, his back to the wall, eyes on Diego. He switched the gun to his other hand to lock the door.

In that split second, Diego lunged forward.

Cristiano whipped around and pulled the trigger.

I screamed when the shot rang through the air, covering my ears as I hit the ground. Diego crumpled, clutching his bloodied thigh.

Men pounded at the bullet-resistant door Papá had specially installed. Fists hammered the wood, followed by what sounded like the butts of their rifles.

Cristiano picked up Diego's gun, stuck it in his waistband, and leveled the White Monarch on his brother's writhing body. "You left me no choice. Loyalty is king around here, but look how quickly it's broken."

"Don't shoot—I know a way out," I exclaimed through my sobs. Cristiano towered over me, looking like the Grim Reaper himself. "I can help you escape," I said.

Cristiano stilled. "It's not possible."

"I know a secret way." My voice shook. I wasn't helping my mother's killer, I told myself, but protecting Diego and me.

"Natalia, no," Diego said, huffing as he made an effort to sit up. "He—he has to pay for this."

"Where is it?" Cristiano asked.

Diego was getting unnaturally pale as if he might pass out any second. I got to my feet and started to go to him, but Cristiano grabbed my arm and yanked me back against his hip. "They'll get in before he dies. Show me the way out."

Diego groaned and closed his eyes, and I inhaled a quick, stuttering breath to keep my panic at bay. "The c-closet," I managed.

Cristiano marched me back across the room and into my old nursery. Once I'd outgrown the space, my mother had converted it into a sizeable walk-in closet that held much more than just clothing. There were walls of shoes, purses, drawers, and mirrors, as well as an island in the center for her costume jewelry and Papá's ties.

Cristiano took a chair from my mother's vanity dresser, wedged it under the closet's door handle, and turned to look at me. "Now what?"

I couldn't think. There was a bullet in my mother's stomach and one in my best friend's leg. My bloodied skirt stuck to my knees. I was going to be sick. "The . . . the dresses."

Cristiano walked to me. He put the chilled metal barrel of the gun under my chin and tilted back my head to get me to look him in the eye. "If they get in here before I get out, I can't promise we'll both make it out alive. Show me the escape, or tell your father I didn't do this. Those are your options."

I tried to swallow, but I couldn't even breathe. I'd never been so sure I would die if I made one wrong move. I shook my head hard. "I won't lie for you."

"Look what loyalty got me, Natalia." He raised the gun higher and I glanced down the barrel. The silver nearly sparkled under the closet's lamp. "Whether I did or didn't do this, I'm dead. If they don't get me here, they'll hunt me down. That isn't loyalty, and there is no justice."

"*Loyalty*?" I was shaking now, but there was no quiver in Cristiano's voice, no tremble in his hand. "You killed my mother. Why? She cared about you—she treated you like a *son*."

His Adam's apple bobbed as we stared at each other. "Show me the way out," he commanded.

"I'll help you, but only to save Diego," I said. "Promise you'll never come back here."

"I can't." His expression hardened as his voice dropped. "Consider this a lesson—never trade your life for someone else's."

I backed away slowly, turned, and went to the safe. Amongst the papers, I found the small metal box I needed. I popped it open, took out a key, and stilled with a *bang* from the next room. If security was breaking down the door, then Diego must not have been able to let them in. I quickly prayed he was still alive.

I hurried to the closet that held my mother's party dresses. They were heavy enough that I had to use both hands to push them apart so I could crawl through them. "In here," I said.

Against the closet's back wall, I felt around for a keyhole. It was dark, but my father had walked me through this plenty of times. There were tunnels under the house all the security knew about, including Cristiano, but *this* secret passageway was only for my parents and me. When I'd pointed out to Papá that the men who'd built it must've known about it, he'd exchanged a grim look with my mother and changed the subject.

I put the key into the hole, but it was already unlocked. I slid the wall open to reveal a dark, dank room. "There."

If Cristiano was surprised, he didn't show it. "There what?"

I pointed to a trapdoor inside. "Go down that hole. There are no lights; you'll have to feel your way."

He stared into the dark. "How do I know this isn't a trap?"

"It's your only choice."

He got closer, his presence looming tall. "Open it for me."

It wasn't a request. Fortunately, my father had ensured that I knew the escape drill well, so entering the small space wasn't foreign to me.

I squatted down to unlatch the trapdoor that led to the one passageway nobody else knew about. Cristiano closed and bolted the door behind himself, extinguishing everything but a sliver of the closet's warm light.

I hoisted open the hatch and it fell with a hard *thud* against the ground. I concentrated on keeping my voice steady. "This also connects to the tunnels the mules use," I explained. "But if you stay to the left, that's a way nobody else knows about. It will take you south."

"To where?"

I glanced back at him. "That's all my parents told me."

The dark turned him into a shadow as he stalked toward me. "I'll have to take you with me."

"What?"

"We're going down there together."

I backed away, but since he blocked the door, there wasn't anywhere to go. "Why?"

He tucked the White Monarch into his waistband with his other gun, grabbed my arm, and yanked me toward the entrance of the tunnel. I flew forward, no match for his strength. My heart leapt into my throat as everything happened in a flash. He couldn't take me. He wouldn't. Nobody dared cross my father—but Cristiano already had, and now, he had nothing left to lose. If he got me into that tunnel, I'd never return. Never see Diego again. My father. I wouldn't attend my mother's funeral.

"I *helped* you," I said as more sobs bubbled up into my throat. I looked down the ladder. Since we were on the second floor, one push would send me flying some five meters down into the pitch dark. "Why are you doing this?"

"To show you that you can't trust anyone. Not me, not Diego, maybe not even your parents. Just because you help someone doesn't mean they won't betray you." He turned toward the ladder. "And because I need a head start. Get on my back."

Once he released me, I switched into high gear. Perhaps he was known for his ruthlessness, but I'd spent my short life sneaking into places I shouldn't, surprising even the stealthiest of my father's guards. I grasped the White Monarch from his pants and stumbled back, leveling the pistol on him with both hands.

With the light at my back, I saw a hint of amusement flash in his eyes. "You don't know true fear, little girl. It puts you in danger."

I *did* know fear. I was staring at my mother's murderer. I couldn't swallow. Couldn't hear over the deafening pounding of my heart.

Wherever Cristiano surfaced, my father would kill him.

Or I could save Papá the trouble and do it myself.

For the first time since I'd tripped over my mother's dying body, calmness fell over me. Nobody had been able to stop Cristiano—not my mother or father, not Diego, and not security. I could, though. He deserved to die for his sins.

I urged myself to act, but something Cristiano had said stopped me. *There is no justice.* Was I sure, down to my very core, that he had done this? What if he hadn't? I didn't know him nearly as well as I did Diego. Cristiano was fourteen years older than me—a man. Despite his reputation as a killer, he had always treated me with kindness.

And my mother too.

But as he'd said—you couldn't trust anyone in this world. Not even your own blood.

"Do it," he invited.

Based on what I'd seen, I was pretty sure in order to shoot, I first had to slide the top of the gun toward me. But the firearm itself was so heavy, I needed both hands to keep it steady. I glanced at the top part to determine the best way to do this.

"Never hesitate, Natalia." Cristiano snatched the pistol from me and pressed the muzzle to my forehead. "See? *Bang.* You're dead."

My breath caught in my throat. *I was dead.* Defenseless. Shivering like the little girl I was.

"And *never* draw a weapon you can't operate. When you aim, kill." He flicked a switch on the side, stuck the gun back in his pants, and grabbed me.

"Stop," I cried and pushed against him as he hugged me to his chest with his arm.

"Hold on." One-handedly, he quickly descended the ladder.

Instinctually, I wrapped my arms around his neck. He was the furthest thing from a safe place, but in that moment, I was no longer concerned with being brave. I was trapped. I gave into my fear, submitting to the warmth of his body, sobbing into his neck as he descended into the dark.

"Is there another key to the secret door?" he asked.

I sniffled. "My father keeps it on him."

"He's probably already on his way," Cristiano said, almost consolingly. "They'll find you eventually, Natalia. This is the only way I'll be able to put enough distance between them and me."

It was cold and black at the bottom. I shivered uncontrollably as he reached the final rung of the ladder and jumped the rest of the way. *Never go down if you don't have to*, Father had said. *You won't be able to reach the ladder to get back up.*

This was it. I was at Cristiano's mercy now.

On solid ground, he took a few slow steps, feeling for a wall. When he found one, he squatted. "Sit here," he said. "Don't move until they come for you."

I didn't let go of his neck. The scent of his sweat and

my tears mixed with the soil around us. I'd never been worried about the dark before, but I couldn't even see my own hand.

"What if nobody comes?" I asked.

"They will. And by that time, I'll be long gone." He pulled at my arms. "You're brave. Let go."

I released him. The next thing I heard was his retreating footsteps. I sat against the wall, wrapped my arms around my knees, and held my breath. Tears flooded my eyes, overflowing onto my cheeks.

I'd always known the love and protection of my parents and their titles. Being the daughter of one of the most powerful drug lords in Mexico meant I'd been in danger since the day I was born—and also sheltered from everything.

No longer.

As the threat of Cristiano receded, I was left alone in the dark with the realization that my mother had kissed my cheek and tucked me in for the last time. Her lyrical voice would never again lull me to sleep and end each night with, "*Te quiero mucho, mariposita.*" There would be no more of her famous homemade "Talia taffy" for the rest of my birthdays, no more riding horses into town to shop for fabric or spices.

That morning, impatient to go, I'd hugged her waist and asked her to hurry up as she'd done her makeup. Now, I wished only to stay with her a little longer. I wished for more time.

But the parade was over.

Death's day had come.

1

NATALIA

I ducked out of the helicopter and into dry desert air as the blades whipped wind through my hair. My father's head of security offered a hand and helped me down. *"Bienvenida a casa, señorita,"* Barto called over the whir of the rotors.

Welcome home.

The pilot carried my bags to a black Suburban waiting on the tarmac. Somehow, the Mexican heat felt stronger than in California, the sun intense and unforgiving. I slipped my sunglasses into place and followed Barto to the car.

"How's it feel to be back?" he asked.

No words could properly convey it. Leaving home for a boarding school in the United States had been my choice, but Father would've shipped me off even if it wasn't. I both dreaded and anticipated coming here. California was safe, clean, easy. Nothing like this place, where danger haunted the streets. It was the thought of seeing Diego that lifted any sense of dread that came with getting into a car headed for home.

Barto glanced at me in the rearview mirror. "If I can say so, you look more and more like *señora* Cruz each time I see you."

I had my mother's light eyes, and her small, sharp nose, but our physical similarities stopped there. "I'm more like my father," I said.

"But you have her grace."

I swallowed. *Regal* was how my father often described her.

"And that determined look she often wore," Barto added.

I didn't doubt that. I wasn't only home to spend time with my dad, catch up with friends, and celebrate Easter. I was here for Diego—my best friend and my love. The boy who knew all my secrets because he'd been there for many of them, if not physically, then a phone call away. But with the distance between us, we'd done enough talking for a lifetime. I couldn't wait to just be close to him for the first time in a year.

Next summer, I'd be graduating, and I was dead set on having Diego in Santa Clara with me by then—permanently. But since my dad wanted the opposite, it would take some convincing.

Barto steered us up the long, winding drive lined with imported banana leaf trees. Men with AR-15s stood along the side of the dirt road, waving us on, smiling at me through the blacked-out windows.

Barto handled my luggage and sent me straight upstairs to see my father. At the threshold to Papá's study at the south end of the mansion, I stopped when I heard his raised voice. "Do you have any *idea* the magnitude of what you've committed us to?"

"We can handle it." When Diego spoke, a kaleidoscope of butterflies erupted in my stomach. "We've been refining our operation for over a decade, and it's as close to perfect as it gets."

"'Close to perfect' is not perfect," came my father's grave response.

"Nevertheless, we're ready. With this partnership, we take things to the next level."

I should've made my presence known. I'd found out at a young age that sneaking around was the only way to get information. Back then, it'd been exciting. Now, information was both powerful and burdensome. People who knew too much were targets. Witnesses. Leverage. The more you knew, the harder it was to escape this life.

And the more dangerous you became.

But my curiosity continued to burn the brightest flame, no matter how I tried to extinguish it. I resisted the old habit of removing my shoes to mute my steps, but I still peeked into the light-filled room, finally laying my eyes on Diego. He was as beautiful as ever. His normally silken brown hair had been kissed by the sun and was long enough to tuck behind his ears. He'd been working outdoors more, and it showed, not just in his skin tone and hair color, but in his broad, muscular shoulders. He stood straight and tall to address my father. I wanted to run and throw my arms around his neck, but Papá wouldn't stand for it.

Patience, Diego had told me a million times before.

It had never been my strong suit.

"This is not a *partnership*." Deep lines slatted across Papá's tanned face. Each time I saw him, he appeared older, but his voice boomed, and his clear, molten brown eyes painted him as more youthful than his fifty years. He was as astute as ever, and his overbearing height defied how the bags under his eyes sometimes made him seem tired. "The Maldonado cartel is not a partner but a master," he said. "With this deal, they'll own us."

I considered entering the room and cutting off the conversation, but the name stopped me short. Even *I* knew —and I made it my business not to know much anymore— doing business with the Maldonados was dangerous.

"Times have changed, Costa," Diego said. "Eleven years ago, you reevaluated your business model, trading risk for security and violence for a quiet life—not that such a thing exists in this world. It's time to adapt again."

With my mother's death, much had changed, and not just in the obvious ways. Father had scaled back his business as newer, more bloodthirsty cartels like the Maldonados had come up the ranks.

"My father would roll in his grave to know we're not as feared as we once were," my dad said, glancing out the window of his second-floor office.

Diego put a hand on his shoulder. "We're still here, and we're just as powerful, but in different ways."

Diego spoke earnestly and with his hands. It was hard *not* to see his passion, intelligence, and charm, but that still wasn't enough to convince Papá that Diego was the man for me. Nobody was good enough in my father's eyes— especially not someone who belonged in this world. My father cared about Diego in his own way; he'd practically raised him. But unless I could convince him otherwise, Diego would always be a soldier, a right-hand man, a cartel member . . . and a threat to my safety.

"Many leaders of the old order have either been captured, killed, or forced out," Diego continued. "Who of your former enemies remains? Not many. I'm going to ensure the Cruz cartel—and the de la Rosas—don't fall to the same fate. We do that by moving forward with the times."

"The de la Rosas don't exist," Father said, warning in his voice as he regarded Diego with heavy eyebrows. "You're a Cruz. And while I know our success is as important to you as it is to me, there's risk in wanting more. There's much to be said for stability."

"With new technology hitting the market each day, there's more risk in staying still. We're number one in shipping and logistics now, but that can always change."

I leaned on the doorjamb, worried Diego was into something he shouldn't be. If I asked either of them why they'd taken a meeting with the Maldonados in the first place, I'd get the same answer I always did.

Don't worry. Todo bien. *Everything's fine.*

My father rubbed his forehead as he frowned. "And making a risky deal is moving forward?"

"We'll deliver," Diego said, crossing his arms with a shrug. "Their requirements are no different than any of our other arrangements. They have a valuable shipment to get across the border. As the premier transportation option in México, we can make that happen. Simple."

"The difference is who we're dealing with. How much product are we moving?"

"More than we're used to," Diego admitted. "But I'm not concerned. As other cartels distract themselves battling each other, we've solidified a nearly flawless, strategic network. I've assured them an eighty-seven percent success rate."

"Eighty-seven, eh?" Papá asked, slipping on his glasses to bend over and read his computer screen.

"Lower than our stellar average," Diego said, pulling back his shoulders. "We've delivered better results countless times, and in less than the twenty-one days they've given us."

"And after that?"

"We make a more permanent arrangement," Diego said. "With the rate they're growing, their business could take us to the next level."

"I've been at that level," Dad said. "It's dangerous up there."

"But those who were once your competitors are now your customers. You've neutralized." Diego stuck his hands in his pockets and glanced out one of the study's wide windows. "We'll use the income the Maldonado deal generates to expand."

Papá grunted. "You didn't say how much we have to move."

"Two-hundred million in product in three weeks."

My father straightened up. "That's almost four times what we normally do."

"The amount doesn't matter as much as—"

Papá held up a hand for Diego to stop when he saw me leaning in the doorway. "*Mija*," he called, removing his glasses and opening his arms. "*Ven aquí.*"

He shut his laptop as I went to him, then surrounded me in a strong, protective embrace.

Over his shoulder, I met Diego's gaze. His face had been pinched, but it eased as his eyes cleared to emerald green. Neither video chatting nor photos did the color of them justice. "Welcome home," he mouthed.

Home. It had been once, but I found no comfort in the word now. Diego schooled his expression for my dad, but I knew him well enough to read his happiness to see me.

"What's wrong?" I asked, reluctantly tearing my eyes from Diego to look up at Papá. "You were arguing."

"Not at all. Don't worry." He kissed the top of my head, then turned to Diego. "Leave us."

Diego didn't flinch, though I knew the dismissal hurt. He yearned for my dad's respect, but I could see age and experience had not fully earned him it. *Yet.* I didn't doubt my father would one day see what I did, but I also knew it pained Diego that the approval he'd so desperately sought since his own father's death continued to elude him.

I hoped during this trip I'd be able to open my dad's eyes to who Diego really was—a sensitive, creative man who'd been trapped by circumstance. My father wanted me out of this life, and I wanted that too, but to Papá, Diego *was* this life. I had to show him the potential Diego had outside of it.

With a short bow and a brief, promising wink in my direction, Diego exited the room.

My father took my shoulders and held me at arm's length. "Let me look at you. *Qué bella.* Turn for me."

"Papá." I blushed. "Please."

"I don't get to see you often enough and want to commit every visit to memory."

"We were together at Christmas."

"But that was in California, not here, where I watched you grow up. Indulge your old man."

Rolling my eyes playfully, I turned in a circle. "All my limbs intact as previously reported," I said. "Fingers and toes too."

"Your hair has grown. Do they not have salons in Santa Clara?"

I smiled. "Of course, but long hair is always in style."

"You're taller too, no? You get that from me."

I had taken after my father's side of the family and was the tallest of my girlfriends at five-foot-seven. He was a sturdy six-foot-two, my grandpa even taller, which had suited his far more menacing temperament.

Father liked to tell the story of an eighteen-year-old girl named Bianca who'd flown down from northern Mexico "like a migrating butterfly." She'd come for a cousin's *quinceañera* and stayed for love, caught in my father's net by the time dessert was served.

As romantic as it was, sometimes I wondered why she'd been stupid enough to trade a safe and happy life as a farmer's daughter for this. It'd been foolish and risky, and it had gotten her killed. I wouldn't share her fate, and neither would Diego.

I had to find a way to free him from the chains of the cartel so he could come to the States and start a life with me. I would convince my dad to let us go and live in peace rather than war, looking over the Pacific instead of over our shoulders.

Diego had been in my father's grip too long, and I was the only one who could ask a favor like this.

Father sat back behind his desk. "Tonight, we celebrate. What're your plans while home?"

"I thought maybe you, me, and Diego could have dinner tonight," I said.

He picked up his folded glasses and tapped them against his temple. "I've already arranged a feast in your honor."

"Tomorrow then, or sometime this week."

"What for? I'd rather just the two of us," he said. "Anyway, my annual party is Thursday night as you know. I'll have my hands full with that, and so will Diego." He frowned. "Why don't you visit the stables? It's been so long since you've ridden."

Eleven years to be exact. I would go see the horses, but I hadn't gotten on one since my mother's death. It'd been our thing, an activity we'd done together almost every day. I nodded so as not to start off my visit with an argument. "Maybe, but it's hotter than Hades here. I'll go to the beach, no doubt."

"No doubt." He patted my hip. "How was the trip?"

"Barto took great care as always. No attempted murders."

"A joke," he said. "I'm glad you see the humor. I don't."

It was important to remember to laugh when traveling with three guards and in bulletproof transportation.

"I need to get back to work," he said, opening his laptop. "Dress well for dinner."

I stooped to kiss his cheek. Out of habit, I glanced at the computer screen for clues as to what he and Diego had been discussing, but I forced my eyes away. I didn't want trouble. I just wanted to get Diego and myself the hell out of there before someone else I cared about got killed.

On my way out, Papá called me back. "One more thing. Don't let me catch you trying to sneak into the ballroom again this year. It's no place for a young girl."

"I know many girls who've been to your parties."

"None of which is my only daughter."

My mom had hosted a legendary annual affair for clients and friends of the Cruz cartel in a ballroom on the property. I'd never made it into a party and had been forced to settle for hearing the music from my bedroom across the lawn, followed by weeks of gossip and folklore. Papá had tried his best to keep me isolated from this world since birth, but that'd bred curiosity.

Now that I knew better, I appreciated his intent. But it hadn't saved me from witnessing my mother's murder.

"I'm not a young girl anymore," I said with a shrug. "I'm twenty."

I left the room and tried not to think about the party. I'd once harbored a morbid curiosity about the life my parents led—until I'd learned firsthand the senseless violence, corruption, and evil that came with it. Since then, I'd been trying to tame the little girl in me who'd been fearless enough to draw a weapon on a man three times her size. The girl who'd equated danger with fun. The one who'd listened to the devil whispering in my ear that there was no escaping this life, not now, not ever.

I had run away from all this, but the devil still tempted that stupid little girl. She knew better than most what could come of that.

After all, she'd ended up locked in a pitch-dark hole for hours, senseless and defenseless, covered in her own mother's blood.

2

NATALIA

In the corridor on my way to the library, a figure sprang from the shadows and seized me from behind. I gasped, but the moment I caught Diego's familiar scent, I relaxed in his arms.

"*Buenas, princesa,*" he murmured in my ear, stealing me toward the library.

As children, Diego and I had scoured almost every inch of the house with the exception of my parents' bedroom. We knew it better than any member of the security team, likely better than my father himself, as he couldn't fit in some of the spaces Diego and I had been known for folding ourselves into back then.

The library was one of the only surveillance-free spots. Papá had built it for my mother's ever-curious mind, but hardly anyone went in it anymore. My dad claimed he wasn't intelligent like my mother and had no use for books, but it was simply too painful for him to spend time in here.

My father was smart in other ways.

Diego left the door open behind us. Since we'd spent so much time together growing up, it wouldn't be unusual for a guard or even my dad to find us alone together. But with the door closed? That would raise red flags.

He spun me around and pressed his lips to mine for a hasty kiss. "Are you really here?"

"I am." I put my hands to the chiseled, lean jaw and high cheekbones of a face worthy of being immortalized on a statue. "Every time I see you, you're less the boy I knew and more the man I love."

He took my wrists and kissed the inside of one palm. "I was a man back then, Tali. I had to be."

"I know." His bravery in a world of danger and a life of loss continued to awe me. "Are you happy to see me?"

"You have no idea." He went to the long window over-looking the grounds, then turned and perched on the sill. His eyes lingered on me. "Every time I see you, you're less the girl I knew and more an alluring creature with wiles that could possess the devil."

"You'd call me a creature?" I asked, smiling as I formed claws with my hands and stalked toward him in my leopard-print flats.

He held up his hands to form a square, looking at me through it. "When you're back at school, I'll remember you this way—a lioness."

"You won't have to remember," I said. "You'll be able to look up and see me with your own eyes."

"I want that more than you know." When I neared, he put his hands on my hips and drew me to him. "I just don't want you to get your hopes up."

"He'll understand once I tell him how much you mean to me. How much you've *always* meant to me," I said, smoothing away dark, golden strands that fell right back over his forehead. "My father adores you."

"Adores?" He arched an eyebrow. "He adores two

things in this world—you, and the memory of your mother. The rest of us hope for his respect and his mercy."

I wrinkled my nose. "You're exaggerating. These days, he's more forgiving than most. At least, more than my grandpa ever was. Papá is a fair man."

"Fairest in all the land," Diego agreed. "But nothing about the land is fair. Except for his daughter. She's both her mother and her father, darkly beautiful with cunning eyes."

My beloved was a poet—a side he only showed to me. I wanted to melt into him, but I could sense the tension in his forearms, the restraint in his touch. Diego followed my father's example, though, and rarely volunteered when something was wrong. I would've happily ignored any problems, except that I didn't want my time with Diego encumbered by the stresses of business. "What was your argument about?" I asked.

"Nothing, nothing, *está bien*." He slid a hand under the hem of my top. I arched into the warmth of his skin on mine while acutely aware of the open door behind me. His green eyes danced as he looked up at me. "Tali?"

"Diego."

"We have to talk about our future."

I grinned. "That's why I'm here."

"I want nothing more than to be with you." He sighed. "This town is a jail cell. A death sentence, even. I'm only alive today. Tomorrow is never guaranteed."

When he talked like that, it hit too close to the truth. So many nights, I'd stared up at the ceiling of my dorm room waiting to hear from Diego, both craving and fearing news. Keeping in touch with someone whose life depended on staying under the radar hadn't been easy. "It won't be for much longer," I said. "You'll see."

"But how can I leave?" He inched his fingertips a little higher. "I have responsibilities here."

I bit my bottom lip as he approached the underwire of my bra. "You'll get out of them."

"This isn't a job I can just quit. Your father took me in when he didn't have to." He removed his hand from my top to rest it on the outside of my thigh. "Costa brought me into this business and gave me a chance."

I didn't want him to stop touching me, but even though our self-control continued to hold, it was thin. "That doesn't mean you're indebted to him forever."

"I'll never be able to leave without your father's blessing, and he won't give me that."

"He brought you and your brother in at my mother's urging, out of a sense of duty for what he did to your parents." I slipped my hand in his and squeezed. "And yes, he could've left you behind, or worse, killed both of you. But he's also the reason you're an orphan in the first place."

Diego's eyebrows knitted. "I've never heard you put it like that. Are you suggesting I hold that against him?"

"No," I said. "He won't feel any guilt. He did what he had to. If he hadn't gone after your parents, they would've come for him. And I don't think the de la Rosas would've taken *me* in if the situation had been reversed."

"They wouldn't have. I miss my mom and dad, but you're right—they weren't so merciful." He glanced away. "Perhaps it would've ended up worse for you than death."

What was worse for a young girl than death, I didn't have to ask. Though our families had been rivals, they'd still abided by a code. Back then, the de la Rosas had trafficked weapons, and the Cruzes had dealt in narcotics. My father and grandfather had imposed a strict pact that neither family would enter into the vile space of human trafficking. And when Papá had discovered Diego's parents had broken that pact, the de la Rosas had needed to be dealt with.

But it was plotting against my father that'd ultimately gotten them killed.

I sighed. "Maybe we should just smuggle you across the border like a brick of cocaine." I leaned in conspiratorially. "After all, that's what the Cruz cartel is known for, right? Our unusually high success rate at getting illegal goods into North America?"

The corner of Diego's mouth quirked. "Where'd you hear that?"

"It's true, isn't it? My father's instinct is unrivaled, but you're the brains behind this business."

"I'm hardly that," he said, but deep dimples appeared with his smile. Once I'd been old enough to notice how sexy they were, they'd proven irresistible. "I just want him to see me as . . ."

"As?"

"More than the others." He kissed the back of my hand. "Someone worthy of being part of his family."

"You *are* worthy. I know that, and so does he."

"But I can't blame him for doubting me after the way my parents conspired against him."

I refrained from pointing out what he already knew. Yes, Papá *had* agreed to take in both boys, but on one condition—that they wouldn't followed in their father's footsteps. In order to ensure the boys never made a move against Costa Cruz, my dad had made them watch as he'd put bullets in their parents—a warning.

"My father knows you'd never go against him," I said. "Their murder ended a decades-long feud between our families—"

"Until Cristiano," Diego said.

I shivered, a natural response to hearing the devil called by his name.

Mamá's hospitality had come with a price—her life. But it had also brought Diego into mine.

He'd understood that my father and *abuelo* had had no choice but to stop his parents.

Cristiano, on the other hand, hadn't.

Eleven years later, he should've been a distant memory. I tried not to think of his tight grip on my arm, his gun tipping up my chin, or the shadowed, divine face of a godless man. But how could I not look over my shoulder? Cristiano de la Rosa still inspired dread, even from the grave. At least, I hoped that's where he was. Despite rumors that he'd been running an underground drug empire in Russia, or that he owned a freighting company in Bolivia, or had become an arms trafficker between America and the Philippines—I'd convinced myself he was six feet under. I didn't sleep well most nights, but assuming he was dead helped a little.

"My father knows you aren't your father, and he *definitely* doesn't think you're anything like your brother," I said.

Diego stuck his hands in the back pockets of my jeans and pulled me closer. We were tempting fate by being affectionate out in the open, but it excited me that Diego couldn't resist touching me. "Your parents treated Cristiano like a son, and he *still* turned on them," Diego said. "No matter how I prove myself, your father keeps me at arm's length—even before the betrayal, I was just another worker to him. I sometimes question whether Costa would've taken me in without my brother."

Even though it hurt to hear that, I understood why Diego felt that way. Both boys had been tossed into the Cruz cartel army right away. Cristiano had taken to it like a child to sweets, while sensitive, creative Diego had struggled to adapt.

"You've shown him almost twenty years of loyalty," I said. "You're now one of the cartel's most trusted advisors. You've helped make this business what it is—one with an average success rate above eighty-seven percent."

Diego's mouth fell open as he scoff-laughed. "How long were you listening at the door?" He narrowed his eyes, playfully scolding me. "You little snoop."

"I just didn't want to interrupt," I said. "But is eighty-seven percent good?"

"The best. Our competitors don't even touch us. Cartels come to us when they need the absolute best chance of getting their shipment over the border." He winked. "That's how we can charge so much."

"See?" I said. "You could never be just another worker. Papá knows that."

"Let's get back to the topic of our future." He squeezed my ass cheeks. "In the States, will we be royalty like we are now?"

Not if I could help it. To be royalty was to put a target on our backs. We already had that here; I wanted to escape it. There was much more to life than wealth and status. "How does a bungalow near the Pacific Ocean sound?" I asked. "Fresh fish, fruits, and vegetables every day. No guns in sight. And California has great schools."

"Schools?"

"For the children."

He chuckled. "We have children, do we? Do they have names?"

"I'm serious," I said. "Once I graduate and start my career, we'll marry in a small, cozy ceremony. Although, the churches there are big and tacky, not like the ones here." Regretfully. Our little Roman Catholic church in the town center was beautifully maintained thanks to my family. Father lavished millions every year on our small *pueblo* nestled between arid desert lowlands and lush mountainside on the west side of the country—a business investment more than charity, as it secured him the loyalty of the townspeople and local law enforcement.

"But how will I show off such a beautiful princess if we have a cozy ceremony?" he teased.

"Oh, my whole family will be there. Show off what you like, but I don't care about being fancy—I just want you and the people I love around." Diego made good money here, and had been saving instead of blowing it like a lot of his friends, but it wouldn't last forever where we were going. California was expensive, and Diego would struggle to find work without experience. I wanted to make sure he knew I didn't need money to be happy. I cupped his cheek, impatient to feel his lips on mine again. "We can throw a party that would blow all other weddings away if that's what you want, but all I need is you."

He leaned into my palm. "If I could, I'd make you mine tomorrow."

Excitement fluttered in my tummy. I'd pictured our nuptials many times. Whether the affair was big or small, blessed by my father or forbidden, the core of it remained the same. Diego was my soul mate. He'd seen me through the dark months after my mother's death, checking on me whenever he could get away from the ranch, making sure I'd slept and eaten and gotten fresh air when I'd only wanted to give up. It wasn't hard to conjure the image of promising to care for *him* too in sickness and in health.

But would my father be there to walk me down the aisle?

Papá was a fair and decent man, but he'd been ruthless

once. He didn't value anyone's innocence but mine. He'd tried to awaken more in Diego, to turn him into the killer his brother was, but Diego remained pure. A peaceful soul trapped in a fight for survival. He wasn't made for this world, but there was no way out—except, maybe, through me.

Diego frowned. "I should go check on things at home before anyone notices my absence."

I sighed, but sulking wouldn't change anything. "When will I see you next?"

"I wish I knew. I have to show my face at the costume party and do some networking. Then this weekend, I'm trapped at the house to oversee some things."

"I've still never seen your place," I hinted. Diego had told me enough about it over the phone that I could picture it clearly. "What if I come over?"

Diego rose from the windowsill and lifted my chin with his knuckle. "You know I'd love that if it wasn't too dangerous. It's a hub. Men come and go from my house all day. And if I know your dad, he'll have security detail on you the next two weeks. They'd never let you come over, and you can't be there without them."

"But *you'll* be there." Everyone loved to remind me how dangerous this life was as if I didn't know. And though staying in the dark felt safer, I also knew ignorance could expose me to danger.

"I'll be preoccupied, though," he said.

"Then what about the party?" I asked. "I promised my dad I wouldn't show up, but if you think about it, isn't it really the *safest* place to be? With all the important people in attendance, there'll be a guard every meter."

"He's not keeping you from the ballroom for safety reasons, Natalia Lourdes." Diego only used my full name when he was serious. "His parties are a cesspool."

"They're attended by the highest government officials in the country."

"My point exactly. Those people are deadlier, greedier, and more corrupt than anyone. They've ruined countless lives and families without ever dirtying their hands." He thumbed my bottom lip. "Promise me you'll stay home. I have no doubt you've already mapped a route inside."

"I don't care about the party. I have no interest in what goes on there." That wasn't entirely true, but the only thing stronger than my curiosity was my desire to disassociate myself from this life. Then again, what trumped *all* of that —was Diego. "I don't have much time here," I said. "I only want to spend it with you."

"I want that too, *princesa*, but not if it puts you at risk." He glanced over my head, then pecked the bridge of my nose. "I'll see if I can steal away for a kiss after the party, all right?"

"You expect me to sit home and wait on the small chance you'll be able to meet me?"

"No, my angel straight from heaven. My Aphrodite incarnate. I don't expect it, but I hope for it." He took me in his arms and brushed his lips over my cheek, then the corner of my mouth. "Promise me you'll stay home," he said in my ear, "and in exchange, I'll tell you a secret."

I was getting exactly what I wanted—a clear divide between myself and this life. But I wasn't getting what I needed—Diego. Maybe the party was wild, but it would also be safe. Security would be tight. If I found the right costume, nobody would even recognize me. "I'll stay home," I said. It wasn't exactly a lie—the ballroom was on our property. "What's the secret?"

"I wrote you something."

"A poem?" I melted against his hard chest. "Let's hear it."

"Not so much a poem as a love letter. A tribute to my princess." He half-smiled. "It's in my pocket, but it's not ready."

I reached for it. "Give it to me."

He laughed, catching my wrists and pulling me close. "If you put your hands in there, I can't promise I'll let them out."

I blushed, at a loss for a response. We'd been best friends a long time, and we were still a little new at the intimate parts. I laced our hands together, admiring his long fingers and the tattoo on the inside of one—a sketch of roses he'd done with his family name and the date of his parents' death.

And inked on his inner ring finger, small enough so nobody like my father would notice, were our initials in black ink. I brushed my lips over his knuckles.

"God, I've dreamed of your mouth on me since your last visit." His voice dropped. "Tell me you're still my girl, Talia."

I knew what he was asking, and although I'd assured him many times that I'd kept my virginity intact at school, there was always an edge to his voice when he asked. I put my cheek to his. It was easier to talk about sex without looking at him. "I'm still your girl."

"Good." The word came out on a growl. "I worry about those fraternity sharks circling someone as sweet as you."

"Sharks don't eat sweets," I said with a smile. "The sharks are *here*—out for blood. Americans are boys compared to you. I've no interest in them." I put my arms around him and nuzzled his neck. "I only think of you."

He sighed. "How have we lasted this long?"

Even though most of my friends, both here and in the States, had lost their virginity, it was easy to save myself knowing I'd only ever give myself to one man—my best friend. As scary as my father's grief had been after Mamá's death, I still wanted what they'd had—an all-consuming devotion to each other, even now. As far as I knew, Papá had never so much as been on a date with another woman in the last decade. "Because it's important to me," I said. "I want to commit myself to you in every way once it's time."

He kissed my forehead. "It's important to me too."

I arched a brow at him. "Only because you're afraid my father will find out we didn't wait."

He laughed lightly. "It's true—I value my life. Luckily, even if we were tempted, the guards keep you in and me out." He ran his fingers through the ends of my hair. "Our first time will be special, *mi sol.*"

I smiled quizzically. He hadn't called me that before. "Your sun?"

"You're always alight. That, and you hate the night."

"Mmm. It rhymes. You *are* a poet."

Diego knew me well, but then, he'd heard firsthand accounts of my night terrors until I'd left for boarding school. The shadows that tried to catch me, the lingering memories of a nine-year-old watching her mother take her last breath . . . and then there was his brother.

"Promise you'll never come back here," I said.

"I can't."

It was hard to believe Cristiano had once been the hero of my nightmares. Like the time, as a girl, I'd woken up screaming, and my mother had come running. She'd smoothed sweat-sticky hair off my face and asked me what I'd dreamed about.

"Monsters," I'd told her.

I hadn't noticed Cristiano, who'd been patrolling the property, standing in the dark doorway, until my mother had turned to him. "Are there monsters here, Cristiano?" she'd asked.

"Yes," he'd said gravely. "But they'll never hurt Natalia."

My little heart had raced as fresh tears had filled my eyes. "How do you know?" I'd asked him.

"Because I'm here to protect you," he'd answered. "And I'm scarier than any monster."

Cristiano had chased away the monsters under the bed until he'd become one.

And Diego was the light.

"Will your nightmares return?" Diego asked.

Not wanting to worry him, I'd told him I didn't have them while at school since they were less frequent and less frightening. Now that I was home, I expected they'd return, but there was nothing he could do about that, so I shook my head.

If I had my way, I'd be on a plane back to California before my nightmares could even catch up with me.

But I knew from experience—I could never completely outrun them.

U nder a starry sky, I walked away from the house, crossing our damp back lawn in heels. Lit from within, my father's ballroom shimmered like a golden paradise to welcome the state's elite. Town cars and limos lined the curved driveway, inching forward to meet the valet. Fountains out front glowed sky-blue, the water shimmering as it reflected hundreds of strung lights. It was how I imagined the gates of heaven—down to the large men in suits and earpieces guarding the entrance and scrutinizing invitations.

Unfortunately, I had to use heaven's back door. Security was heaviest at events like these. Armed men patrolled the perimeter of the property, keeping certain criminals out and others in. The main house was off-limits.

I took cover in the garden between the house and ballroom, crouching behind a fountain with a statue of Poseidon.

Your curiosity is an affliction, my father had often said to me. *And there's no cure,* I'd teased him. Being forbidden from the party was like being sent from the dinner table as a girl when conversations had turned to business. Or like when my father had put up a fence in our backyard to keep me from exploring the grounds beyond the trees. Most of the time, finding ways around the blockades was more fun than whatever lay on the other side.

Once one of the guards had turned back the way he'd come, I hurried through the courtyard. Intricate, lifelike butterfly wings, strapped over a black bodysuit, flapped at my back. My best friend, Pilar, had been too skittish to sneak in with me, but I'd convinced her to help me make an elaborate black-and-orange eye mask with feathers and glitter before streaking blonde extensions through my hair. She'd then clipped handmade, delicate monarch butterflies throughout my curls.

Full costume required. It'd been printed there on the invitation, and from what I'd heard and glimpsed of these parties, anything less than an extravagant, costly costume, and I'd stick out.

"*Alto,*" I heard behind me. I stopped and turned as a guard approached. "*¿Qué hace?*"

I swallowed and disguised my voice with my best North American accent. "*¿Hablas inglés?*"

"You are not permitted here," he said in broken English. "*¿Invitación?*"

I pulled a sharp-cornered card from my pocket and handed it over. I'd looked at the guest list earlier to forge an invite with the names of one of the few attending couples from the States.

"*Señor* Matthewson?" the guard asked.

"Husband." I flashed a small diamond ring one of my uncles had gifted me at my *quinceañera*. "Inside. Waiting."

He picked up his two-way radio, but as he was about to speak, a voice came through asking for security at the front. He handed me back the invitation. "*Adelante. Quédate en la fiesta.*"

Stay in the party. I continued around the side of the house. A Playboy bunny with red lipstick and a cigarette held open the door for me on her way out, and I entered the hall to "Walk Like an Egyptian." As my eyes adjusted to the glittering affair, waiters circled with trays, passing between rooms. To my right, disco music vibrated the chandeliers that looked as if they'd been dipped in gold and crystals and hung to dry.

Belly dancers rippled through the crowd. Walking toward the main hall, I crossed the imported Moroccan tile Mamá had bought on a trip to Africa, hypnotized as a heavyset man took the stage for an emotional aria.

Partygoers showed off their costumes—a black vinyl catsuit that hugged every curve. Cleopatra in a metallic leotard with layers upon layers of necklaces over her breasts, her nipples poking through. A bare-chested Tarzan with nothing but a cloth covering his genitals. Marie Antoinette walked in on the arm of Two-Face. Even some of the security guards wore painted masks or had gold-plated machine guns.

A waiter stopped and lowered his tray for me. It wasn't canapes or mini quiche as I would've thought but an assortment of pills and powder. Growing up in the world of drugs, I had little interest in them, so I opted for a fizzing drink instead. With a sip, bubbles tickled my mouth and made me smile.

This wasn't the ballroom in which I'd grown up playing hide-and-seek or had taken piano lessons, but an opulent show come to life. I walked into the next room, my heels solid on the floor even as music muted them. On a balconette overlooking a dancefloor, a row of women in lace corsets, bejeweled thigh-high stockings, and vibrant feather boas kicked slender legs for the can-can. A man in an open-collared suit and gold chains stood beneath them, likely hoping for a glimpse of heaven. I turned in a circle, taking in the spinning dancers. Men wore women's clothing, ladies dressed as animals, and caged birds sang. In one corner, a tiger paced its gilded pen for partygoers' amusement. Nearby, a woman in black leather also wore a leash.

The affair lived up to its tales of opulence and extravagance. I could hardly believe all this had been happening a hundred meters from my bedroom.

Glancing up, I spotted Diego in a long-sleeved denim shirt, a brown suede vest, and a cowboy hat. He surveyed the room from behind a second-floor railing. When our eyes met, he narrowed his. I bit my bottom lip as recognition crossed his features. He shook his head at me to signal his disapproval but tipped his hat with a small smile. After a quick scan of the room, he started down to the ground floor, but a security guard stopped him to speak in his ear. Diego looked at me, checked his watch, then turned back up the stairs.

I walked toward a pair of fire dancers twirling on the patio, their flames making shapes against the backdrop of night, but my attention snagged on a scribbled *Fortune Teller* sign. One corner of the room had been sectioned off with hung purple fabric. *How strange.* My father became more devout in his faith the older he got and held nothing but contempt for the occult.

I heard Papá's booming voice before I saw him. I craned my neck, but he was a head taller than most and easy to find. He shook hands with a governor. If Diego recognized me, my father probably would too, and I'd be banished back to the house.

I ducked behind the fortune teller's curtains to watch through a sliver. Papá carried an ornamental staff and wore a heavy looking jeweled crown that flattened out his black and gray hair. A ruby-red velvet cape with ermine trim weighed on his big frame.

"All these riches will be yours one day," said a craggy female voice.

Startled, I turned around. The partitioned area was shrouded in crimson light, but a glowing purple crystal ball illuminated the deep-set wrinkles and dark eyes of a woman at a small table. On the exotic tapestry, a stack of tarot cards sat by her slender, veiny hand. A convincing actress, she certainly looked the part. "I'm sorry?"

"You will inherit all of this. Not just material things."

"I don't want my fortune read," I said, peeking back through the curtains.

"You don't believe in it?"

"No."

"Then what's the harm?"

Damn. I'd lost sight of my father.

"It's no use hiding. He'll find you." She spoke unevenly, her words jagged.

I glanced over my shoulder. "Who?"

She stared at me from under thick black lashes and a shimmering gold headdress. "I see a man . . ." She tapped one nail on the table, squinting. "The man of the rose."

De la Rosa. It wasn't unusual that she'd have heard Diego's name somewhere—he was well-known around here. "You're wrong," I said. "I'm not hiding from him."

"I'm rarely wrong, *muñeca.*" She gestured for me, calling me a doll and treating me as one, too. "Come. *Siéntate.* The monarch wills it."

I turned to face her completely as chills covered my shoulders. It occurred to me that up until my mother's death, she'd planned every detail of these parties. Maybe she'd known this woman. "What?"

She said nothing more, waiting. Father would never have a true oracle here, if such a thing existed. As she'd said, what harm could it do? I took the cushioned folding chair across from her. In the light, her eyes were as ultraviolet as they appeared shrewd. One look told me she had seen things, knew things, but that didn't scare me. The past was the past. It was impossible to tell the future.

"Did you know Bianca King Cruz?" I asked.

"Only from afar." The woman lifted up and fixed the pillow on her chair. "*Perdón*. My achy back."

"I'm sorry," I said, unsure of the appropriate response. Her musky, floral perfume wafted across the table. When she didn't offer anything else, I held out my palm. "Well? Are you going to read it?"

"You're a young girl," she said.

"That's obvious to anyone with eyes." My gaze drifted to the deck of cards. "Aren't you going to tell my fortune?"

"I don't need to. It's clear as day." She reached out, her bracelets jangling as she took my hand in hers. She wore rings upon rings on each finger—amethyst gemstones set in gold, a silver snake coiled to the knuckle of her right thumb, a pearl cradled by a tiny pair of intricately carved, pewter hands. "With so few years behind you, you've already met your true love."

"Yes, I have."

"You know who he is?" she asked. "He's close by."

I nodded. "He's here tonight."

"I see great love for you."

Diego had taken a bullet for me all those years ago, and he'd saved my life many times since as he'd seen me through brutal pre-teen years without a mom. We already possessed a deep devotion to each other, and we hadn't even been intimate yet. I nodded. "It is a great love."

"I see pain," she said in the same flat tone.

I shifted in my seat. That was a given considering the circles my father moved in. He and I had already gone through tragedy—that was, if there was such a thing as going through it. Grief ebbed and flowed, but it never truly receded. Now, he ran a more respectable operation, but for those who dealt in vice and contraband, risk would always be present. The fortune teller saw pain? She could've been speaking to anyone in the room.

"I see betrayal and violence," she continued. "And much death."

The grandfather clock in the main ballroom chimed. How long had I been sitting there? "I've already experienced all of those."

"And at such a young age," she said, clucking. "There's more to come, I'm afraid."

Whether I believed in her powers or not, that wasn't what I'd hoped to hear. I took my hand back to put it in my lap. "Whose death?" I asked, touching the diamond on my finger.

Her rings clinked against the glass ball as she palmed it, but she didn't bother to look, as if that was just the most convenient place to rest her hands. "You will die for him, your love," she said.

"I would, yes."

"No. You *will* die for him."

Goose bumps pebbled my skin. I thought of the barrel of Cristiano's gun pressed to my forehead. *"Bang. You're dead."*

The dark came next. The pitch black, my cries, and the scurrying rodents, the smell and feel of blood that didn't leave me for weeks. A shadow, the same one that often haunted my dreams, rose in me.

My heart raced. In the warm glow of the red and purple light, I couldn't tell if the woman looked on with sympathy or delight. Either way, I didn't like her face just then, or any of this. It was silly. Child's play. She was wrong to hide behind a costume for a night and play with people's lives.

"This is stupid," I said and stood to return to my post at the curtains. I willed my heart rate to slow so I could focus on finding Diego. I spotted him standing in the entrance hall. He looked like he belonged in an old Western in his cowboy getup, yet blended perfectly amongst Mexico's upper echelon. At the same time, he was utterly out of place. I could give him an escape. I could give him everything.

Was *I going to die for him?*

I slipped out from the make-believe lair, and like a hawk to a mouse, his eyes set on me. The worry in them eased, replaced with the same longing surely reflected my eyes. The soothsayer's dark words lifted, and I saw them for what they were—generic, baseless, fearmongering senti-ments, a one-size-fits-all likelihood that more than the majority of this room would encounter death, pain, violence—and *riches*. That was the point of all of this, anyway.

As if plotting his route to me, Diego rubbed his jaw. He'd be blamed if we were caught together. That didn't stop my craving to feel his lips on mine. He started toward me, but after only a few steps, my father appeared, slapped him on the back, and pulled him away to introduce him to a couple.

I moved through the crowd, catching and losing Diego's gaze as people passed between us. He shook the hand of an Elvis impersonator as I ducked by a man in a toga. He kissed Catwoman's cheek but winked at *me*. I touched my neck in mock-offense and stopped short of face-planting into a wall of a security guard.

"*Perdón*," I said as I went to go around the man.

The guard moved to block me, and in an instant, the energy around me shifted. I tilted my head back until I was looking straight up at a monster of a man and into the face of a ghoulish black-and-white skull. The blackened eye sockets, rimmed in deep red, didn't hide the menacing way his eyes focused on me. Nor did the drawn-on teeth, shaped in a sinister grin, disguise his frown—or the flawless bone structure beneath his veneer. Raven-black hair had been slicked back, as stark against the chalky face paint as his tie cutting down the center of a pressed white dress shirt.

Standing as still and straight-backed as a mannequin, and looking as polished as one too, he inclined his head toward me. "May I have this dance?"

4

NATALIA

I t wasn't a request.

The stranger costumed as a brooding *calavera* sugar skull wasn't *asking* for a dance. There was more than simple bass and gravel weighing down his words—he spoke the way a lion growled, with a snarl and a gaze as powerful as the muscles rippling under what appeared to be an expensive custom suit.

May I have this dance?

No. Neither my gut nor my brain left any room for argument, but my body drew toward his, as if he were the sun pulling me into its orbit. I forced myself to step back. He wasn't security; he wasn't here to protect me, but the opposite. He was the danger my father had warned me of. This was a man who walked into a room and left with what he wanted—revenge, money, women . . .

Me.

No one in the room matched his obvious strength. It would take a bullet to stop him.

He'd asked my permission, and though I declined in a

whisper, he put a large hand on my waist anyway, drawing me in, towering over me like a threat.

The dancers gave him a wide berth, staying just outside the span of his long arms—as if he might reach out and snatch one of them. He placed my hand on his solid bicep and engulfed my other with a gentleness that contradicted his hold on my side and the severity of his costume.

"I don't know how to tango," I said as a Gotan Project song started.

"You've been away from Latin men too long," he said. "Follow my lead, *mariposa*."

What made him think I'd been away at all? I'd lived in North America eight years, but the Latina in me would never fade. I did, in fact, have some basic knowledge of the dance and fell into step with him.

"We're a match," he said, his eyes drifting over the butterflies in my hair.

"I'm sorry?"

"Our costumes."

There was no obvious correlation between a sugar skull and a butterfly, but I didn't dare contradict him.

"Why the monarch?" he asked.

I turned my cheek. Beside us, a minotaur and a French maid danced a beat faster. I wasn't going to tell this calavera what monarchs meant to me, so I resorted to facts. "It feeds on poison."

"Milkweed—to render itself unpalatable to predators," he said, sliding his hand to the center of my back where my leotard dipped. I stiffened as he dug his fingertips under the straps of my wings, into my exposed flesh. "One bitter taste, and the hunter backs off."

His skin touched mine and stole my focus, just like that. It had taken Diego years to make his first move. Against my will, my nipples hardened between us. "I—I think it's clever that they do that."

"It's just nature," he said. "Monarchs also represent the souls of the departed. Like me."

I looked up at him, unnerved at the way his black eyes drank me in. "You're very much alive."

Leaning in, he lowered his voice. "It's said if you whisper your desire to one, it can deliver your wish to the gods on quick and soundless wings."

I realized he was dancing me farther from the other partygoers. "I should get back," I said.

"To?"

"My . . . fiancé," I said, hoping it would fizzle his interest in me.

He stopped dancing. "Your fiancé? What about California?"

My mouth fell open, but I quickly closed it. I should've known better than to look caught off guard, having been raised by masters of schooling their emotions. "Do I know you?"

He hesitated before resuming our tango. He danced with precision and a peculiar grace, like a hunting lion. "I detect an American accent."

Somehow, that didn't give me any relief. "I have to go," I said, trying to pull away.

He tightened his grip on me, and with what I suspected was hardly any effort on his part, kept me where I was. "But I haven't whispered my wish in your ear yet."

I swallowed dryly, wondering where Diego had gone. Surely, he wouldn't like to find me pressed against another man. "People are waiting for me."

His roughened hand constricted around mine. I followed his gaze to the diamond ring on my finger. "Which people?" he asked.

Would my father's wrath be safer than where I stood now? The mystery around this man stopped me from telling him who I was. "People who would not like me to go missing."

"Then perhaps they shouldn't have left you all alone, *mariposita*."

"Don't call me that." Sometimes, my parents had called me their little butterfly. Even my father knew better than to use that nickname anymore. I looked around the man, panic rising the more tightly he held me.

He drew me flush to him, the warmth of his body contradicting his cold stare. "Then what should I call you?"

My gaze locked onto Diego as he separated from my father and scanned the room.

"And nobody left me alone," I said, ignoring the man's question. "I can take care of myself."

"Is that so?" he asked. "Regardless, I wouldn't take the chance if you were mine."

If I was his. My chest rose and fell a little faster, but this time, it wasn't in fear. His tight, possessive hold made it feel as if he already thought I belonged to him. For a split second, the thought of being at his mercy both scared and excited me. "But I'm not yours," I said to gauge his reaction.

"Are you suggesting I remedy that?"

How bold. Nobody in this world had ever come on to me like this. "You could try," I said, "but I can promise it wouldn't go well for you."

"I like a challenge. Because it doesn't sound to me as if your *fiancé* deserves you. He'd be wise to recognize that someone else might come along and show you that."

I didn't know many men around here who would speak

so shamelessly about another man's fiancée. "You're worse than that hag of a fortune teller," I bit out.

One dark eyebrow rose, his interest obviously piqued. "What'd she tell you?"

I looked around his shoulder and saw Diego wipe his temple as he started toward the dancefloor. He still hadn't spotted me, but his movements became agitated. I tried frantically to make eye contact. "She told me not to dance with masked strangers."

The man moved so I could see nothing but him. He had tangoed us into a dark corner, away from anyone else, and my heart started to thump. He lowered his mouth to my ear. "What if I'm not a stranger?"

He was playing games. As he isolated me from the crowd, all I heard was Cristiano de la Rosa's threats to my nine-year-old self. *You don't know true fear.*

"What are you doing?" I asked, trying to see around him.

"Tell me. Are you willing to die for your fiancé?"

The eerie echo of the soothsayer's words made my face heat with anger. "Are *you* willing to die for *me*?"

"Excuse me?"

"If you don't let me go," I said, searching for the most menacing threat I could, "I'll scream."

"I thought you could take care of yourself."

"I'm no match for your size. I wouldn't scream to be rescued, but as the fastest means to get a gun in your face."

"I see. Do you think they'll hear you over the music?" he asked, sounding amused.

"I'll scream as loud as I can, for as long as I can, until my vocal cords give out or I can no longer keep my mouth open."

A disarmingly slow smile moved over his face, the teeth

of his disguise spreading ear to ear. "I admit, I *am* curious to see how long you can keep your mouth open."

I shivered at the insinuation and pulled back, this time unable to hide my shock. "You've threatened the wrong person. I can have you killed in seconds without lifting a finger."

"Then I'd like to change my order. Please tell the heavens it is my dying wish to hear you scream."

He spoke with a rumble so deep, I felt his voice between my legs. And I was sure, by the way his eyes bore into mine, he'd meant me to. He wanted my screams, and to scare me, but it didn't come from a place of menace. I couldn't put my finger on his intention, but it was something much more carnal.

We were no longer dancing, but his hand still clenched mine as his fingers buried into the skin of my back. He held me like I was an instrument to be played, one he would snap in half before he gave it up. Not even Diego held me so greedily.

"Then I'll grant you your wish," I threatened.

"Your loyalty to him is admirable if not baffling." He checked over his shoulder, then released me with a bow. "We've been discovered anyway. If you'll excuse me, I'll have to take you with me."

I'll have to take you with me.

I'd heard those words in my nightmares and any place I was alone in the dark too long. "What?" I asked, my throat suddenly dry as I was transported back to the tunnel.

"I said, I'll have to take my leave. Excuse me."

He walked away, leaving me in darkness as I hung on his words, torn between never wanting to see him again and a temptation to call him back—in a way that felt all too familiar.

Diego pushed his way through the crowd. "Who was that?" he asked when he finally reached me.

"I don't know," I said, hugging myself. "I told him I didn't want to dance."

"And the bastard put his hands on you anyway? I should get Barto so we can hunt that *cabrón* down and teach him some manners." Diego searched the space around us. "I told you not to come."

"You knew I would anyway."

He paused, then glanced over my costume, and his expression relaxed. "In a mask that didn't fool me for a second. You make a liar of an innocent butterfly, Natalia."

"I didn't lie," I said, cozying up to him, pulling gently on his bolo tie. The braided leather was held together by a metal shield with his family name in decorative script. "I said I'd stay home, and I did. This is my home."

He drew his brows together, something unfamiliar sparking in his eyes, but then he glanced away.

"What is it?" I asked.

"Nothing."

I ducked my head to get him to look at me. "No, it's something. Tell me."

"I promise, it was a passing thought."

I crossed my arms. "Diego."

He took my shoulders and brought me close to kiss my forehead. "It's nothing bad. I just had this weird . . . sense of joy hearing you call this place home again."

His sense of joy was my sinking feeling. Diego's attachment to this town was stronger than mine; he'd never lived anywhere else. There were times I questioned how devoted he was to leaving here. He said he wanted a life in California with me, yet he continued to embed himself in the cartel and ingratiate himself with my father.

"This place will always be part of me," I said, "but I

can't call this home again. Not knowing that every day I'm here, every day *you're* here, death is a possibility."

"I know, and of course, I'm in complete agreement that the U.S. is where we belong." He pecked me briefly and ghosted his thumb over my bottom lip. "Let's not argue about something we both agree on. We should move before someone recognizes you."

I ran my fingertip over the curling, cursive letters of the *de la Rosa* engraved on his metal tie. "You won't make me go back to the house, will you?"

"Not if you swear you'll stay by my side every moment."

"An easy promise to make." I smiled as he guided me through the crowd by my shoulders until a friend waved at us from the main room.

"There's an announcement coming," Tepic called. Dressed in a Hawaiian shirt, fanny pack, and aviators, Tepic was as wild as the curls on his head and only as tall as me, but compact and mighty nonetheless. As we approached, he took an entire tray out of a waiter's hands. "Come one, come all," he said, showing us an assortment of narcotics. "What kind of night do you wish to have?"

"A sober one." Diego waved a hand. "None for us, *compa*."

I glanced around the room for the skull-faced stranger. There was something about him my mind tried to grasp on to, like a word at the tip of my tongue.

"Aren't you going to introduce me?" Tepic eyed me when I looked back at him. "I'm Tepic, like the city I come from."

"You don't say." I laughed and shook his hand. "*Mucho gusto*."

"You must've missed the gossip," Diego said, sliding an

arm around my shoulders and looking into my eyes. "Should we let him in on our secret?"

Tepic lowered his sunglasses, gaping. "Talia? I didn't recognize you in that mask."

"That was the plan."

"Costa will be happy to have you here for Easter," he said, looking up as the music lowered. "Speak of the devil."

On a large, wide balcony overlooking the main room, dancers stopped the can-can and parted, gathering on both sides of the gallery. My dad appeared through red velvet curtains and came to the railing, scanning the crowd and waving as his staff herded everyone into the same room. I moved behind Diego but kept my eyes on Papá, who looked almost cherubic with a cheeky grin, red face, and his crown tilted to one side. He tapped his scepter against the tile to get everyone's attention, but the effect was muffled by a clear tarp on the ground. Soon, silence fell over his audience.

"Thank you all for coming to celebrate tonight," he said almost drunkenly yet maintaining the sense of calm and composure he'd become known for in a world of chaos. "I know you're all eager to get back to the party and to the drinking,"—he paused for some laughs—"as am I. But there's a quick matter I want to resolve while all my closest friends and colleagues are in one place."

Diego glanced over his shoulder at me, his eyebrows drawn in question. I shrugged.

A waiter handed Papá a champagne glass. "On this day, the Cruz cartel welcomes back an old friend."

A murmur moved through the crowd as Tepic whispered to Diego, "*¿Qué está pasando?*"

Diego kept his eyes up and shook his head to say he didn't know what was happening. "*No sé.*"

If Diego didn't know about this, I wasn't sure who would. I slipped my hand into his and squeezed.

"Years ago, a wrongdoing was committed, and I intend to make it right before all of you tonight." Papá looked over his shoulder, into the wings. "Let it be known that a Cruz doesn't cower from his mistakes or turn his back on *familia*."

What family did he speak of? I looked to Diego, but his gaze was still trained on my father.

Papá turned forward again, and any belligerence vanished as he fell serious. "And that in the Cruz cartel, no betrayal goes unpunished."

The audience clapped, ready for a show.

"It gives me great pleasure to present you the leader of the *Calaveras*," my dad said. "But more importantly, to accept back into our lives a man who was once like a son to me and my wife."

"Calavera?" Diego asked. "He can't be serious."

"Who are they?" I asked.

"One of the new order cartels that has come to power over the past few years," Tepic explained quickly.

An "old friend" Diego knew nothing about—and an unknown cartel that had to do with my family? I struggled to connect the pieces. "Why would he . . . who is more like a son to him than you, Diego?"

Papá half-turned and beckoned the suited man in face paint I'd danced with. He stepped forward, surveying the room with black eyes that landed on Diego and me. My heart slammed against my chest as the pieces clicked and the puzzle finally revealed itself.

Father raised his champagne glass. "Welcome home, Cristiano de la Rosa."

"*Puta madre*," came Diego's slow curse.

Fear flooded my limbs with the same force and speed it

had in the closet eleven years earlier. My mind stripped away the face paint and I saw Cristiano clear as day. He was harder, angrier, an indisputable man who'd seen things. With a rippling red curtain at his back, he appeared like a devil looking down on us from hell.

No betrayal goes unpunished. My eyes fell to the tarp. Would he make an example of my mother's murderer here in front of everyone?

Instead of putting a bullet in Cristiano—who'd had a considerable bounty on his head for more than half my life —my father shook his hand.

My stomach turned over.

Flashbulbs popped as reporters captured the moment.

My father drew his shoulders back. "The Calaveras have risen to success faster than any cartel in México's history under the guidance of Cristiano."

The crowd remained silent at first, as if unsure of how to react. Cristiano's role was widely known in Bianca King Cruz's death; Diego had led the charge to hunt Cristiano with the help of most people in this room for years.

"Friends, *por favor*," Papá said in a less jovial tone. "Show my *compadre* some respect so we can get on with it."

People applauded as Diego and I stood frozen. He squeezed my hand until it hurt, but I couldn't speak, even if I wanted to. I would not show dirt respect.

"If my wife were here, I know she would feel the same," my father continued.

What? My gut smarted as if I'd been sucker punched.

"This cannot be," Diego said, staring up at his brother. Cristiano watched us back, still as polished as a mannequin.

I had danced with him. Let him touch me, hold me, whisper in my ear. A crook, a ruthless monster, and a cold-blooded killer.

Did I know somewhere deep down it was him?

I silenced the thought. I wouldn't have danced with him knowingly.

By the way he set unforgiving eyes on me, Cristiano knew exactly who I was—and he hadn't forgotten anything about that day eleven years ago.

Diego followed Cristiano's heated gaze to me, then pulled me possessively into the crook of his arm.

"Cristiano has come to me with new evidence in the death of my beloved wife," Father said, passing his drink to a member of the staff. "*Que su alma descanse eternamente en paz,*" he added, making the sign of the cross as he wished eternal peace on her soul. "Cristiano de la Rosa did not kill my wife."

I covered my mouth to silence my gasp, but it didn't matter—everyone around me was just as shocked. What was my father saying? Why was he dishonoring my mother this way?

Cristiano looked out over the crowd. "It's good to be welcomed back to a home I have missed," he said. "But there's a more pressing matter to address." He held up a gun. The warm light of the chandeliers flashed off burnished gold, sleek silver, and milky pearl.

White Monarch.

I grabbed onto Diego's arm. "What's he doing?"

Cristiano handed it to my father, then disappeared behind the curtain. He returned dragging a bloodied-and-bruised older man whose hands were bound in front of him. He released the man's bicep with a push, and he stumbled to the railing, next to my father. Blood soaked his light t-shirt.

Diego stepped backward. "Fuck."

"Who is that?" I asked.

"I don't know," Diego said without removing his eyes from the balcony. "Look away, Natalia."

"This *sicario*, who doesn't even deserve to be named, defiled and killed Bianca Cruz," Cristiano said, "and he is my gift to her family."

I covered my stomach. It wasn't possible. I'd never seen that man—

My father put the gun to the hitman's temple. To the thrilled screams and cheers of the crowd, he pulled the trigger and blew up his head like a firework.

5

NATALIA

My bare feet sank into the soil of my mother's garden as I emptied the contents of my stomach onto one of her rosebushes. Diego held my heels in one hand, dodging my wings as he tried to keep my hair off my face. Everything was a blur. I didn't remember screaming with the crowd, running out, or ripping off my mask and shoes.

"Careful for the thorns," Diego said about the bushes.

My eyes watered, blurring the roses' blood-red color. A man's head had exploded. His brains had splattered across the tarp. His body had crumpled at my father's feet. I held onto Diego's arm until I could stand without wobbling.

Loitering by the fountain, Tepic pushed his aviators to the top of his head and chuckled through the cigarette in his mouth. "You okay, Talia?" he asked. "What a show, eh?"

At least Diego still possessed enough compassion to look as ill as I felt, his face colorless and drawn. He smoothed my hair off my forehead gently but said to Tepic, "Shut the fuck up. Can't you see she's sick?"

"What's the matter, Diego?" Tepic asked, getting another cigarette and his lighter from his fanny pack. "You look like you've never seen a man's head blown off. Or blown it off yourself."

Diego rubbed the inside corners of his eyes. "Not in front of Natalia."

In front of me, my father had once dragged a drunk out of a restaurant by his hair for waving a gun near my family. My mom had told me to stop crying; that was how Papá handled his business. Dad had returned ten minutes later and ordered a towel and ice for his bloody knuckles followed by a slice of *tres leches* cake. Over the years here and there, I'd witnessed him knock his men around or order to have people "taken care of" and "made an example of." I was no stranger to the stories about him, either—like the one where Papá had supposedly addressed a package with an army general's fingers in it to the mayor and dropped it in a public mailbox.

I had always known my father to be feared, but to me, he was just Papi. Now, because of him, I'd seen a man's brains. I breathed through another urge to vomit.

Careful to avoid where I'd gotten sick, Diego stooped to pick up some of the butterflies that'd fallen out of my hair. "I'm sorry you saw that," he said to me.

"Sorry?" Tepic asked. "She just watched her father take the sweetest kind of revenge. Anyone who's lost a mother should be so lucky to witness what Talia just did."

"It should've been Cristiano," I heard myself say. It had been a long time since I'd wished death on him.

"Not if he didn't do it," Tepic pointed out.

I quelled my shaking and tried to piece together my thoughts. "There's no way he didn't," I said to Diego as he stood. "You were there. You saw. There has to be an explanation."

"I know. Come on out of the dirt," he said, extending a hand to me.

I took it, wiping my bare feet in the grass before I stepped over a row of tiny lanterns. Diego led me to the glowing fountain, set my delicate hair clips on the ledge with my mask, and helped me out of my wings.

"How is Cristiano back?" I asked. "And why does Father believe he didn't do this?"

"I don't know." Diego crouched to strap my shoes back on. "But I'm going to find out."

I stood. "I want to hear it from my father."

Diego pulled me into a hug, shushing me. "Just take a minute to calm down," he said, rubbing my back. "Breathe."

I buried my face in his chest, where it was familiar, where his shirt smelled like soap, suede, and cigars—where it was safe. Warm. I wanted to stay in his arms and pretend I hadn't just watched my own father brutally murder a person. That Cristiano hadn't just reentered our world. That everything I knew about my mother's death hadn't just been called into question.

How had Cristiano pulled this off?

How could my father shame my mother's memory this way?

"I need to see my dad," I said, disconnecting from Diego.

He held my elbow. "Not tonight, my love. You're not even supposed to be here."

"I don't care." I frowned up at him. "I want answers. I demand them."

"Cool off. Let Costa do the same. Can you even look him in the eye right now?"

That hadn't occurred to me, but Diego was right—even though I wanted answers, the thought of facing my dad made my stomach roil again. It would be too hard. Diego knew my mind better than I did in that moment, so I surrendered to the safety of his arms, deciding to wait until the morning to approach my father.

But I wouldn't let him off the hook. Not for this.

I shifted my focus to the other side of the equation— Cristiano. Why was he back? Where had he gone? What had given him the confidence to return with a million-dollar bounty on his head?

"I didn't even know Cristiano was still in the country," I said.

Tepic tapped ash from his cigarette. "Me neither."

"Who are the Calaveras?" I asked.

Diego and Tepic exchanged looks. "You mind if I smoke?" Diego asked me. "I could use one."

"I don't care," I said, drawing back. "Are they a cartel?"

"Stay," Diego murmured, one arm around my shoulders while Tepic passed him a cigarette. As he stuck it in his mouth and lit it, he nodded. "Calavera is a cartel that came to power while you were away," he said, exhaling smoke, "and has been growing at an exponential rate. They move narcotics too, but they're mainly in arms trafficking, like my father was, and extremely private—"

"As they are violent," Tepic added.

"They're like a gang of misfits from all over," Diego said. "Tightly knit. Supposedly make big decisions as a whole. But also a little cultish over their leader."

"Cristiano?" I asked. "And you didn't know it was him?"

"I didn't even know he was back." Diego shook his head. "Their leader was anonymous until now. Most likely hiding behind a front to keep his identity secret."

"Because of my family?" I guessed. "If we'd known

where to find him, it would've been Cristiano up there on his knees just now."

"I assume so." Diego took a drag, squinting ahead. "The question is why Cristiano's back, what he wants, and how he pulled this off. I have no doubt he's filled Costa's head with lies."

"Even with that display, you still think Cristiano's guilty?" Tepic asked.

"I don't think it." Diego pressed his lips into a thin line. "I know it."

"You would too if you'd seen what we did," I told Tepic. Cristiano had killed my mother. If I'd walked in a couple minutes earlier, I probably would've witnessed it. Why was Father denying it, and in front of such important people? "It must be blackmail."

"Wow, Tali. Good thinking." Tepic stopped pacing, looking from me to Diego. "That's got to be it, hasn't it?"

"I wouldn't put it past my brother." Diego nuzzled my hair. "He was always dangerous, but if the rumors are true, Cristiano became something else entirely after he fled here."

I kissed Diego's cheek. Sometimes I forgot that the day I'd lost my mom, he'd essentially lost a brother. "What rumors?" I asked. "The ones I heard were mostly in regard to his whereabouts."

"It's, ah,"—Diego grimaced—"not really suitable for your ears."

"If you don't tell me, I'll find out another way," I said. It brought me no joy to hear graphic details about the man who continued to haunt me, but if he was back in our lives, then I had to know what I was dealing with.

"The Calaveras aren't like us," Diego said. "We grew up here. Our home is our identity. These transients from all over the world are here to take advantage of our market." He waved smoke from around my head. "They have no loyalty and no home—literally. Since they didn't have a location to operate out of, they took a town about an hour north of here."

"What do you mean they *took* it?" I asked.

"Like a hostile takeover. The Calaveras seized it to run their operations. Raped the local women, pillaged and stole businesses, enslaved their people." Diego checked my expression. "Now, the whole town is walled off on three sides, and the back abuts a mountainside. Some sadistic shit goes on in the Badlands, I'll bet."

"Badlands?" I asked.

"That's what some people call it. Rough terrain." Tepic wiggled his fingers like a witch. "*Las puertas del infierno.*"

The gates of hell. That sounded familiar. Suddenly, the designation *Badlands* rang a bell. I'd heard it before but couldn't remember where. "He made his own town?"

"More or less. There are homes and businesses within its walls, but who knows what's true or legitimate. As far I know, nobody has ever escaped, nor has anyone infiltrated and lived to tell the tale."

"They're like a cult," Tepic said, waving his cigarette toward the house with a grimace. "Satanic rituals and shit. They eat snails, speak in tongues, sacrifice virgins, throw rotten fish at whores, that kind of stuff."

I widened my eyes. I'd heard a lot of cartel-related fact that better resembled fiction, but nothing involving any of that. "How do you know all that if nobody's ever escaped?"

"Who knows how rumors start?" Tepic said. "But I don't doubt what I've heard. I just feel bad for the women trapped there who—"

"Tepic," Diego warned. "Stop. You're scaring her."

I would've had to believe all that to be afraid, and I

wasn't sure I did. Rotten fish? Speaking in tongues? It sounded pretty far-fetched. Although, I started to vaguely recall a news story from years earlier about a foreign cartel that operated differently than others. Its boss had a long, international reach and an even longer rap sheet. It'd claimed he'd never been photographed or named and had taken more bullets than he had drugs in his lifetime—and survived.

I stared at the fountain, comforted by the sound of running water. Why were women trapped, and how come nobody had freed them? Did Cristiano really have something to do with that? Until the dark day in question, he'd always been respectful of my mother, and she had cared for him. As a girl, I'd caught Cristiano watching me many times with something that'd felt akin to affection. Nothing that'd made me fearful. Maybe I'd just been too young to know better, though.

"What about the women trapped there?" I asked to stop my mind from filling in the blanks.

"It's terrible, Tali, really," Diego said. "You don't want to know. It's my father all over again, which is why I don't understand how Costa could go into business with Cristiano. He represents the same things my parents did."

"Human trafficking?" I asked quietly.

"It's fucked up." He knocked ash from his cigarette, looking somewhere over my head. "But not all that surprising, I guess. Cristiano and my dad are a lot alike, which is why they never got along."

"The women are mostly foreigners if that makes you feel any safer, Tals," Tepic said.

Who could feel anything but disgusted hearing that? My stomach churned. Had there ever been anything redeemable about Cristiano? Why had my mother not only taken him in, but, as I remembered it, treated him with tenderness?

"It makes *me* feel like shit," Diego said, glancing down at me. "I don't want you anywhere near him. If he ever gets you alone, you scream, hear me?"

I had screamed—and screamed and screamed. And nobody had been able to stop him. Not in my parents' bedroom, nor their closet, nor the tunnel beneath it.

I removed my arms from around Diego, suddenly warm. "He can't get away with this," I said. "If any women, from my country or another, are being held by Cristiano, my father wouldn't accept him back."

"And yet it seems he has," Diego said. "It's just another business to Cristiano. He traffics some, and other women are there for him and his gang's use."

I couldn't keep my disgust at bay any longer. Bile rose in my throat, even as I tried not to let my imagination wander down that path. This was the side of my father's world he tried to shield me from, but I was in it nonetheless. Did that make me complicit? What about Diego? Could either of them even stop someone like Cristiano?

"Are you sure?" I asked.

Diego glanced at me and flicked his cigarette butt away. "Jesus," he said, taking my shoulders to hold me at arm's length. "You're pale again. I told you not to ask."

"It's okay," I said. These were things I had decided long ago I didn't want to know about. But now that I *did* know, I was less frightened than I thought I'd be and more quietly enraged. What about the millions of women in my country who didn't have access to the defenses I did? Who was on their side?

Cristiano had always been a calculating killer, that was no shock—but apparently, he'd grown into a disloyal degenerate, a callous crook, a master of mind games. Hades of the Badlands.

Diego massaged my shoulders. "Relax. This is not something you need to worry about. I will always protect my sun—without you, I'd live in the dark. I won't let anything happen to you."

"Cristiano can't get away with all the things he has," I said. What did he have over Papá? It had to be big for him to ignore the horrors I'd just heard. After all, he'd taken down Cristiano and Diego's father for similar offenses. "He must have a reason."

"Who, Costa? He has none. He's lost his mind," Diego said and gestured at Tepic. *"¿Tienes otro?"*

Tepic passed him another cigarette, then dropped his and used his heel to stamp out the butt. "I'll see what I can find out from Barto and the guys."

Diego nodded him on. "Go."

I tried to wrap my head around why Papá would do this to us. To *himself.* Just seeing Cristiano brought back scores of memories better left to rest.

Had he manipulated my father? Or could there be any truth to his claims?

Was there even a sliver of possibility that Cristiano was innocent?

It was a thought I knew I should ignore, because if he was or wasn't, either answer would only incite more questions. And if my curiosity was an affliction, then my curiosity about a man like Cristiano could be of the fatal sort indeed.

6

NATALIA

Some details from the Day of the Dead eleven years earlier were hazy, and some crystal clear, but I'd never doubted that Cristiano had left my mother for dead and had been about to take off with our valuables.

As Tepic returned to the ballroom on a quest for information, and Diego removed his arm from me to light a fresh cigarette, I paced by the fountain and tried to figure out the riddle before me.

Cristiano had forgotten the duffel on the bed, but enough cash and jewelry had gone missing from the safe to set him up for a long time.

Then there was the fact that nobody else could've come or gone from my mother's bedroom that day without being seen. And that the mansion's security system, including the cameras, had been magically disabled, which Barto claimed could only be done quickly and by someone familiar with it. Cristiano, who'd been one of the only guards with the highest security clearance at the time, had known it intimately. Then, getting access to my parents' safe was nearly impossible—it would've taken someone close enough to the inside to find out the combination.

That was as far as I let my mind go. Whatever struggle had caused the tear in Mamá's dress and the bruises on her face—whatever had happened between the intruder entering the bedroom and me skipping in—I couldn't think of without getting sick, so I never did. I knew it tortured Papá enough for the both of us.

And the final detail that didn't add up was the small fact that a *sicario* didn't kill of his own volition. He would've been hired. So if Papá believed Cristiano hadn't done this, then who did? Who had the hitman worked for?

Some of the more conspiracy-minded newspapers back then had speculated rival federations had done it instead of Cristiano, but growing up, I'd dismissed those theories without a second thought.

I stopped pacing. "Could any of this have to do with the Maldonado cartel?"

Diego frowned from a couple meters away. "Cristiano's return?"

"No. My mother's death."

"The Maldonados didn't exist back then." Diego sat on the edge of the fountain, placed his cowboy hat next to him, and scrubbed a hand through his disheveled hair. "They're newer. What do you know about them anyway?"

"Mostly what I've read in the news or what I overheard in the study the other day," I said.

"I thought you wanted to stay out of all this." He sucked on his cigarette, squinting at me as silky strands of his dark-cocoa hair fell around his cheekbones. "Yet as soon as you got here, you were already hiding in hallways like you did as a kid."

"I want to live a respectable and honest life away from all this, but that doesn't mean I want to be ignorant." I couldn't blame his quizzical look. When I was away at school and we spoke on the phone, I *was* ignorant. I'd ask about business because it was his life, but then I'd let him get away with cursory answers.

After my mother's death, I'd no longer wanted to hear about the things I'd sought to know growing up—the handshake deals made over caramel flan with men visiting from exotic-sounding countries. The foreign sports cars, endless vices, and other spoils that came from feeding the world's various drug addictions. The lost boys of the town that the cartel took under its wing, protecting and feeding them while training them like wards.

Back then, I'd do more than hide. I would seek information, curious about the dangers I was always kept from. I'd sneak away from the house and ride my bike a few kilometers to the sprawling, private ranch house on our property that housed boys and men like Diego and Cristiano. There, they'd learned everything about the business—including how to protect and kill for it. From a distance, I'd been introduced to the different kinds of arms and how to carry them. Other things happened in those training camps too, but those I didn't stick around for. I hadn't wanted to learn what could be worse than death.

As far as I knew, the ranch house had been empty since Papá had traded all that for less violence, going from rival cartels' competition to their solution. They now paid him top dollar to move contraband across borders, and since he'd nearly monopolized the shipping market, he could be more discerning than most.

"My father can pick and choose who he associates with," I said. "If he worked so hard to minimize risk and violence, why are we suddenly involved with two of the most dangerous cartels?"

"Calavera and Maldonado have nothing to do with each other," Diego said, raising his eyes to mine.

"Are you sure?" I resumed pacing in hopes that moving would help the uneasiness building in me. "Maybe there's some connection between them."

"I don't see how there could be. Maldonado is my thing. I brought them in."

From what I'd heard in the office, it hadn't sounded as if Papá had been completely on board. "It wasn't my father's call?"

"I brought the contract to him once it had all been arranged." The orange tip of his cigarette flared with a drag. "He would've said no otherwise. Your dad wants to keep doing things as he's always done, but that's dangerous."

"Dangerous or wise?" I stopped in front of Diego and crossed my arms. "If it works, why tempt fate?"

"What do you think happens when a wild animal slows down to rest or to tend to his wounds, or if he gets sentimental about his prey—the way Costa has about Cristiano? Nothing good." He put out the smoke on the ledge, picked up his hat, and leaned his elbows on his knees. "If you're not moving forward, you're going backward," he said. "Adaptation is the key to survival."

I could see Diego's point. We'd done case studies in business school about insolvent companies—those that'd changed too fast, or in the wrong ways. Those that had been left behind.

"Why does adapting have to mean taking on more risk?" I asked.

"Working with the Maldonados isn't any more dangerous than what we normally do—it just sounds that way because they're . . ." He scratched his temple. "Let's just say they're less forgiving than most."

"What does that mean?"

"Can you come here, please?" He reached for me. "We don't get much time together as it is. Why waste it on talking about stuff we can't control?"

It was all I had wanted in the last year—to have Diego's hands on me again. To be ignorant of the dark side of this business. This was exactly why I tried to stay out of these things. Now, I knew too much and had too many questions to overlook what was happening.

Not only that, but I couldn't ignore how invested Diego was in the future of a cartel he was planning to leave behind soon.

I stayed where I was. "What does 'less forgiving' mean, Diego?"

He looked down at the hat as he turned it over in his hands. "They don't do business the way your dad and his friends did. If they don't like something, they get rid of it. They kill unnecessarily and without regard for the rules."

"There *are* no rules," I pointed out.

"Not true. As you know, up until the past decade or so, there was a code. There were *agreements*—like the one my family broke. But older cartel leaders are being replaced with ones who think they're above the law of the land. With the Maldonados, there's no justice—only the word of those in charge."

Justice. In a strange way, it did exist in this world. I thought back to what Cristiano had said to me about justice and loyalty before he'd forced me down the tunnel. My father or his men would've killed him without trial based on the damning evidence they'd had. I could almost see Cristiano's reasoning. If the Maldonados murdered who they wanted when they wanted, then that bred more distrust, disloyalty, and violence within their own cartel and amongst others.

"And you made a *deal* with them?" I asked, spinning the diamond on my ring finger. "What happens if you don't deliver?"

"I will, Talia. I've done my homework. I'm talking over fifty percent more profit for maybe nine or ten percent more risk. How can I refuse those odds?"

"Because if there are no rules, how do you know when you've broken one? Or what they're capable of?" I paused. "What *are* they capable of?"

"Things you've asked me not to tell you before."

This was the kind of information I could never forget once I knew. And yet, if it involved Diego's life, remaining in the dark didn't feel like an option. I stilled my fidgeting hands. "I'm asking now. You're caught up in this. So is my father. I want to know what happens if something goes wrong."

"You're overreacting, Tali. I've got everything under—"

He stopped when he picked up on my glare. "Life or death is overreacting?" I asked tersely.

Sighing, he looked away from me. "What happens if something goes wrong with the Maldonados? Death if they're merciful. If not, it's because they can do worse. Enslave a man to do their bidding, hold his family hostage, torture him by killing off his brothers, sell his women and kids."

My heart rate kicked up a notch. It wasn't as if I had no clue of the reach these criminals around me had. But it scared me that although Diego was most likely smarter than the people he did business with, he'd never be as ruthless. "You have to cancel the deal."

He whipped his gaze to me, brows drawn. "I can't do that, Tali. What's done is done, and we need their business anyway. If this goes well, then an ongoing arrange-

ment with the Maldonados would set all of us up for
life."

"What kind of life is it if you're looking over your
shoulder every day? If you're never allowed to make
mistakes?" I ran my hands over my face. "No amount of
money is worth that."

"You can't even comprehend the kind of money I'm
talking about."

"I don't *care*," I said, throwing up my arms in exasperation. "This is exactly the life I don't want—one I'm trying
to help *you* escape. Why are you even worrying about an
ongoing deal if you're trying to get out?"

"I have to make as much money as I can before I
leave," he said adamantly, imploring me with his eyes.
"When I get to the States, I'll be back at square one. What
will I do for work? I need a bank account with enough
zeros to take care of you."

"Diego." I squatted in front of him, set his hat on the
lip of the fountain, and took his hands. "That's not how I
need to be taken care of. I could have that life if I wanted
it, but I don't. I chose to leave, and I thought you wanted
the same." I swallowed, searching his eyes. "Do you not
want to come to California?"

"I do. I want that so much, but I have to know I can
provide for you first. Whether you ask me to or not, it's my
responsibility as a man, and I won't be happy anywhere if
I can't do it." He moved some of my hair behind my ear
and tilted up my chin. "It's not just about the money. This
first run will net me enough to come with you, and then
you and I will be set until I get on my feet. But if it goes
well, it'll also secure the most profitable deal your dad has
ever made. It'll prove to your father that he can bring his
business into the present, and . . ."

"And?" I asked.

He looked at me with cinched eyebrows, as if in pain. Diego felt everything. I hated arguing with him, but it was important that he see that money and status meant less to me than being with him. I was tired of living a country apart.

He glanced toward the house, avoiding my eyes. "It'll show your dad what I'm capable of. That I'm more than some lackey on his payroll. That I'm good enough for you and can care for you—not just financially, but in every way."

"Oh, Diego." I cupped his jaw, and he leaned into my hand. "He doesn't doubt what a strong, smart, skillful man you are. He just doesn't want me near any of this. It wouldn't matter who you were."

He put his hand over mine, turning his face into my palm to kiss it. "I'm sorry."

"For what?"

"All of this. Worrying you about Maldonado and Calavera. I'm sorry you had to see my fucking *pinche* brother." He brushed his lips up my wrist and forearm, smiling against my skin when I shivered. "I know how those memories of Cristiano affect you," he said softly, "but I'm not going to let him anywhere near you."

Diego *didn't* know. Not entirely. My nightmares were not limited to the horror of finding Mamá in a pool of her own blood. Cristiano had taught me that the gilded fortress I'd grown up in wasn't as secure as I'd thought. He'd robbed me of my carefree childhood. I'd sat in the dark, my nine-year-old mind growing more and more paranoid I might never be found, trying to think of how I could reach the last rung of the ladder without the height or vision I needed. Even if Cristiano hadn't killed my mom, I didn't know if I could ever disassociate him with the fear he'd inspired or the lessons I'd learned too early in life.

Trust no one.

Never draw a weapon unless you meant to kill.

Loyalty didn't guarantee loyalty, even to your own blood.

Anyone, even the most loyal disciple, could turn.

And I had danced with him tonight, aroused by a possessive touch and menacing words that should've sent me running into Diego's arms. I could've screamed like I'd threatened—but I hadn't. What was wrong with me?

I stood, pulled Diego up from the fountain's ledge, and wrapped my arms around his neck. "Thank you for protecting me," I whispered as I brushed my cheek against his. "For wanting more for us. For taking a bullet for me all those years ago. I love you."

"I only wish I could do more." He slid his hands down my back, lowering his mouth but pausing before our lips touched. "I would erase that day for you."

I hugged him more tightly, breathing him in as he pecked me once. Twice. His tongue slid between my lips, tasting me. "My sweet Natalia," he said on a moan.

I loved how he said my name. Even as Diego and I had changed, as our relationship had grown and our devotion to each other had solidified, he continued to say my name the same way—as if he owned it. As if nobody else knew it like he did.

I deepened the kiss. The world fell away, and we were just two people in love who hadn't had enough chances to show it.

His hands moved everywhere—searching, finding, claiming. He cupped my ass and pulled my hips against his, and I groaned.

"God, I want you," he said, his voice hoarse. "I don't know how much longer I can wait."

In that moment, I felt the same. I'd preserved my

virginity for him—that part was easy. But keeping it *from* him? I struggled to be good. I wanted to do right by my faith, act with grace as my mother had, and be a woman she would've been proud of. But sometimes I wondered if it even mattered since I would marry Diego no matter what.

His hand dropped lower than it ever had, and the wrongness of being groped outside where anyone could happen upon us made something pull deep in my tummy. From behind, Diego cupped me between the legs and held me in place as he ground against me, rubbing a sensitive spot that made me moan up at the sky. "Oh, *god*. That . . ."

"Hmm?" he asked, running his tongue along the shell of my ear.

"That feels so good," I breathed.

"For me too. I'm getting hard, Tals."

Desire washed over me. This was still new territory for us. It wasn't easy to talk dirty to my best friend over the phone when we'd only ever stolen a few kisses here, a few intimate touches there.

"Tell me something too," he said in my ear. "Are you wet?"

I curled my fingers in his hair, taking two handfuls of honeyed downy strands. I hadn't known a question like that would excite me so much. "I think I am now," I said.

He smiled against my cheek. "You're pulling my hair."

"Oh—sorry." I released my fists.

"I don't mind it. How about you?" Keeping one hand under my ass, he tugged on my curls with the other, causing a butterfly clip to fall out. "Or is it too much?"

He'd been gentle, but I bit my lip as a passion we rarely got to explore warmed the space between us. "It's not too much."

His eyes darkened. "Tell me you love me, Talia."

"You know I do."

"But *say* it, *princesa*." He growled a little, in a way I'd never heard from him. "When I ask, that means I want to hear it."

I was taken aback by the tremor of frustration in his voice, especially because I couldn't think of a time I'd ever denied him anything. That was one thing he and I had never experienced—a chase. We played the games that had been forced upon us by keeping our romance a secret, but maybe the hungry look in his eyes now meant Diego also wanted to hunt a little.

What would happen if I didn't give him what he wanted every time he asked for it?

"No," I said softly.

"No?" He pulled me against him once more, bringing me to the tips of my toes. "Don't keep your love from me, Talia. Ever."

He sounded angry, but his excitement was growing more and more obvious against my stomach. And something about refusing him was equally as exhilarating for me.

I shook my head.

"You don't love me?" He nipped my earlobe. "All I want is to take care of you. Protect you. Love you. And you'll deny me?" He took my face with one large hand, his grip rough but his dancing eyes boring into mine, challenging me in a way that sent a thrill down my spine. His hand under my buttocks crept lower and locked between my legs. He had me trapped, my face secure, while his fingers were centimeters from my most intimate spot. "Tell me how much you love me," he demanded. "I won't ask again."

With footsteps at Diego's back, I jumped back as my heart launched into my throat. We'd let down our guards, which might've made our fondling more thrilling, but that was never smart around here. I hid behind Diego, adjusting my neckline, even though we hadn't been doing anything.

Diego turned just his head to the side. "Move along," he called over his shoulder. "Pervert."

No response. I looked around him and swallowed at the skull in the shadows. One that both arrested my gaze and inspired my instinct to flee. Cristiano had found us vulnerable, away from the team that protected us. I wasn't even sure if Diego had his gun. Cristiano could shoot me. Take me. Hurt me.

But would he? Who was he now? How was he different from the protector I'd grown up with? I couldn't even be sure that version of him was the same man who'd murdered my mother.

If he had at all.

Was I really questioning what I'd seen?

God. Cristiano hadn't even spoken yet, and he was playing mind games with me. His composure and coded words from earlier put a match to the embers of curiosity I continually tried to extinguish.

Diego turned, standing protectively in front of me.

The figure stepped into the moonlight. "You were going to take her out here for everyone to see," Cristiano said with an inviting gesture. "Don't let us interrupt."

I shivered at the thought, wondering how long he'd been watching.

Diego put a hand back to stop me from reacting. "What the hell are you doing here?" he asked Cristiano.

Even Cristiano's shrug was threatening. "I came outside to say hello to the brother I haven't seen in years."

"You know what I mean," Diego said. "Why are you in town?"

Cristiano turned his glare on me. "It's time for you to go home."

And leave Diego alone? "No."

"You haven't changed." Cristiano's eyes scanned my body, lingering on my breasts and hips. "And in some ways, you're entirely different."

"Fuck off," Diego said, moving to block me from Cristiano. "She has nothing to do with this."

"So send her away, as she doesn't seem to listen to me. Never did." A whistle sounded over our heads, and I jumped with its visceral *bang*. A burst of shimmering gold lit up the sky. Cristiano shook his head at me, as if disappointed. "I can see your fear from our last encounter has worn off, Natalia. What a shame."

I bit my tongue to stop from retorting *what a shame* it was that he'd lived to see anything at all. It was enough that Diego and I had his attention; it wouldn't help to anger him.

"Tell me," Cristiano said, moving to see me better. "Have you learned how to shoot a gun yet?"

When you aim, kill. "Hand me yours," I said, "and let's find out."

"*Cuidado*, Talia," Diego said through his teeth. "Careful. You don't know what he's capable of. Go back to the party. I'll find you."

I kept my eyes on Cristiano as his stayed on me. "What if he tries to hurt you?" I asked.

"Not unless the traitor strikes first," Cristiano said. "Go back to the house, and I promise you my brother's safety."

A second firework sailed through the night sky and exploded blood red. "He's not a traitor, and he's not your brother. I don't know what my father wants with you, but you're not family."

I immediately wished I'd kept my mouth shut. Cristiano came closer, tilting his head as his black eyes took me in. "Natalia Lourdes," he said, drawing out my full name in a way that made it sound sinful, like wisps of breath against a neck that didn't belong to him, and dangerous, like sharpening a knife.

With a sudden movement from Diego, Cristiano turned his head, focusing on his brother. "If you're going to draw your gun on me like you did back then," he said, "aim well. You'll only have one shot, and this time, you'd better be willing to die for it."

Behind him, the shadows stirred. Two shapes with two sharp pairs of eyes took form. Were these the misfits Diego and Tepic had spoken of?

Before anyone could make a move, voices from the lawn made me turn.

Barto approached with two members of our security team. He looked between Cristiano and Diego. "Costa wants to see you both in the ballroom. Now." Barto turned to me. "And you, Natalia. What are you doing here?"

"I was just taking her back to the house," Diego said.

Barto frowned at him, shaking his head. "You'd do better with the truth, Diego."

"Meaning?"

"Costa's likely to be less angry that she snuck into the party on her own than that she came to spend time with you."

Diego licked his lips. "Had I been *informed* we were hosting a known murderer and rapist, I would've obviously sent Tali straight back."

Cristiano barely noticed the insult. Instead, he was watching me. Listening. He'd always been that way, taking in everything around him, processing it like a computer, keeping his observations to himself—to what end, God only knew. Was he plotting ways to terrorize me more? Reminiscing about the life he'd had here?

Fantasizing about dancing in dark corners?

Or worse?

A small part of me couldn't reconcile the human trafficker to the Cristiano I'd known before he'd fled. He'd been next to impossible to get to know back then, even putting aside our fourteen-year age difference. But having only ever been under his protection growing up, I'd never seen him as the vicious killer everyone else had.

Until that day.

Barto nodded at the brothers. "Costa is waiting. Tonight, he's not feeling patient."

Cristiano and Barto exchanged an unfriendly look, which reminded me that before all this, they'd been close. They had come into the cartel around the same age and had risen in the ranks together. Barto, an important member of our security team even then, had been away on business with my father during Cristiano's attack on my mom. Like Cristiano, Barto never said much, but I knew he constantly beat himself up over it.

Barto had lost not only my mother—a member of the family he'd been hired to protect—but Cristiano too, his closest friend and comrade.

"Send someone back to the house with Talia," Diego told Barto.

"It's okay," I said, even though Cristiano still hadn't removed his eyes from me. "I don't need an escort."

As Cristiano passed me on his way toward the house, he stalled. "I'll see you to your bedroom if you like," he said so only I could hear.

The suggestive offer, not made out of graciousness, made me think of our tango. Or perhaps it was more appropriate to call it a mind game than a dance. It was becoming clear Cristiano liked to play. With Father demanding his presence and Barto watching on, I was safe. Instead of cowering at his suggestion, I called his bluff and offered my elbow as I would to an escort. "Let's go."

"Let's go indeed," he said with a hint of a smirk before he walked off with Diego and Barto.

Apparently, my discomfort amused him—but so did my fight.

That didn't surprise me.

Cristiano would pinch a butterfly's wings together just to watch her struggle.

7

NATALIA

A romas of coffee and cinnamon-raisin toast preceded the *pop* of a toaster as I entered the open, airy kitchen. Papá sat at the breakfast counter with a newspaper as Paz filled a mug with spicy *café de olla* from an orange enamel pot.

"*Buenos días*, Natalia," Paz said as she served him.

"*¿Cómo está?*" I greeted, pulling my damp hair into a ponytail so it wouldn't get my t-shirt wet. Despite my shower, I still had flecks of glitter embedded into my hairline and arms from the night before.

Paz responded, nodded at my father's half-eaten plate of eggs and *pico de gallo*, and asked if I was hungry. When I told her my stomach was still uneasy from the night before, she got me a warm can of Coke Light.

"Good morning, *mi amor*." My father held up the front page to show me a picture of himself with the governor and his wife. Lower down the page, Papá shook hands with the head Calavera himself. I couldn't even bring myself to think the devil's name. "You wouldn't believe the morning's headlines," he said. "Everyone says it was a great party."

No mention of the murder within its walls? Whatever "journalists" had been in attendance should be stripped of the designation.

"*¿Hace mucho calor, no?*" he asked as Paz set down his toast.

With his complaint about the heat, she set to work opening the windows.

Papá sipped his coffee as I stared at his scabbed knuckles and slightly swollen right hand, remembering how he'd gripped the gun. I knew he'd killed before as sure as I knew my own name. That was no surprise. But to see it with my own eyes, and so carelessly, like plucking an orange off a tree or tossing aside a piece of junk mail. No warning or word of acknowledgment.

A breeze passed through the room, alleviating the heat. "I saw what you did," I said.

"Hmm?" He looked up at me. "What?"

"Last night, at the party. I was there."

He stared at me a moment, then stood and carried his silverware and plate of eggs across the kitchen. He threw them in the sink with a clatter. "Goddamn it, Natalia."

"Why?" I asked.

He turned to the maid as she tried to salvage the cracked dish. "*Gracias*, Paz."

She hurried from the room.

When it came to me, my father's bark was much worse than his bite. I stood my ground. "How could you let that monster back into our lives?" I asked.

"I was going to talk to you today. I didn't want you to find out that way," he said. I knew his scolding frown all too well. "I told you not to go to the party. You defied me."

"If I hadn't, I'd be reading lies for headlines." I picked up his picture with Cristiano and thrust it toward him. "My father, shaking hands with my mother's murderer? How were you going to explain this?"

"With the truth." He came back for his coffee, took the paper from me, and looked at the photo. "Cristiano is innocent."

"It's impossible." My voice broke, but I did my best to swallow down my grief. If I got emotional, his instinct to protect me would prevent him from sharing anything beyond the fundamentals. "Cristiano killed her, stole from us, and left me in a tunnel to rot."

"I should belt you for doubting me. My father would've," he said without any conviction. From my grandfather, that threat would've scared me. He'd had a temper. My dad wasn't like that, though.

"Is he blackmailing you?" I asked.

He put down the newspaper and slid his toast toward him. "No—"

"Papá." I pleaded with him. "Tell me the truth. What does Cristiano have on you?"

"Nothing." Leaning one hand on the counter, he took a bite, then tossed the remaining bread back on the plate as if he couldn't stomach it. "And spreading a rumor like that makes me vulnerable, so watch your mouth."

"What is it then?" I asked, undeterred.

He sighed into his coffee. "If you'd let me get a word in, I'd tell you. You're like your mother, storming in here yelling at me for things I didn't do."

"You shot a man in the head," I cried. "I saw it."

Even as his color drained, he straightened up. "Cristiano has proven his loyalty, Talia. For the last decade, he's done more than built himself a strong, successful cartel—"

"How can you say that?" I fell onto a breakfast stool. "I've heard the kind of 'business' he runs, and it's vile."

"His business isn't anything you should worry about. All you need to know is what Cristiano has done for your mother. For *us*." Birds chirped outside, and a sparrow landed on the sill. Papá shooed it away. "When Cristiano left here," he continued, "he ruthlessly and relentlessly hunted your mother's murderer. He made it his mission to find the motherfucker who entered my house—my *bedroom* —and took almost everything from me. I've had dark moments since learning this. I question Our Lady of Guadalupe for letting this stranger into my home, but I thank her you didn't come into the room any earlier."

With my elbows on the counter, I put my head in my hands. I didn't know what to think. "Who—"

"Let me finish. Cristiano delivered the *sicario*, forced him to his knees, and made him beg me for his life. It took a lot of time and resources to find that man you saw up there. Shooting him in the head in front of everyone was probably the kindest way to kill him."

If Father believed that, I didn't doubt a lack of mercy had been shown behind the curtains. It explained his battered hand this morning—and the man's swollen face and blood-soaked clothing. "And you believe it?" I asked.

"I heard it from the rat's mouth."

"Of course the hitman would say anything Cristiano told him to if he thought it might save his life." I nervously *pinged* the tab of my soda can. "Cristiano wants to clear his name and stop running."

"He doesn't need to be protected from me. He's built himself a cartel that surpasses my own. He has his own success, money, and status now. His network spans the world, and he could've built his business in Colombia, Russia, Bolivia—anywhere. But he returned."

He could've been anywhere, but he was here, turning my world upside down. I gritted my teeth, wishing he'd stayed lost. "Why?"

"Because this is his home. There's greater risk for Cristiano to return than to stay hidden. *Dios mío, me duele la cabeza.*" As he grumbled of a headache, he went to the fridge and removed leftover tostadas and a small *talavera* bowl of salsa. "If I hadn't believed Cristiano about the *sicario*, I wouldn't have hesitated to execute him on the spot. I almost did."

"Why even stop to let him explain?" I asked. "And what lies could he have possibly given to change your mind?"

"Cristiano managed to track down some of your mother's stolen jewelry. Each piece told its own story, and each ending eventually led him one place—to this *sicario*."

"It was jewelry *Cristiano* took," I said, not bothering to keep my cynicism from my voice. "He didn't need to look further than himself."

"If he'd taken the jewels, he would've sold them to survive, wouldn't he?"

"Yes," I agreed. "No question he did."

"And then tracked all of it down again?" Papá shook his head as he stuffed his face with chicken and refried beans. "They were one-of-a-kind pieces," he said as he chewed and swallowed. "The diamonds, rubies, and other precious gems Cristiano returned to me have unique settings I designed for your mother myself. He wouldn't have kept them when he had nothing and could sell them." He wiped his mouth with a paper towel. "The hitman was hired, Natalia. Someone wanted my wife dead."

Hearing it in such certain terms, I touched the base of my neck. At the time, Costa Cruz had been a feared drug lord. It would've been no small thing to hire a hit on a family like ours. I only knew of one other cartel who'd tried that, and the de la Rosas no longer existed, considering the leaders were dead. There was something as sinister about that as there was Cristiano killing the woman who'd acted as a second mother to him. "Hired by who?"

He massaged his temples with one hand. "A rival cartel, apparently."

"But why? Who? And how did the man get in? How would he have disabled the—"

"Slow down, Tali." He shut his eyes and took a breath. "Your old man can't drink like he used to. I have a hell of a hangover."

I went to a junk drawer, found painkillers, and tossed him the bottle. "Which cartel?"

"They're no longer in existence." He fiddled with the childproof cap until it popped open. "I'd deal with them if I could, but they've disbanded already."

"How convenient you can't confirm Cristiano's story." I got him a water bottle from the fridge. "It could be an elaborate scheme."

"To what end?" He shook some pills into his palm and tossed them back. I placed the water in front of him, but he washed down the drugs with a gulp of coffee. "I know you were young and may have forgotten," he said, "but your mother trusted Cristiano above anyone except me, and he cared for her. You too."

I hadn't forgotten. Cristiano had been her protector, but that didn't mean her instincts couldn't have been wrong about him. "He knew how much you loved her, and he wanted revenge for what you did to his parents."

"It wasn't revenge. Take my word for it." He replaced the cap on the pill bottle and looked at it pensively, as if lost in a thought. "It was a confusing time. I fell prey to my rage," he said finally. "I needed someone to blame, and Cristiano had fled, so it was easy to convince myself he'd run out of guilt. There was no other possibility, no evidence but what I had in front of me, and what you and Diego saw. But looking back, deep down, I questioned how it was possible he'd done what he'd been accused of. To assault Bianca and steal from us—it was out of character for him."

"But he did that for a living—he was a *hitman*."

"For us. Not against us. Never did he so much as raise his voice toward either me or her."

My throat thickened. Why couldn't he recognize that his devotion to Cristiano might be misguided? I could admit there was a *sliver* of possibility another explanation existed for that day—but to blindly trust him after all this time? "I know what I saw. I know what felt. I see it in my nightmares, Papá—*please.*"

"I'm sorry, *mija.*" He reached out for my hand and squeezed it. "It must be hard to see him again, and maybe I should've warned you, but I was trying to—"

"Protect me, I know." I took back my hand and covered my face. "He put a *gun* under my chin. He *shot* Diego. He left me in a *tunnel.*"

"He knew I would find you," Dad said. "He was desperate. He understood I would've had no choice but to kill him with the evidence I had at the time."

"I don't know if I can believe any of it," I said, my throat thick as I tried to control my emotions. "I don't trust him."

"You don't have to. You just have to trust me." He returned to the sink for the clay pot and refilled his drink. "I'm sorry for what you saw last night," he said with his back to me. "If I'd known you were watching . . ."

"You wouldn't have done it?"

He turned his head over his shoulder, giving me his profile. "I would've had you removed from the party."

I swallowed. He didn't regret it.

A question I'd been fighting since the night before struggled to surface. If *I'd* believed that was the man who'd brutally attacked and killed my mother, would I have been as horrified?

If it'd been Cristiano up there with his hands tied and face beaten, would I have tried to stop it?

Or would I have reveled in his murder?

"You were there with Diego last night?" he asked.

Papá had heard my questions—now I'd have to answer some of his. I'd implicated both Diego and myself. "Yes."

He dumped sugar into his coffee. "I'll have to have a little chat with him then," he muttered.

"Have the chat with me," I said. "I want to talk to you about Diego anyway."

"Don't bother." His spoon *clinked* the sides of the mug as he stirred. "My answer is no."

"*Papi, por favor—escúchame.* You can't tell me what to do anymore. You have to listen."

"*Bueno.* Go ahead," he said, with an inviting gesture. "But it will fall on deaf ears."

"I love him." He froze, his mug halfway to his mouth. "Don't look so surprised," I said. "You know I do."

He lowered his drink, staring at me. "I know you *think* you do."

"Why do you doubt it?" I asked. "Diego has been there for me practically since I was born. He takes care of me. He treats this family and me with respect. He *loves* me."

"He is dangerous, Tali. Everyone here is. I wouldn't let you date the fucking chief of police."

I looked out the window. Two sparrows played in the

terra-cotta birdbath Mom had hand-painted brown and green to look like a tree. Though the landscapers maintained it along with her garden, much of the paint had chipped off. "He's not like the others," I said, turning back. "Diego is sensitive. Sweet. Creative."

My dad seemed to think a moment before he burst into laughter. "My sweet girl. You're smart like your mother. She could teach me about everything from Shakespeare to how to have patience. She'd philosophize on the nuances of morality and ethics, then help me devise the best plan of attack against those who'd wronged me. She'd explain expressionism versus impressionism in a way that made me care."

I had not fully gotten to know that side of my mother. By age nine, I was only beginning to learn the many facets of her personality. But I still understood her innate warmth and intelligence exceeded that of most people. "Do you still think of her every day?"

"What a question, Tali. Of course I do. The day I don't is the day I never think again. But her heart was too pure," he continued. "She could never pull one over on me. When it comes to character, that's where *I'm* smart."

"What are you saying?" I asked, nesting my hands together in my lap. "You doubt Diego's character?"

"No—he has been a good addition to the cartel, and faithful to me. But I wouldn't call him 'sensitive' or unlike the rest of us. He is very much an active part of this world."

"Then why would he want to leave it?" I asked.

My father drew back, looking amused as he dipped crust from his toast into the salsa. "Does he?"

"That's what I want to talk to you about." I wrung my fingers. "Diego's and my plans."

"Your plans." He sighed, reclining a hip against one counter. "Which are . . . ?"

I stilled my hands. This was why I was here. Asking my father to accept us might not be an easy conversation, but it was a necessary one. The thought of leaving here knowing Diego would follow gave me strength. I steeled myself with a breath. "I want you to let Diego leave the cartel so he can come to California and be with me," I said. "I—*we*—want to start a new life there. Together."

He took the sip of coffee I'd kept him from and said simply, "It can't be, Natalia."

Expecting he'd say that, frustration rose in me quickly. I set my jaw. "You're not even listening. He's only dangerous *here*. With *you*. Once he's away from all of this, he'll be free to start over. To reach his full potential."

"As what?" He set down his mug and rapped his knuckles on the counter as he intoned, "This is in his *blood*, Tali—it will follow him wherever he goes. He can run away from México, but not from this life."

"Then maybe it's better to have him by my side," I argued. "Diego is a natural protector. He confronted Cristiano when he could've run away. He knows how a criminal thinks and won't let anything happen to me."

He chuckled. "I'm impressed with your efforts. That debate class has paid off. But my answer is no."

My head began to throb. I slid out my ponytail holder and scrubbed my hand through my hair. "I know Diego is an important part of your business, but he isn't happy—"

"Maybe that's what he tells you, but it isn't so," Dad said, crossing his arms. "There's no escaping this life for me or him. What would he do in California? Bag groceries? That's all he's qualified for."

I frowned, stung and perplexed that he was around Diego nearly daily and somehow didn't see what I did.

"He's smart and resourceful," I reasoned. "He can do anything."

"That means nothing to a man like him. We're cut from the same cloth. Here, he's respected—a businessman, a top advisor. In the U.S., he'll be powerless. He will be nothing."

"He'll be with *me*," I said, rising from the stool. "That's all we care about."

"Diego will never have a normal life. And I know him better than you—he doesn't *want* one."

"He does," I shot back. It earned me a look that made me lower my voice. "You're wrong. He's not made for this world. You're the only thing keeping him here."

Again, he laughed, and it echoed flatly off the tile floors. "You couldn't be more wrong," my father said. "Diego's in too deep. People's fortunes, futures, and *lives* are in his hands. Once a man gets a taste of that kind of power, he can never walk away from it. Not even for a woman."

"But—"

"Enough." He pressed his mouth into a firm line. "Your safety is my number one priority, and Diego can't offer you that. A peaceful, simple life would be death for him." He turned to dump the rest of his toast into the sink. "Go back to school," he grumbled. "Meet someone who can offer you more. Someone worthy."

"He is."

He turned abruptly. "Diego has been an asset to me in many ways," he said evenly. "He's shrewd, and a better businessman than most—even without an education. He's good, but for you, good isn't enough. I want someone great." He paused as he balled and flexed both hands. "These things are not to be taken lightly, Natalia. I loved your mother very much. There is no higher honor in my life than to be called her husband and your father."

"Then you're taking that honor from Diego."

He finished off his coffee and placed it in the sink too. "You will thank me one day."

My face heated. Did he think he was *God*? That he could control love? That he had any right to decide who was great and who wasn't? "I'm sorry you don't see the truth about us," I said, "but you can't stop me from loving him. I'm going to marry him someday, with or without your blessing."

He leveled me with a glare. "No."

"*No*?"

"Marriage is sacred. You will do it once, and only once," he said, raising his voice. "You're too young to know how you feel about him."

"You were twenty when you married Mami," I accused. "She was even younger."

"What your mother and I had was one-of-a-kind. Special. By comparing it to you and Diego, you make a mockery of my marriage."

As he spoke, frustrated tears heated the backs of my eyes. I lowered my gaze to hide them from him. What else could I say to convince him Diego and I had something real? Papá was leaving me no option but to find a way to *show* him.

"When you talk about building a life with someone," he said, "it should only be with the person you're going to die next to."

Shiny black and orange specks blurred on my arm. I fruitlessly tried to pick off the glitter. "Diego *is* that person."

"I don't want you around him anymore. He's already let things get too far with you. You're on the verge of getting your heart broken, and if that happens, I'll have to kill him. Do you want me to kill him?"

I choked back a sob. It was an empty threat, I knew. But for him to react so vehemently was like a slap in the face. I had no misconceptions that he'd disapprove, but he didn't *actually* think he could forbid me from Diego—did he? "He's my best friend," I said. "I don't want to stay away."

Papá sighed, then came around the counter and pulled me into his arms. I fought him at first, but his comfort was exactly what I needed just then—even if he was the cause of my distress. "I'm sorry." He kissed the top of my head. "But nobody risks their life for puppy love."

"Mami did. She cut off her family knowing the danger it would put them in to be associated with the cartel, and she traded small town security for—for *you*."

"And look what it got her, eh? Is that the fate you want?" He took my shoulders and peeled me off. "You have much to learn yet about manipulation, Talia. It won't work on me. I'm your father."

"Please," I begged as he stomped away in the direction of his study.

He turned back. "Diego is this life no matter where he lays his head at night. You might think it's romantic what your mother did for me, but let me tell you—the pain of losing her plagues me every day. You might think you'd die for him, but I won't permit it."

"It doesn't matter what you want," I said. "At the end of the day, we're adults. And you can't keep us apart."

On his way out of the kitchen, he snorted. "Watch me."

My father's blessing meant as much to me as his opinion. He was *the* rock in my life. The one who'd done everything in his power to protect me, and not just physically.

After Mamá's death, I could sense how badly he'd wanted to shut down, but he'd pushed through as a newly single parent—for me.

But Diego had been there too. He'd proven his love through a lifetime of standing by me. I had to believe with all of my heart our love was enough for him—even if my father didn't.

8

NATALIA

It was a good thing Diego had described his home to me in such detail—it made it easier to find and show up uninvited. A large concrete wall enclosed the property, but the custom look of the wood-and-steel gate and the natural stone driveway gave away Diego's eye for detail.

I rang the buzzer at the end of the drive. Diego had told me not to come, but if I didn't take things into my own hands, I'd never get time alone with him. On top of his work obligations, now I couldn't even spend time with him at home, where Papá might see.

After a few moments, movement in the top right corner of the wall caught my attention. I waved into a security camera. With some yelling inside the house, I heard a door open on the other side of the gate.

"*Por Dios*, Natalia Lourdes," Diego called to me. The gate rumbled as it slid open. He stepped out with a scowl —slightly disheveled and totally sexy in a cream-colored Henley and camouflage cargos. He glanced both ways, pulled me inside, and typed a code on the keypad inside the wall. The gate stalled, then creaked as it reversed closed. "What the hell are you doing here?" he asked.

His exasperation was nothing after what I'd endured from my father the day before. I crossed my arms. "We have to talk, Diego."

Where our compound was a more traditional Spanish-style hacienda, Diego's was sleek and modern. The single-story house was a third the size of Papá's—not even counting our hundreds of hectares of land—but still a mansion for these parts with stacked stone columns, a flaw-lessly smooth, white exterior, and manicured bushes around the yard. He led me up the walkway to the front door. Floor-to-ceiling glass windows showcased a cloud-like, puffy leather couch, flat-screen TV, and brass-and-mirrored coffee table atop a neutral geometric-patterned rug—plus the armed men who guarded all of it.

"You can't just show up, *mi amor*," Diego said, opening the door. "That's one way to get a bullet in your head."

"I tried texting, calling, e-mailing—everything," I said. "I miss you, and I'm tired of sitting around watching the clock tick down."

"I know. I had to get rid of my last burner." He shut the door behind us and dismissed a guard from the entry-way. "I've been trying to make it to the house to see you. Because *obviously*, I miss you too—but it's no excuse for putting yourself in danger."

He was right. I was being stupid for love like my mother. Knowing I'd anger my father wasn't enough to keep me away, though. He wanted to separate us, but that didn't mean he got to. Nobody was immune to love or resistant to the blindness it could cause. I shrugged helplessly. "I'm in love's grip."

Finally, he opened his arms, and I walked into his embrace. "I'm in *your* grip," he said, smoothing his hands down my backside. "I like this summery dress. Where are you supposed to be?"

"Shopping with Pilar."

"And how did you get here?"

"A cab. Security will be looking for me."

"*Ay*, Tali. If you don't get me killed, you'll give me a heart attack. I know Pilar is your best friend, but she's weak. She will give you up."

"She won't," I said. "She's easily spooked, but loyal as they come."

I needed to let her know I'd made it safely. We'd spent the morning in town, browsing the shops before an early lunch. We'd attended a service at the church—a gothic-style structure modeled after Spanish cathedrals with Oaxacan *cantera verde* stone and a domed bell tower. Saints looked over the altar from panels of floor-to-ceiling stained-glass windows, centered by a Virgin Mary. It was one of the only places that reminded me of my mother without inflicting pain.

There were *some* things I missed about Mexico. Grand parades and festivals that shut down the town. Unbreakable loyalty that put family above all else. Goods made by hand with love and attention to detail I could never seem to find in the States.

And Diego, of course.

I craned my neck to look around the place where Diego both lived and conducted business. I hadn't been anywhere the cartel operated aside from home and had only seen photographs and heard descriptions of safe houses, warehouses, and labs. "Can I have a tour?"

"You shouldn't be here," he said. "Someone could tell Costa."

"So send them away. You're the boss, aren't you?"

He shook his head slowly. "I can't. There's too much work to be done."

I played with the placket of buttons at his collar. The ribbed style of shirt only seemed to highlight his tanned neck and muscular pecs. "I've been worried."

"I know, but this is different than sneaking around your own property in a flimsy costume."

My mouth dropped open. "It wasn't *flimsy*. Tepic didn't even recognize me."

He reproached me with a frown not unlike the one Papá had worn at breakfast the day before. "Ditching your security detail leaves you defenseless against anyone who might be looking for vulnerabilities in the Cruz family."

I blinked up at him. "*You* said we no longer have enemies. Most of our rivals were incarcerated, overthrown, or died, and we never made new ones because we're no longer competitors."

"Don't question that the Maldonados—or other cartels we do business with—know who you are. Our enemies won't come looking for weak spots or collateral *after* a fuck-up—they already know who and where to strike to deliver the most pain." He glanced through the entryway windows. "We especially have to be careful now that my brother's back in town."

"What happened when you and Cristiano met with my father during the party?"

Diego inhaled deeply. "How about that tour?" he teased.

I smiled. Because I was also curious about the house, I let him change the subject—for now. He walked me through the living area to a state-of-the-art kitchen with glossy, handleless cabinets and a black-quartz island square under a rack of hanging copper pots and pans.

He pulsed his eyebrows at me. "Want to see the bedroom?"

"I thought you'd never ask."

We linked hands, and he led me down a long hall to the master, a large but mostly bare room with a dresser under a TV, a walk-in closet, and two bedside tables. Dove-gray sheets rumpled his king bed. "Well, now I know—you sleep on the left side," I said and grinned. "I sleep on the right."

"Match made in heaven," he said. "If I'd known you were coming, I would've made the bed. Nobody ever comes in here but the maid, and I gave her two weeks off for Easter."

"I don't care," I said, looking over my shoulder at him as I walked farther into the room. "I like tidying. I'll make the bed when we live together."

"When we live together, there'll be no point in ever making the bed."

My cheeks heated at the fantasy of waking up next to Diego each morning, lounging, laughing, and making love until we were forced to get up. "I can't wait," I murmured, stopping at the nightstand on the left side. It had only a phone charger, two business textbooks, and a picture frame. I picked up a photo of Diego and me smiling at my parents' pool. "I remember this day," I said. "It was the first time I'd ever worn a bikini."

"I remember it too, believe me. The bikini best of all."

I half-gaped at my white bathing suit, grateful it at least wasn't sheer. Diego hadn't yet grown into his broad shoulders, and his chest was smooth, not muscular like now. "How old were we here?"

"You were fourteen," he said.

"Which would've made you . . . a cradle robber."

He laughed. "You know it wasn't like that. You were

like a younger sister to me. I remember that bikini because I almost punched my friend in the face for staring at you in it."

I glanced back. "You never told me that."

He stuck his hands in his pockets and shrugged. "And I never told you that when you came home from school two years later, every *puto* within a kilometer radius was talking about the beauty you'd become."

I wrinkled my nose. "You're exaggerating."

"I wish I were. I'd hear them talking about you. '*Qué linda, Natalia Cruz,*'" he mimicked. "That was when I knew."

I bit my bottom lip. "Knew what?"

"I felt more than just protective," he said. "I was jealous."

At times it felt as if Diego and I had talked about everything under the sun. That didn't mean I didn't love hearing all of his thoughts when it came to him and me. "But no other boys ever even *looked* at me," I said.

"I made sure of it."

A pleasant warmth crept over me. With his golden-brown hair in disarray and amusement dancing in his gemstone-green eyes, it was sometimes hard to reconcile the boy he'd been with the man he was now. He'd always been older to me—I'd turned sixteen only four years ago, when he was twenty-three. But he seemed much more comfortable in his skin now at twenty-seven.

"I remember being sixteen and already *crazy* over you, but I thought you'd always see me as a little girl."

"I did," he said. "Until I didn't."

"I'll never forget when you finally began to notice me," I said. "I used to sit on the sidelines and watch you and the guys play outdoor basketball. Then one day, I showed up, and you walked off the court to come talk to me. You'd never done that before."

"The guys teased me for it," he said. "I didn't care. It meant they knew you were mine."

"I never noticed anyone else," I said, glancing back at the picture. "But you know that. When we took this, you were both a best friend and like a brother to me—I didn't really know what was happening, but I was falling in love."

"Then why'd you leave me?"

I set down the photo and perched on the bed to face him. "The same reasons I always get back on the plane. I don't want to end up like my mother. And I don't want to lose anyone else. Papá never gave me a choice anyway. He *still* isn't giving me one."

He furrowed his brows. "Did you talk to him about us?"

"Yes. He doesn't understand that we're serious, no matter how I explain it."

Diego pursed his lips. "I warned you he wouldn't."

"But he wouldn't hear *anything*. He doesn't even want me seeing you anymore, like at all. Not even while I'm home."

He ran his hands over his face and looked to the ceiling. "Let me guess—I'm not good enough for you."

"According to him, nobody is—you know that. It's not personal." I stood and crossed the room to him, wrapping my arms around his middle. "It doesn't matter what he thinks, though."

Diego lowered just his eyes to look down his nose at me. "You know it does. He's your dad."

I shook my head hard. "Not enough to keep me away from you. I'm more worried about other things he said."

He nodded once to prompt me. "Like what?"

I rolled my lips together, trying to think of how to put it

in a way that Diego wouldn't get defensive. "Papá thinks men who've only known this life can never leave it behind. Even if they want to."

"Of course he'll say that," Diego said. "It's to plant a seed of doubt in your mind about me." He used both hands to smooth my hair back from my face. "Is it working, Tali?"

I hadn't thought of much since yesterday except the new information involving my mother's death, and what Dad had warned about Diego's entrenchment in this world. I'd fought my father on each point, but with some distance, I worried his arguments might hold some validity. "Could you be happy in Santa Clara with me?" I asked. "It's nothing like here."

"My love . . ." He held my cheeks and pressed his lips to my forehead. "Are you *seriously* asking if I can endure a life where I'm not in danger of being killed—or killing—each day . . . *and* I get to sleep by your side each night?"

I smiled a little. "It does sound ridiculous when you put it that way, but still. What would you do for work?"

"That's why this Maldonado deal means so much to me," he said. "The money I'll make off it will set us up for a long time, Tali. And if your father makes an ongoing arrangement with them, even if I get a small percent for brokering the contract—it will be enough that neither of us will even have to work again."

"But I don't want that," I said. "I want an honest job and clean money. I'm not working this hard for a business degree I'm not going to use."

"It's not about the money, Natalia. It's important to me as a man that I provide for you. That means gifting you the freedom to follow your dreams, whatever they are, free of any financial burden."

"And what about your dreams?"

"I'm afraid to have any until I know I can." He smiled sadly and hugged me to him. "Once I pull this off, I can do anything. Including marry you. I want your father's approval, believe me—it would mean everything to have him see me as a suitable son-in-law. But at the end of the day, once I can support us no matter what, Costa doesn't *have* to agree."

I shook my head. "I could never abandon him," I said.

"Then we'll stay in California or wherever you want, but we're old enough to decide for ourselves. He'll have to learn to accept our plans if he wants you in his life." He smiled. "Because I'm not going anywhere. You will be my wife."

Excitement tickled my tummy the way a sip of champagne fizzed in my mouth. The idea of walking down the aisle to him made me giddy.

"Let's finish this talk over food. I'm starving." He pulled me by my hand. "Did you eat?"

"I had lunch with Pilar," I said as we walked back through the house. When I noticed Diego humming Led Zeppelin, I gave him a quizzical look.

"I've had it stuck in my head since this morning," he said. "There's this new drug in development, and it's called *Escalera al Cielo.*"

"Stairway to Heaven," I translated.

"*Sí.*" In the kitchen, he disappeared into the pantry. "You remember that guy Juan Pablo Perez?"

"The really good chemist from Nogales?" I asked as I sat at the dining table.

"He's more than really good. He's one of the top scientists in the country now. Probably the world." He returned and handed me a Coke Light. "Tepic told me yesterday he invented a sedative with tetro-something. It's a neurotoxin that comes from . . . *¿cómo se dice? Botete?* What's the word in English?"

"Puffer fish," I said and tabbed open my soda.

"*Sí.* Anyway, it's poisonous to ingest, but Tepic says in the right dosage, it's not fatal."

I sipped my cola. "Why would anyone want to take that?"

"Because, as Tepic put it," Diego said, gesticulating with flourish to imitate Tepic, "it's supposed to be a high more *addicting* than coke. More *life-altering* than ayahuasca. More *euphoric* than ecstasy."

I giggled, raising my soda can. "But is it more satisfying than Coca-Cola?"

"Apparently."

"But why the name?"

"Juan Pablo says it's a round-trip ticket to heaven." Diego came and hugged my neck from behind. "It's peaceful. Euphoric. It starts with tingling in the lips . . ." He kissed the corner of my mouth, then brushed his lips over my neck. "Then moves down to your fingers and arms. It puts you in a trance, and . . ." He tapped me once between the breasts with his fingertip. "Slows your heart . . ." He waited several seconds, then tapped again. "Like that."

I put my hands on his forearms, keeping him close. "That sounds dangerous."

"That's the price for a high like no other." He kissed my cheek and returned to looking in the fridge.

"And with the wrong dose?" I asked.

"What?"

"You said with the *right* dose, it's not fatal. What happens if Juan Pablo gets it wrong?"

Diego leaned out from behind the refrigerator door and cut his finger across his neck. "*Te mueres.*"

"Death. It's literal then—a stairway to heaven."

"He wouldn't put it on the market until it was safe, but I'll be honest. *I'm* not about to risk it." He shut the fridge door and grabbed a mango from a fruit basket. "We don't have shit to eat."

I toed off my flats and pulled my foot onto the chair to hug my knee. I fixed the skirt of my dress even though I wore boy shorts underneath. "Are you going to tell me about the meeting you and Cristiano had with my dad? I talked to him the next morning."

Diego picked up a small knife from a drying rack on the counter. "How much did he reveal?"

"Everything, I hope." If there was more to the story my father had shared, then Papá probably didn't know it. I picked invisible lint off my dress. "He said Cristiano found and returned jewelry that the hitman had sold. And that the *sicario* admitted to being hired by another cartel."

Diego rested his hip against the counter. "That's what he told me too."

"Do you believe it?"

"I . . . I'm skeptical. I'm not sure how—" He blinked at me and shook his head. "I don't know why I'm making excuses. No—I don't buy the story. I don't trust Cristiano, but I've never known Costa to be gullible."

"Exactly," I said. "My father *isn't* gullible. He's trusting his instinct with the evidence he has."

"Something he's known for," Diego pointed out. "Strong intuition. But I'm afraid he's too close to this."

Like my mother had been? She'd trusted her life in Cristiano's hands and had lost it.

"You heard what Costa said at the party—the prodigal son returns." Diego balanced the mango on a plate and sliced a clean curve along the skin. "I think it's obvious he has never been a good judge of Cristiano's character."

"What if Cristiano's telling the truth, though?" I asked.

"Why would he come back knowing my father's been hunting him?"

"It's been years. Maybe he thought the old man had softened."

"Papá made it sound as if it took Cristiano that long to track down the jewelry and the hitman." If that was true, I could see why my father had said Cristiano had proven his loyalty. But I'd spent so long hating him, acknowledging anything positive about him felt foreign. And disloyal to my mom.

Diego's knife slipped, and I jumped as it slammed the plate. He glanced at the table, barely noticing, as if lost in a thought. "Whatever Cristiano's reason for returning," he said, "it must be worth risking his life."

"But if the Calaveras are as successful as you say, what could he want from us?"

Diego resumed skinning the fruit. After a few moments, he responded quietly. "Once a man gets a taste of power, his need for it surpasses hunger. It's a sickness that demands more."

Papá had said something similar about Diego. Because he was *somebody* in this life, he couldn't ever be *nobody*. "What's the *more* that he wants?"

He twisted his lips. "He was Costa's star quarterback, as the *gringos* say. Cristiano never failed at any task. Other cartels tried to lure him away, but he stayed true. He was the only one who could talk back to your father and not get punished for it." Diego gently separated the mango's skin, but his knuckles whitened around the knife handle. "Maybe Cristiano thought he'd one day partner with Costa—or even take over the cartel."

Picturing Cristiano at the helm wasn't that hard to do. He'd worked side by side often with my father and had sat with us at the family dinner table far more than anyone else in Papá's business. "If that's true," I said, "then Cristiano probably felt he lost all that when he had to flee."

Diego nodded. "And now he wants it back."

Even if Cristiano hadn't killed my mother, he'd been blamed for it. What did an accusation like that do to a person? He'd had eleven years to nurse his grudge. I'd never forgotten what he'd said to me before we'd descended into the tunnel: *"Look what loyalty got me."* Those weren't the words of someone who wanted to be accepted home. They were those of a man who felt he'd been wronged.

Certainly Cristiano's definition of loyalty had changed that day.

And that made him dangerous.

Diego raised his voice as he ran the garbage disposal. "Do you know the real reason for the nickname *El Polvo*?"

The Dust. That was what some had called Cristiano when he'd worked for my father. "Because he arrives on a cloud of dust, delivering death before the dirt clears."

"That's what people say, but no." He flipped off the disposal and washed his hands. "It's actually because of how he executed his first kill."

"How?" I asked.

"It's gruesome." He dried his hands on a dishtowel. "On second thought, maybe I shouldn't say."

At this point, I was in too deep not to ask. My curiosity was being stoked at every turn and fighting it just made my imagination run wild. "Tell me," I said.

"He got a bucket of sand from the desert," Diego said, rubbing his palms together. "Then tied up a man twice his age and poured it down his throat until he choked to death."

I gripped my neck, suddenly unable to breathe. "No."

Diego nodded. "I've seen him do it. No screaming that

way. No blood. No marks. And the bonus of a slow death .
. ."

My nostrils flared as I inhaled. I felt that sand in my
throat, strangling me. Death by torture—that was worse
than death itself.

"After the party, I started looking into the Calaveras
more. I've heard all kinds of inhumane things." Diego
brought the plate of fruit to the table, removed his shoes,
and sat across from me. "Apparently they have a soundproof dungeon where they keep one body part from each
person who has betrayed them."

I stopped the question on my tongue—why. *Why* was a
dangerous word. I didn't want to know. Dungeons and
soundproof rooms and body parts could only mean bad
things. Despicable, torturous things. But what was worse—
to know the truth, or let ignorance leave me vulnerable?
Where Cristiano was concerned, I never wanted to be in
the dark again.

"What else have you learned?" I asked. "And don't tell
me not to ask. I can handle it."

He shifted in his seat. "The worst, I guess, is abducting
children to do his bidding."

As horrifying as that was, my father had taken in Diego
and Cristiano for similar reasons. They had food and a
place to sleep at night, but also an obligation to the cartel
that they could never escape. "Is that different than what
you guys do?" I asked.

"The kids in our cartel are like family. Your father
never treated us like slaves. I'm talking bigger stuff. The
Calaveras have gone as far as to purchase an entire shipment of children for labor."

I recoiled, clamping a hand over my mouth. What even
was a shipment of children? And how did someone *purchase*
one? Bile rose up my throat, and I pushed the mango slices

away. "What . . . but how? How can he get away with that?"

Diego ran his sock along my inner calf. It was a small gesture, but still comforting. He lowered his voice, leaning in although we were alone. "Cristiano is powerful. He has even the most pious of government officials in his pocket and within Badlands' walls are all kinds of businesses, big and small. From *supermercados* and hardware stores to drone security centers and freight shipping offices."

"But shipping is your business," I said. "Isn't that stepping on your toes?"

"We own ports and plazas and have arrangements all the way from individual fishermen to fleet management companies, which reduces our risk." He ate a piece of fruit. "Cristiano invests but also has solutions in-house—"

"*Con permiso, señor.*" A boy who couldn't have been more than sixteen stood in the doorway. "*Hay un problema.*"

Diego nodded as he wiped his fingers on his pants. "Speak."

"Tepic is trying to reach you. It's, ah . . ." He glanced at me with anxious eyes. "*Es importante.*"

Diego stood and kissed the top of my head. "I'll be right back," he said, taking out his phone. "Feel free to snoop around the kitchen—unless it's not as much fun when you have permission?"

I stuck my tongue out at him as he left, then texted with Pilar to update her.

By the time Diego returned, I'd finished all the mango. "Sorry," I said as he stayed in the doorway, typing something into his phone. "I guess I was hungry after all. Want me to cut another?"

He glanced up but looked past me, staring off as if he hadn't quite registered that I was there.

"Diego?" I asked, sitting up straighter.

He blinked, and recognition crossed his face. "What?" he asked. "Did you say something?"

"What's the matter?" I got up and went to him. "What was the problem?"

He ran a hand through his hair, then looked at his cell. "Ah, it's nothing, but . . . I have to get back to work." As soon as he stuck the phone in his pocket, it started to ring, and he took it back out. "I'll have someone take you home."

"I can get a cab."

"Hmm?" He checked the screen and ran a hand over his mouth with a curse.

"You're getting pale," I said. "What'd Tepic say?"

"I have to take this, Tali. Don't get a cab." He kissed me quickly on the lips, then retreated. "Sit tight, and I'll send someone in to drive you."

"But—" He was already halfway out the door. "When will I see you next?" I called.

"Soon, *mi amor*. I'll be in touch." As he exited the room, he answered the phone with, "Jojo? There's been a theft."

Despite his unusual behavior, my shoulders relaxed with a small degree of relief. Stolen goods didn't sound like much to be concerned about when a phone call could mean anything from a kidnapping to a RICO charge to the death of a family member.

I put my shoes back on and sat to wait for a ride, feeling slightly comforted.

As far as bad news went, I would take a theft over the alternative any day.

9

DIEGO

O ur waitress looked between my brother and me in the low light of a steak restaurant, trying to decide which one she liked better. It'd been a while since we'd been sized up that way. Women had started comparing Cristiano and me once I was old enough to get female attention.

"Brothers?" she asked, placing Cristiano's mezcal on the table.

Don Costa sat back in his dining chair, reveling in the show. "What gave it away?" he asked her.

She twisted her red lips at Cristiano, her eyes glimmering. Apparently, she'd chosen him, not that I cared. With a long nose and features that didn't quite register as feminine, she was no Natalia. "The height," she answered. "Dark hair. Same smile. You look a lot alike, but there's also something very different about you."

"What do you suppose that is?" Costa asked Cristiano.

Who gave a shit? I checked my phone for news from Tepic. We'd been in constant contact with the increasingly dire events of the past couple days, but it'd been a few hours since I'd heard anything.

I prayed that was a good sign.

"One of you is lighter." The waitress returned her eyes to me as she served my tequila. "Must be the eyes."

"Or Diego's soul isn't as charred as mine," Cristiano said with a half-smirk. "Yet."

She laughed. "Enjoy. I'll be back soon to take your orders."

When she was gone, Costa looked me over. "You like her?" he asked me. "We can send a chopper back for you tomorrow if you want to stay the night in the city."

I bit my tongue to keep my temper in check. Anything to keep me from Natalia. I unfolded my napkin onto my lap. "No, thank you."

"All right then." Costa leaned his elbows on the table. All mirth drained from his features as he lowered his voice. "You have fucked us, Diego."

We'd taken a helicopter all the way here, to an exclusive restaurant that topped the city's tallest building, for him to say that. Two tables away, Mexico's attorney general dined with his wife. At the bar sat a rep for one of Bolivia's most pervasive cartels. *Comandante* Trujillo laughed with cronies across the room.

It was no accident that Costa, Cristiano, and I were showing our faces here tonight.

"Two stash houses were hit in two days," Costa said. "Millions worth of product stolen. What do you have to say, Diego?"

No excuse would do. I hadn't slept much and needed to return home to help prepare the next few deliveries, but instead, I was here, putting on a show. "It can only be explained as bad luck," I said.

My brother picked up his drink. "Two direct hits less

than forty-eight hours apart? Nothing to do with luck. You have a leak."

"Unlikely." A rat inside the walls would fall on my shoulders, and having a solid team I could trust was one of the things I prided myself on. "My men wouldn't do that."

"Until they would," Cristiano said.

I looked to my brother. Over the last decade, I'd worked side by side with Costa to strategize and build a more advanced tunnel system, to secure long-term relationships with border agents, to arrange reliable shipping via land, air, and water in all corners of the Americas, and more. Cristiano hadn't been there for any of it, so why was he here now?

"How much is gone?" Cristiano asked.

"We're still within reach of what I promised the Maldonados," I said, "but that means we have to be especially careful going forward. No hiccups at the border."

"There are always hiccups at the border," Costa said. "You know that better than anyone, Diego. When have you ever gotten every last kilo across? It can't be done."

Costa spoke with a smile for anyone who might be watching. Rumors were likely starting to circulate, and the first sign of trouble would only breed more of it. Our current clients would pull their cargo until they heard more. A broken link in our system would expose us to weakness. And most importantly—the Maldonados would start asking questions.

Questions they wouldn't like the answers to.

We were here tonight to reassure those around us that we weren't worried, and to crush any rumors that might start circulating about our business or our relationship with Cristiano.

"We have some leeway still," I said, massaging my eyes

as they burned from lack of sleep. "I just have to take extra precautions with the transport."

"That's not acceptable." Costa struggled to keep his voice level, but anyone paying close attention would see the tension in his posture. "Failure to deliver means more than retaliation. It's complete obliteration."

That wouldn't happen. If I'd thought there was a possibility of it, I never would've made the deal. I'd even accounted for bad luck. With the odds I'd calculated, doing business with the Maldonados had been a no-brainer. A little risk was good, but there was a point where it became reckless, and we hadn't reached that. I knew my business in and out.

Still, I paired a long sip of tequila with a quick prayer. "I'll handle it."

"Did you see yesterday's news?" Costa asked. "A potential witness in the latest case against Ángel Maldonado was found at the top of a pyramid."

I frowned. "A pyramid?"

"*Of human bodies*," he said. "Every member of his family from Chihuahua to Oaxaca."

There was a time when that mental image would've made my stomach churn. Now, gruesome death was sadly routine.

"This happened while the witness was under twenty-four-seven government protection," Cristiano added. "That's not the Maldonados handling a problem—it's a clear message to anyone thinking of flipping."

I wasn't flipping. I was costing the Maldonados money —equally bad if not worse.

With a vibration in my pocket, I put down my drink and read Tepic's text: *Emergencia*.

Shit. What now? Forcing my shoulders down, I excused myself and dialed Tepic as I wound through the tables toward the windowed perimeter of the dining room.

"Diego," Tepic answered breathlessly. "Have you talked to Jojo?"

"I'm still in the city with Costa." I stopped at a floor-to-ceiling glass wall overlooking the city. "What is it?"

"An explosion at the Juárez-El Paso tunnel."

I closed my eyes and clenched a fist. *What the fuck?* That tunnel had been a million-dollar construction in itself, not to mention a crucial channel into the States. "Tell me that's the only news."

"No." He hesitated. "Mike and Felipe were inside. And they didn't make it."

I looked down, massaging my temples with one hand. I was no stranger to losing people on my crew, but it never got any easier. It was personal. Mike and Felipe were more than workers—they were friends. I refrained from making the sign of the cross only so I wouldn't draw attention. "This wasn't an accident," I said.

"No, *patrón.*"

"What happened? How much did they have with them?"

After some static on the line, Tepic said, "I'm finding out the exact amount—"

"How much?" I repeated.

"Jojo says they were mid-delivery. Some made it but not all. Five, maybe six containers gone."

"*Puta madre,*" I said under my breath. "Make sure every border agent on our payroll knows we have no margins. Pay them more if you have to. And get *every* man we have guarding *every* stash house."

"Some are en route to Guadalajara to meet with Nuñez's guys."

"Bring them back. We need all hands on deck." I

glanced at the table to find Cristiano watching me as Costa picked a cigar from a box the waitress offered. "Keep me updated," I told Tepic and hung up.

The cityscape glowed against a starless night sky. I tried to figure out how to break this to Costa. This wasn't human-pyramid bad, but now we'd hit our absolute limit. That was a serious problem in itself made worse by the fact that whatever was happening, it was calculated. And it was in front of Cristiano. Or because of him?

He'd been back less than a week, and things we're starting to fall apart on the most important deal I'd ever made. Natalia had drawn the right conclusion—Cristiano had lost the only life he'd known when he'd been forced from the compound. A life he'd felt he'd deserved, even if it'd been built on betrayal. And now he was back—but *I* was the one who had Costa's trust.

Was my brother here to earn it back?

And how would he regain it?

I didn't doubt he had come home with a plan. Did the Maldonados somehow play into it?

I pocketed my phone and returned to the table. There was no use in drawing out bad news, so I resumed my seat at the table and dismissed the waitress.

"What is it?" Costa asked, puffing on his Montecristo. "I was about to order."

I placed my elbows on the table, leaning in. "A tunnel has been compromised at the border," I said.

Costa nearly choked. As he coughed, smoke billowed around him, shrouding his reddening face. As I sensed his temper mounting, I glanced around to remind him we had onlookers.

When he'd calmed, at least in appearance, he spoke. "We're under attack."

I nodded. "Yes."

Costa looked to Cristiano. "It has to be one of the Maldonado cartel's many enemies who don't like the idea of us working together. Don't they know fucking with us means severing ties to our network?"

"I can find out." Cristiano spun his glass on the table. "But right now, you need a plan."

"Damn right we do." Costa scrubbed a hand over his face and pulled at his long chin. "What are you thinking?"

Why was he looking to Cristiano for guidance? How easily they fell into old patterns. After our parents' murder, Costa Cruz had set us up at the ranch house on his compound, far enough away that gunfire wouldn't draw attention, but close enough that the main house was only a short drive. At the ranch, Cristiano had been fed choice food, armed with the finest "toys," and boarded in a private room while I'd shared everything with the others adopted by the cartel.

Costa and Bianca Cruz had favored Cristiano up until her *untimely* death. But now, I was the one who ate at Costa's dinner table many nights. I had over a decade on my brother of unwavering loyalty to Costa. Of standing by his side to build a business with limitless potential—and profits. And of being there for Natalia whenever she needed me.

Failing the Maldonados could take all of that from me. And if my instinct was right—Cristiano knew it.

"I can still salvage the shipment," I interjected. I couldn't dwell on what was gone. I needed to protect what remained. "We won't exceed the Maldonados' expectations as I'd hoped, but we'll still be within the percentage we promised."

Costa raised his cigar to a comrade across the restaurant. A signal that we had things under control.

But over the past two days, we'd lost more than just control.

"How close?" Costa asked.

"Some of the drop was made." I looked to the ceiling to subtract what we'd potentially lost and the containers that had made it. "If we move everything left, we're likely still within a percent or two of what we guaranteed the Maldonados would make it across the border."

"So you need a ninety-nine percent success rate for what's left." Costa set his jaw. "Not *one* seizure at the border. It can't be done."

"It can if I move slowly, carefully, and strategically," I said.

"You've run out of time for that," my brother said. "You're being targeted, and you need everything in the States immediately."

Cristiano had to comprehend the scope of that operation, even for a company in supply chain management. To mitigate risk, product was stored all over town, then moved in small batches across the border, mostly by individual vehicles. "I can't just send it across all at once," I said.

"And what if another stash house falls tonight? Tomorrow?" Cristiano asked. "You'd be a dead man walking. You, and everyone associated with you. Including Costa."

I pulled at my collar feeling suddenly parched. The situation was dire, yes, but Cristiano was just trying to rattle me. "That won't happen," I said after gulping some water. "I've called in all our security and alerted them to the gravity of the problem. It's all under guard."

"By men who have inside information about where everything is kept," Cristiano pointed out.

"*You* have inside information," I shot back at my brother. "And you were the last to show up around here. So how the hell do I know you're not behind this?"

"*Tranquilo*, Diego," Costa warned. "Calm down."

Cristiano took a slow sip of his mezcal, watching me over the rim. The Cristiano I'd known had never touched alcohol and wouldn't have cared enough to distinguish top-shelf tequila from sludge. Then again, I'd never seen him in a suit until his return, either, and definitely nothing near the fine, custom-made ensemble he currently wore. What was the point of a gangster like him in a bespoke suit that'd surely be ruined by the blood of his enemies? He could show off all he wanted, but while some of us did what was necessary to get by, Cristiano thrived on being a natural killer.

"I've spent the past decade trying to get back in Costa's good graces," Cristiano reasoned. "Why would I immediately turn around and jeopardize that?"

"That's what I intend to find out," I said.

The corner of Cristiano's mouth ticked. "There's no ruse. I can tell you the truth of it. It's that I've missed this —strategizing under fire. Enjoying a meal with the great minds at this table. Spending time with *mi familia*." He said *family* with an edge that Costa seemed to miss. That, or he didn't want to see it. Cristiano looked between both of us. "It has been too long."

"It has," Costa agreed.

I bit my tongue. What Cristiano missed wasn't family —he'd given that up long ago. It was the prestige and power he could gain by partnering with Costa.

Prestige and power I would earn by pulling off this deal.

"Your brother is right," Costa said. "You need to get every last kilo over the border as quickly as possible."

That was easy for Costa to say. He had nothing but constraints to contribute to the process. He was asking for complete accuracy on an impossible schedule. It wasn't as if he'd be down in the trenches with us. "Even with a full crew, I don't have the manpower," I said.

Cristiano drank some mezcal and studied his glass. "I do."

Of course he did, but I wouldn't allow him to insert himself in my deal. "I'll make it work."

"Then at least let me try to reason with the Maldonados," Cristiano said. With his elbow resting on the back of his seat and a passive expression, he could've been discussing anything from wine varietals to horse racing.

"Why would that make any difference?" I asked.

"We have history," he explained, "and they need my guns more than I need their money."

As Cristiano and I locked eyes, his plan began to take form before me. His timing *wasn't* a coincidence. Cristiano wanted in on this deal. But if I knew him, it wasn't about the money. He wanted the credit. By saving *my* Maldonado deal, *he'd* be the hero. He'd win back Costa's favor. And he'd undercut me in the process. Everything he wanted with one fell swoop.

"I can't guarantee anything," Cristiano continued, "but perhaps it'll help ease the sting if I tell them they might not get the results they were promised."

The results *I* had promised was what he meant. Results that were challenging but should've been attainable. Unless someone with a motive to bring me down had interfered.

Costa nodded along as if Cristiano spoke the word of a patron saint. "That's a generous offer, but a last resort," Costa said. "I'd rather not get the Maldonados involved until we have to. We'll take you up on help consolidating what's left, though."

"I'll make some calls," Cristiano said. "Get your most trusted men together, and I'll get mine. We can store the product in one of my warehouses. Nobody will know the location, and if they do, they wouldn't dare cross me."

Cristiano was hijacking my deal in front of my eyes. How would it look to Costa that I needed to be rescued? How would it look to *Natalia*? With a deep ache in my jaw, I unclenched my teeth. "You expect me to trust my livelihood to you and your unhinged *cabrónes*?" I asked.

"Cristiano is offering to help," Costa said. "Where is this warehouse?"

"At the border of town where the desert starts," Cristiano said and glanced at me. "Nothing to do with the Badlands if that's what you're referring to."

"Sounds like a plan," Costa said. "With both cartels working together, we can pull this off."

"With our two cartels working together," Cristiano said, returning his gaze to Costa, "we can pull *anything* off."

I narrowed my eyes on him. *Aha.* There was more to it than I'd thought. The Calaveras had their own solutions for trafficking, but if they joined forces with us, they could move double the volume *and* restrict their competitors from our services.

But that would mean a merger—one I'd be excluded from.

And not just any merger, but one between the de la Rosas and the Cruzes.

Anyone at the helm of both the Calavera and Cruz organizations would be afforded a power few others could match. Did Cristiano feel he was owed that after the decade he'd lost? Was it not enough that he'd taken our parents from me? Now he was back to take the rest? If so, his endgame was bigger than I'd guessed.

He had reason to push me out . . . but no—it was impossible for him to know that. I was nothing if not careful and always had been. Cristiano would've gone to

Costa by now, and this conversation would be happening atop a fresh grave.

"*Perdón.*" Cristiano rose from the table with his cell phone in hand. He started to turn but paused. "You may want to consider putting Natalia on a plane, don Costa. In case things get any worse."

I wondered, not for the first time, why Cristiano was concerned with Natalia at all. I hadn't missed the way he'd looked at her at the costume party, first predatorily from the balcony, then later, the way a man regards a woman who has something he likes.

I recognized his interest in Natalia because I shared it as well.

She was more than an interest to me, though. I loved her. She was my weakness.

Did we share that as well?

Did Cristiano have a tender spot for her that he might not even be aware of . . . until someone stepped on it?

As Cristiano left the table, Costa turned to me. "*Are* things going to get worse for my daughter, Diego?"

He said everything he needed to in that one question. It had nothing to do with how the Maldonados could hurt her, but how *I* could. "Natalia is my best friend," I said carefully. "I'd do anything to protect her."

"That won't be necessary. The best thing you can do is put her safety above all else and release her."

I didn't have to be explicitly told to stay away from her —that had always been implied. But it was the closest Costa had come to acknowledging my relationship with her. I wasn't going to get his blessing. Which turned the question from how to get his approval . . . to whether I needed it.

"So I ask you again," Costa said. "Are things going to get worse for Natalia?"

I shook my head, looking into my glass. "No, *señor*."

"Good. As for your brother," he said. "He wants to help."

"And you don't wonder why?" I asked.

Costa sucked his teeth, charting Cristiano from across the restaurant as he made a call on the patio. "No. Because he is grateful I have welcomed him back to his home," he said. "Finish your drink. Then go and express your gratitude for your brother's offer to help."

Cristiano wasn't here to help. He was here to hurt. Or worse . . .

No doubt he thought I'd turned my back on him eleven years ago and blamed me for everything he'd lost. It occurred to me that I hadn't even considered the worst Cristiano could do.

It was true that by saving my Maldonado deal, he'd get credit for it, win back Costa's favor, and potentially replace me. I'd assumed that was the fastest way for him to get everything he wanted.

But perhaps I'd been looking at the wrong side of the coin.

He could sabotage the deal instead.

If it failed . . . the Maldonados would see to my demise quickly and swiftly. Cristiano wouldn't even have to get his hands dirty.

And I'd be removed from the picture entirely.

Art belonged to my mother. Trying to read brushstrokes or create my own wasn't something I understood. I learned about the world from books or travel, found nature by cantering a horse, and studied history by passing on legends through *corridos*—Mexican ballads.

Art, to me, was living in the world, not observing it. Floating on my back in the ocean on a hot day, finding shapes in the clouds. My aunt's laugh when my nephew took a bite straight out of his birthday cake and came up with a face full of icing. Art lived in people.

It was the way one look from Diego could warm me to my core.

My mom's studio spanned the top floor of the house. With a glass dome in the center and large corner windows facing southwest, it had the best light.

When I was younger, I'd hide in here to see how long it would take Diego to find me. We'd dip our hands in paint and make colorful prints on the tarp Mamá had put down.

But most commonly, we'd look at the constellations with a telescope, our own private planetarium.

All the paint and easels had been removed, but the telescope sat on the deck. Tonight, I opened the doors and windows and watched the sun set while I waited for Diego.

When tires crunched dirt, I jumped up and leaned over the rail. A convoy of three cars kicked up dust as they wound up the driveway and parked out front. Cristiano and Diego got out, moving almost lethargically up the walk until my father stepped out of the house to meet them. It was strange, after all this time, to see Cristiano and Diego casually standing next to each other. I leaned out farther to try to piece together their conversation.

". . . forty-eight hours."

"No word . . . Maldonado."

"*Antes de que salgas . . .*"

Before you leave? My heart dropped at the thought of Diego disappearing again when I hadn't seen him in three days. As if sensing my anguish, he looked up, met my eyes, and winked discreetly. I watched until they moved inside. As tempted as I was to run downstairs, I waited where I was, knowing Diego would come to me.

Paciencia should've been my second name—it was all I seemed to do. Wait. Bide my time. Bite my tongue. A sitting duck, as Americans said.

I killed time by peering through the telescope, but it wasn't dark enough to see much yet. Eventually, the door to the studio opened. I sprang to my feet, hurrying across the wood floors to meet Diego. He caught me in his arms and lifted me for a kiss.

"Why have you stayed away so long?" I rushed out in a whisper, even though we were alone. "I'm set to fly home in a week."

"I'm sorry, Talia. I haven't had such a bad week in

recent history. I shouldn't be up here, but I texted because I needed to see you, even for a moment, to get me through." He set me on my feet and gripped my waist. "But if your father catches me here, he'll put you on the next flight out of México."

"He wouldn't. Easter is Sunday."

"Believe me, he would."

Papá wouldn't ruin our holiday for that reason. I touched the brown, coarse stubble on Diego's face. He stank of alcohol, sweat, and cigars, but I was comforted just to be in his presence. "Where have you been? Have you even slept?"

"No." He loosened his already sagging tie. "We went to the city for dinner last night, then flew back. Cristiano and I worked through to just now."

To hear about cartel life over the phone was one thing, but the evidence of its non-stop demands stood in front of me. I hated to think of Diego overworking himself. "You need rest. Come. Sit and tell me everything."

"I can't stay, Tali. If Costa finds me here after dark—"

"He won't." I pulled him to the deck by his hand. Even his palm seemed rougher. "He never comes up here."

"Your father's serious about keeping us apart." Diego sat in an Adirondack chair, following me with his eyes as I went to the linen closet. "It wasn't an idle threat," he said. "At dinner, Costa said he's thinking of sending you back early."

I stopped short, clutching a blanket. "But I've barely spent any time with you! I see you for a few hours, and then you disappear for a few *days*."

He stood to take the wool throw from me. "Sit down," he said.

I fell into the chair next to his. "He didn't mention anything today, and we had lunch."

"Does he ever? He keeps you in the dark to protect you. If he wants you gone, he'll put you on a plane. He wouldn't ask your permission first." He unfurled the blanket over me. "I'm starting to think Costa will never come around to the idea of us. And then what?" He swallowed as he focused on tucking me in. "Would you still want me?"

I reached up to grab his cheeks. "*Yes*," I said, forcing him to hold my gaze. "I'll never give up on us. We'll find a way."

He searched my eyes. Though his were alight, the dark circles under them betrayed his lack of sleep. What had brought on his sudden doubts, and why did my father want me gone so soon?

"I have to ask, Tali . . ." Diego went as still and quiet as the sprawling night around us. "Could you be happy without your father in your life?"

To choose between my dad and Diego? It would be impossible. "He's already lost too much," I said. "If it came down to it, he'd be forced to accept us. I don't think he'd ever make me choose."

"But if he did?" Diego pressed his lips to my forehead before pulling his chair closer to mine to sit. "I just want you to start considering that possibility."

I couldn't imagine not calling Papá whenever I had a question, missed my mom, or simply had the urge. He always spent Christmas with me at school. And just because I only visited once a year didn't mean I wanted to give up the possibility of coming home one day. Having one parent taken from me, I would never willingly give up the other. At the same time, I'd chosen to leave this life as much as I had been sent away.

But not once did I ever *choose* to be separated from Diego.

"And his approval is only half of the issue," Diego added.

Diego didn't want to be separated from me, either. It just wasn't necessarily up to him. I opened the blanket, and he pulled part of it over himself, checking to make sure I was still covered. "You mean leaving the cartel," I said.

"It's not as if I can just put in my two weeks' notice. If Costa thought I was abandoning the cartel without permission or trying to steal you away . . ."

My father raised the White Monarch, put it to the sicario's *head, and* bang!

It was an image I doubted I'd ever be able to scrub from my mind.

What would it take for him to "handle" Diego? He'd leveled a threat in the kitchen days earlier, but I hadn't taken it seriously. Diego was practically family to him.

"He wouldn't hurt you," I said. "He has to know what that would do to me." I believed that, but there was another truth I couldn't ignore. Papá hadn't gotten to where he was by letting offenses slide, no matter how sentimental he might feel.

"As long as he doesn't take us seriously, he'll go out of his way to put up a wall between us," Diego said. "He has to realize this isn't a game to us, *princesa*. That we're in this for life."

Diego spoke with such conviction that *for life* inspired a thrill in me. I was his princess, but I was also that to my father—and in his eyes, Diego was just a ward of the cartel, forbidden from entering the proverbial castle walls he guarded.

"Then we'll have to make sure my father understands that if he doesn't let you go so we can start a life together, he will lose me."

"You've told him how you feel. *I've* tried to broach the

subject, but he won't hear me. What else can we do to get him to see?"

It would have to be something that couldn't be ignored, dismissed, or stopped. I thought back to my conversation with Papá in the kitchen about loving one person and being willing to risk everything for them. About the ties my mother had cut for my father. About how marriage was sacred and should only happen once. With the person you were willing to die for.

"If we can't tell him, then we'll have to show him," I said. "Even if it means something drastic."

"Such as?"

My heart began to race. I looked out toward bruise-colored mountains as dusk swallowed the day. I was too shy to say it directly to Diego's face in case it wasn't anything close to what he was thinking. "We could always elope."

When he didn't respond, I finally chanced a look at him.

He stared at me with a tenderness that melted my insides, leaving me a puddle of need and longing. This was the art of life—the art of Diego—and what I would risk my father's wrath for. Diego possessed a potential he would never reach here. He'd supported my decision to go away knowing he'd be left behind. And he wanted the best for me, even if it meant the worst for him. *He* would never make me choose between the two of them.

"Marriage, Tali?" he asked softly, almost reverently.

"It's a lot, I know—"

"It's everything." He took my hand under the blanket. "You're the only one who believes in me enough to trust me with your love. With the *world*. I have tried and tried to show your father the man I can be. I have no one else—my parents gone and a brother I no longer recognize. You and

Costa are my family, but he continues to deny me. And you have never once failed to accept me."

Moved by his openness, my throat thickened. "He won't be able to deny you once he sees how devoted we are."

Diego slid his hand up my arm and massaged my shoulder. "I don't understand how Costa freely respects Cristiano but continues to hold me at arm's length. Last night, we were three grown men drinking and talking business, and yet, it's like I was a teenager at the ranch again."

I hated that Diego had grown up feeling second best to Cristiano, who'd been treated like a prodigy just because of his size and capacity for brutality. "There's no way my father can just switch his trust for Cristiano back on."

"It feels that way—like I'm being replaced."

"Never, *mi amor.*" I stretched over the arm of the chair to kiss him for all the times we'd had this conversation and I hadn't been able to physically comfort him. "I'll show you so much love and respect that you won't need it from anyone else."

He held the back of my head for another peck. "We will be married," he said, "but I can already declare that I intend to love you until death do us part."

And death would *do us part.*

The soothsayer's unwelcome warnings shivered through me. Damn her and her bullshit fortune. I forced her voice from my head and replaced it with a glowing vision of myself in all white, facing a suited Diego. We stood before an altar, hands intertwined as we committed our lives and love to each other. I'd dreamed of it many times at school, but for the first time, calling him my husband felt within grasp. "I wish the day were tomorrow," I said.

"Don't tempt me." He released me to recline back. "I may steal you away and officially make you mine."

"*Stealing* implies I wouldn't go willingly." Under the blanket, I folded my hands in my lap and squinted up, hoping for a shooting star. We needed all the help we could get. "I'll be on a plane soon, Diego."

He nodded slowly. "What're you suggesting?"

"I don't know. Just pointing out that we don't know when we'll be together next, so if we were going to do something drastic . . ." It would have to be now. I absent-mindedly picked at my fingernails as I thought. "If the Maldonados gave you twenty-one days, then you only have less than two weeks left until you're out of that. Then it's over, right? But I'll be gone."

He fell quiet as he stared at the night sky, but he didn't seem to be marveling over its wonders. He was working through something in his head, and the longer it took him to figure out his response, the more concerned I became. "What is it?" I asked.

"You know what this reminds me of?" he asked.

I studied his profile. "Catching insects in the rose garden?"

"I don't know why I'm still surprised when you read my mind," he said with a sad smile.

"Up here and out there were the two places you could sneak to for a little bit to keep me company."

"Your mom would always find us and send me immediately back to the ranch."

"She had to. My dad would've been upset. You were supposed to be working, and I wasn't supposed to be around you guys."

"I got to have a childhood through you, hearing about your adventures while I was off doing unimaginable shit to my own people. I never told you this because you were so young, but once, Cristiano used me as bait to kidnap a friend we grew up with."

"What?" I asked, lifting my head. "How come? What happened to him?"

"What do you think?" Diego asked. "He ended up at the bottom of a wash."

"But why?"

"Cristiano found out the kid was paying for his drugs by pimping out his underage sister. To Cristiano, that was enough reason to make our friend disappear."

Good, I thought, and immediately covered my mouth. Who was I to say who lived or died? Who was Cristiano to play God? But who was anyone to pimp out a young girl? Around here, justice wasn't always served through the channels it was supposed to be. Most of the police were corrupt, and the ones who weren't were overwhelmed by either trying to prevent or clean up near daily murders.

"I'm sorry," Diego said, removing his hand from under the blanket to take mine from my face. He intertwined our fingers. "That was too much."

"No," I said. "I just didn't realize . . . I didn't think the cartel would handle something like that. Did your friend work in the cartel?"

"No, just a customer. I mean, your dad would never stand for underage prostitution," Diego said. "He might've ordered it done or cut off his dick or something. But Cristiano didn't even go to him. He just popped the kid on his own time."

I rested my head back against the chair with a mental image I could've done without. Had Diego's friend automatically broken some imaginary law my dad held that Cristiano had enforced? Or had Cristiano done it out of compassion toward the girl? Considering the kind of cartel Cristiano ran now, I wondered if any of that benevolence remained. "Do you think the kid deserved it?" I asked.

Diego ran a hand over his stubble and scratched his chin. "Yeah, it had to be done. But I was a kid too, like thirteen or fourteen. I'd known him my whole life."

"That's messed up," I agreed, grateful my dad had moved on from that kind of business.

"You were my break from all of it." Diego kept my hand in his but put his other arm behind his head. "You'd tell me about your adventures of the day. Your mom would take you to the outdoor *mercado* and you'd sneak fruit right from the stands. You'd come home with an orange-stained tongue or dirty fingers from picking wildflowers on the way back. Bianca loved to be outdoors."

"My mom grew up helping my grandparents on their farm." It was strange to call two people I didn't know *grandparents*. They'd wanted no affiliation with anything illegal, and my mom had respected their decision in order to keep them out of danger.

Diego and I had nice memories, but the past couldn't distract me from the fact that he was clearly avoiding the subject of his very dangerous arrangement. "Is something wrong with the Maldonados?" I asked, taking my hand back. "Don't lie to me."

"I wouldn't lie. I just don't want to worry you." He removed his arm from behind his head and shifted to face me. "It's just that—I . . . it looks like someone's sabotaging the deal."

My heart dropped. After what Diego had told me about the Maldonados, even the *threat* of a problem would worry me. "Why didn't you tell me?" I asked. "And what does 'sabotaging' mean?"

"Just how it sounds. There's no reason we shouldn't have been able to deliver what I promised the Maldonados, but *a lot* of their product has been compromised. And it's no accident." He rubbed his eyebrow. "The majority hasn't even crossed the border yet, which is usually where it gets confiscated or stolen. Someone has to be messing with us, but not many would on our own turf."

"How exactly did they target you?" I asked, trying to ignore the sudden tightness in my chest.

"There were thefts at two secret locations and an explosion in one of our tunnels the *exact* time my men were passing through."

Thefts. The phone call Diego had gotten when I'd been at his house came rushing back to me. In this case, a theft wasn't better than the alternative. It could mean death.

"Your dad and I have a plan in place to make sure nothing else happens to the rest of it. That's why I was up all night. But until everything has crossed, I'm going to be on edge."

"How could you not be?" I asked. "What happens if anything else goes missing?"

"This is the most we've ever undertaken," he said. "Millions of dollars' worth of drugs. It's not like we can afford to cover it. So that means it's gone."

Gone.

I had the same shortness of breath I got whenever I thought too long about Cristiano forcing me to the brink of the tunnel. It had taken no effort on his part. Despite every ounce of fight I'd had, no matter what argument I'd put up, he'd still gotten me to the edge. And then down, down, down.

"What's the plan?" I asked. "Please tell me it involves taking out whoever's behind this."

"It would if we knew who it was. Costa and Cristiano think it's one of the Maldonados' rivals . . ."

I frowned. "But you don't agree."

He flicked his thumb and middle finger a few times, then flexed his hand. "There are pieces of the puzzle that don't make sense."

The only new variables in Papá's business were the Maldonados and Cristiano. But Cristiano was more than a puzzle piece. He *was* the puzzle. Nothing about him was clear—not his involvement in my mother's death, his unusual business practices, his patched together past, nor the men he surrounded himself with. "Cristiano is the wild card," I said.

"Exactly." Diego sat forward and looked back at me. "Jesus, Talia—I swear, you're the only person who gets it. You should be in charge around here."

I blushed. "It's not that big of a leap to make."

"You'd think."

Cristiano had once been the best man to protect us. He'd known our weaknesses. Then, possibly, he'd exploited them. Had he returned to right the wrongs he felt had been dealt him as Diego had suggested? Did Cristiano actually hope to reposition himself in our family?

A pit formed in my stomach at the thought that he had a greater plan. I didn't trust Cristiano, but I *did* trust he could accomplish anything he set his mind to. "So how does your Maldonado deal fit into his plan?"

"That's what I'm trying to figure out. My gut tells me it's some kind of power grab. Like we talked about the other day, an alliance between the Calaveras and the Cruzes would be formidable." Diego leaned his elbows on his knees and ran both hands over his hair. "My father plotted to steal your family's territory. He would've done it if Costa hadn't put a bullet in him." He glanced back at me. "History repeats itself."

"But your father's plan was to kill mine," I said. "Not unite."

Diego shrugged, but not casually. "What's to stop Cristiano from *anything* once he's gained your father's trust?" He gestured toward the darkness concealing the compound before us. "If they merge, Cristiano will replace me. And once I'm out of the picture, there's nobody in his path."

"His path to what?"

"It's a tale as old as time, Natalia. It's only a matter of time before a prince fantasizes about being king."

"He's king of his own cartel," I said.

"Cristiano's anger has been simmering for many years. Maybe he still feels like a prince who never got what he was owed. The taste of power lingers eternal on a man's tongue. Now that Cristiano has his own kingdom, I have no doubt he hungers for a second."

"Are you saying . . ." My throat went dry, and the first image that popped into my head was Cristiano and his bucket of sand. I grimaced. "Are you saying Cristiano wants to usurp my father?"

Diego balled his fists, still leaning forward in the chair. "He'd have to earn Costa's complete faith first. Then, Costa wouldn't worry about turning his back to him. And that's when Cristiano slips the knife in."

With a sharp pain in my jaw, I unclenched my teeth. Cristiano had already taken one parent from me. History would *not* repeat itself. I wouldn't let it. "We have to tell my dad," I said.

"Costa won't hear it. I've tried. Cristiano's reach is too far and too deep. He has to be cut off at the root."

"You have no time left." I knew how stubborn my dad could be, but if I caught him at the right time, maybe he'd listen. "I could talk to Papá."

"And say what? The minute you start asking questions, he'll assume I sent you, put you on a plane, and come looking for me."

I massaged my palm with my thumb as I thought. "What happens if I return to school and one day, I get a call that Cristiano succeeded in taking out everyone who means anything to me? And I'd done nothing?"

"What you did was keep yourself safe. That was the whole purpose of you going to school in the first place." Diego bit his bottom lip, looking over his shoulder at me. Anxious as I was about what he was telling me, his concern for me was kind of *sexy*. "You're out of this life, Natalia. Why dip a toe back in?"

"To help you," I said quietly.

Diego blinked at me, then reached over and tucked my hair behind my ear. "That's not your responsibility. I shouldn't even be worrying you over this—it's just that nobody else sees the truth."

"If I'd defy my own father to marry you, why wouldn't I do everything I could to save your life? Even if it meant going to Cristiano myself?"

"Going to *Cristiano*? No. I'll figure this out, Natalia," he said with conviction. "Believe me. Just the thought of building a life with you fuels me. I'd marry you tomorrow if only I could predict how this deal will end."

Cristiano had taken my fate into his hands once. He'd changed my life in moments. I wouldn't afford him that kind of power again. If he stood between Diego and me, if he deigned to think he could lay a hand on my father, then I had to do something.

I wouldn't lose anyone else I loved to him.

Ever since I'd fallen in a puddle of blood at his feet, our every interaction had been a mind game. Somehow, he'd known who I was at the costume ball and instead of keeping his distance, he'd danced with me. Toyed with me. Touched me. I couldn't deny the rush that had accompanied his hands on me. Maybe I could use that to my advantage.

He wanted to play. I could play too.

The deep distrust Diego had for his brother was most likely reciprocated. That day eleven years ago, Cristiano had denied any part in my mother's death, yet Diego had chosen truth and honor over his own blood. To many men in this world, that was an unforgiveable sin.

And if Cristiano had considered my parents family, then I'd committed the same offense against him with my own accusations that day. But could there be any trace left of the man my mother and father had trusted? Was there more to Cristiano than a ruthless killer?

If so, then there was a chance I could scratch his cold exterior and find the warmth beneath. "I'll talk to Cristiano."

"*Jamás*. Never." Diego frowned. "I couldn't ask you to do that."

"You didn't." I took a breath, hugging myself as the night began to cool. "I need to know for myself why he's here, and what he's planning."

"How? He's not easily cracked, Talia." Diego bit his thumbnail. "And yet . . . I sometimes wonder if he holds a soft spot where you're concerned. Like maybe he cares about you."

That was a stretch. If there was anything between Cristiano and me, it was more carnal. More savage. A thirst for power and a knowledge that the most effective way to hurt my father would be through me. I was a tool for him. After so many years, it likely ran deeper still—an obsession with my family, and maybe even my mother, that had been fostered and stoked to the point that not even an eye for an eye would be enough. Perhaps he longed to defile me while my father stood helpless. I didn't doubt Cristiano possessed a craving for me, even if it was just as simple as a man desiring a woman. But a fondness? No. The only soft spot between us was whichever part of my body he held in his grip. My girlish bicep years ago. My defiant gaze. My arched back as a woman, my hair tickling his forearm during our tango.

My breath sped thinking of the possibilities. Instinct alone had told me as a nine-year-old girl that being the subject of Cristiano's attention was as thrilling as it was dangerous.

I didn't know what exactly tied me to Cristiano, but I understood I could tighten the knot between us if I wanted. If I had the courage. "I think I can get in his head."

"You probably could, but I won't let you." Diego flipped the blanket off himself and stood to pace. "It's too risky."

"I *want* to," I said, following him with my eyes.

He glanced over at me. "But you've always feared him, and with good reason."

What I knew about Cristiano scared me as much as what I *didn't* know. Somehow, the more I learned, the more mysterious he grew. A perverse side of me wanted to test that fear to see if I could glimpse what he never seemed to show anyone.

Nobody ran toward a man like Cristiano de la Rosa. How would he react if I did?

"I have as much reason as anyone to want to bring him down," I said.

Diego raised his eyebrows at me. "I know, but—"

"What other choice do we have?" I asked. "You were right. My father wants my head in the sand. He won't respond well to me asking questions. And Cristiano doesn't trust you."

"You think he trusts you?"

He'd handled me like I was a child once but had spoken to me the opposite. He'd warned me of loyalty and justice and hadn't shielded me from the reality that he could kill me if I didn't help him. "He has no reason to trust me," I answered, "but I think he did once."

Diego ran his hands over his face and looked up at the sky. "I'm corrupting you."

I wrapped myself in the warmth of the wool and got up to stand in front of him. "It's a means to an end. Let me see if I can figure out why he's back, and what he knows about the Maldonados."

Diego rubbed my arms through the blanket as his eyes drifted over my face. Resignation crossed his features as he nodded. "Okay. But you couldn't just go to Cristiano or he'd suspect something. He has to come to you."

"How?"

He blew out a breath. "Well . . . since I've been looking into him, I've discovered that he goes to this nightclub a couple towns over on Thursday nights. If you show up, he'll want to know why you're there. Then, you get him talking."

My heart pounded at just the thought of being alone in the dark with Cristiano again.

"I'd be there of course," Diego said, lowering his voice as he put his forehead to mine. "Watching from afar. Keeping you safe. Believe me when I say—he doesn't lay a *finger* on you."

I nodded slowly. I was walking into the fire. Was it naïve to think I wouldn't get burned? That I could possibly use the unidentifiable, twisted bond that had solidified Cristiano and me years ago to control a conversation with him now?

"Won't he be suspicious if I show up at a place out of town?" I asked.

He twisted his lips. "No. Your father has a lot of eyeballs here who will report your whereabouts back to him, and Cristiano knows that. He'll think you snuck out, because that's what he *wants* to see."

"What does that mean?"

"My brother is a born hunter. He'll assume he caught you out in the wild. Let him hunt. Let him chase. If you make it easy, he'll see right through you." He squeezed my shoulders. "And be careful, Natalia. He's a master manipulator. He'll try to twist your memories or your perspective of him, but never forget what he's capable of or what he did."

If he did it. I pushed the unbidden thought from my head. How could I doubt what I'd seen with my own eyes? What I knew in my gut? Cristiano had spoken of justice all those years ago, but nobody had ever imposed it on him.

"I won't forget," I said.

"He's hurt too many people, and he will continue if we don't stop him. Let your fury burn." Diego clasped my hands and brought them to his mouth. Pressing a kiss to my knuckles, and with fervor in his words, he added, "Let it drive you toward the answers we need to stop him."

"I will," I said.

It was a promise. It had to be. Because even if I harbored the slightest doubt about what Cristiano had done, there was no question of what he *could* do.

I feared I hadn't even begun to imagine what he was capable of.

And that if he caught me trying to cross him, I would learn.

11

NATALIA

I n the States, there wasn't much of a rush in trying to get past a bouncer who studied my tits harder than my fake ID. But here, at *La Madrina*, while the doorman inspected my license, I could only think about how I was putting my life on the line to get information from one kingpin to save another. And I hated that each time my heart palpitated with trepidation, a tremor of excitement followed.

The bouncer gave Pilar and me a once-over before he unhooked the velvet rope to let us pass. I entered the night-club with nothing on me but a credit card stuck into the neckline of my black, strapless mini dress and oversized gold hoops that swung each time my platforms hit the ground.

The windowless club had three levels with VIP railed off and overlooking the dancefloor from three sides. A large, rotating disco ball had been hung for the 70s theme, and it reflected white light from a DJ booth against the wall opposite the entrance. The club was dark enough for someone to hide in corners, but lit enough that a person could be seen if she wanted. Somewhere up there, Diego waited in the wings, hidden from everyone, including me. I felt his eyes on me, though—watching, waiting, guarding.

Pilar and I hit the bar first and the dancefloor next. Diego was convinced I didn't need to do anything to capture Cristiano's attention except show up and dance, so that's what I did, dangling myself out in the open like a fresh piece of meat.

When a gut feeling spurred me to look up, I met a dark and burning gaze from the floor above. In a white dress shirt with rolled sleeves and an open collar, Cristiano leaned his elbows on the rail with a drink in hand. A cigarette dangled from his lips. He'd clearly been staring but didn't flinch or pull away.

I sipped from my straw. *Will you come?*

He shifted against the rail, narrowing his eyes on me.

I turned slightly, holding his gaze as I moved my hair off my neck.

Oh, yes. He stubbed out his cigarette in an ashtray and turned away.

He didn't come at first, but I felt eyes on my every move. Was it only Diego? Or both men? To have Cristiano's interest was to put myself in the line of fire, and I was in his crosshairs now, wearing nothing more than a bandage for a dress.

Pilar had picked up a dance partner, and the man's friend slid up behind me.

Before I could react, Pilar grabbed my arm and yanked me to her. "I-I think Cristiano de la Rosa is here."

"He is," I said. "I saw him."

"Then that's him coming over here? Why?" The cubes in her Long Island Iced Tea rattled against the glass. "What does he want?"

"Nothing with you," I assured her.

"This is *Cristiano* we're talking about, he——" She jumped when her dance partner touched her waist. Her drink fell and shattered at our feet. "*Perdón*," she said, bending to pick up the glass. "I'm sorry. It slipped."

"Don't touch that." I stopped her, urging her back up. "What's wrong?"

"He's a bastard, Talia." Her eyes widened into saucers. "He nearly beat *mi primo* to death, remember? In my mom's shop."

"Your cousin was skimming off the top," I told her. "*And* bragging about it."

"I was there," she whispered. "I ran into the stockroom to hide, but that was where Cristiano took him to do it. I saw the whole thing from behind some pineapple crates."

"I know." I rubbed my eyebrow. "But that was years ago——"

"And your mother?" she asked, raising her voice over the music. "Do you tell yourself it doesn't matter because it was so long ago?"

The man Pilar had been dancing with closed in again as his friend slipped an arm around my waist. I swatted at him, and he backed off. "I didn't mean it like that," I said to Pilar.

"That *monster* is ten times worse now—*why* did your father bring him here?" She took my arm, trying in vain to pull me away. "Please, we have to leave."

"He won't do anything, Pila. We're in public."

"Do you think that matters?"

I didn't have to answer. Cristiano probably got off on taking a life in front of an audience. "Go get someone to clean this mess. I can handle Cristiano," I said, even as a wave of doubt coursed through me.

"He has to be two meters tall. He could pick you up

with one hand, Tali." She shook her head. "You can't be alone with him."

"I'm not alone. Look at all these people." My dance partner tried to slip between Pilar and me. "*Déjame en paz*," I said, pushing him off, hoping Diego wouldn't get jealous and blow his cover. "Go away."

The man showed me his palms but continued dancing near us.

"But—" Pilar began.

I pulled her to me and whispered, "I'm *fine*. Diego's here—no, don't look for him. Is Cristiano still coming?"

"He's walking onto the dancefloor—"

"Go to the bar," I pleaded. "Now."

She was trembling. "I shouldn't leave you."

Within moments, Cristiano's unmistakable presence warmed my back. I inhaled slowly to calm myself, even as my palms sweat. I hadn't knowingly been alone with him since the tunnel.

I wasn't alone, though. Diego was here.

"*Vete*," Cristiano ordered from behind me.

With the command to leave, the man circling me looked over my head and left the dancefloor.

"Go," Cristiano said to Pilar next.

She nearly tripped over herself as she scurried to the bar.

After a moment, he spoke near my ear. "You're more courageous than your friend."

It went against my every instinct to keep my back to him. The hairs on my nape rose. The mix of my pounding heart and the drink I'd had formed little stars in my vision. I tried to pass off my swaying as dancing rather than nerves. It would serve me right to fall on my face for toying with the devil. Could Diego even stop Cristiano from doing what he wanted? I'd never been scared of the dark while surrounded by this many people.

"More courageous?" I asked. "Or more foolish?"

He grunted. "Where are your guards?" When I didn't answer, he added, "Can you turn around and look at me, Natalia?"

A wild animal like him would sense my fear. I wasn't sure if vulnerability would help or hurt me. I turned just my head over my shoulder but didn't look at him. "*Por favor*. Go. I'm just here to have a girls' night."

"You're a little far from home."

"We didn't want to run into anyone we might know. We're not supposed to be out."

"Ah. You're unsupervised then." He lowered his mouth to my ear. "I won't ask twice. Turn . . . around. Look —at—me."

It was no longer a request. I obeyed, facing broad, pulled back shoulders, somehow both severe and elegant. They squared off to the lean, muscular arms that had pinned me to his body as a girl, that had held me tight as we'd danced a week ago. His skull face paint had enhanced his bone structure then—or so I'd thought. Even without the mask, his angular jaw sharpened with high cheekbones and caved cheeks. A darker, more demanding beauty than his brother's left me breathless. They had similar faces arranged like Greek gods, but where Diego's features yielded to sun-kissed, smooth skin, Cristiano was harsher, weather-beaten with crow's feet around his eyes. His neatly parted hair and clean-shaven face contrasted his stern expression.

I sipped my drink, hoping to calm my nerves. "Why bother asking for anything if you're just going to demand it?"

He licked his lips as his eyes drifted over the short, tight dress Diego had picked out for me. Though Cristiano's eyes were as black as a starless sky, they still glimmered behind his hooded gaze. "It's the polite thing to do."

Had I been brave enough, I would've snorted in his face. He'd just shooed off Pilar with no regard for her obvious anxiety. "Is it *polite* to make a woman tremble with just a word?"

"Very." One hollowed dimple appeared as the corner of his mouth rose. "Sometime I'll demonstrate on you."

My face flushed. He wanted to make me scream and tremble. Despite what I'd heard about his brutality, my mind descended into a shameful vision of being trapped underneath his wide shoulders, begging for a different kind of mercy.

He took my Long Island Iced Tea from me and handed it to a random woman. She started to protest but then looked up and disappeared like the others. "Let me get you a real drink," he said to me.

Diego was right about playing hard to get. It was working. "I have to check on my friend," I said. I took a step, but he wrapped his hand all the way around my upper arm and pulled me back against his wall of a body. "Watch your step, *mamacita*," he rumbled before he picked me up by my waist, turned, and set me down.

I lost my breath, disoriented by being repositioned like a doll. "What are you doing?"

"There's glass all over." Cristiano signaled across the bar, alerting them to the mess.

He kept one hand lightly at my hip. I shifted to see if he'd let me go. He flexed his long fingers against me, pressing the pad of his thumb into my hipbone. A few degrees south, and he would've found a pistol strapped to my upper thigh—if only Diego hadn't made me leave it behind, rendering me defenseless.

Cristiano started to pull me closer, but I moved away. He dropped just his eyes to mine. If he wasn't six-foot-five as Pilar had guessed, he was within centimeters of it. "What's the matter?" he asked. "You only dance with men in costume?"

"You looked friendlier then."

He pursed his lips as if suppressing a smile. "I wasn't."

"Did you know it was me at the party?" I asked, even though I could guess his answer.

"It's too loud down here. Come with me." He nodded behind him. "Arms up."

Reflexively, I raised them when he cupped the sides of my breasts and slid the deadly weapons he called hands down my waist and hips. "What? Where?"

"Upstairs." He squatted to clasp one of my ankles.

"What are you doing?" I asked, trying to free my leg.

"Security check."

"My legs are bare."

"Nevertheless." One dark eyebrow quirked. "People are creative about where they hide their weapons." He grazed both palms along my outer and inner calf, higher and higher, until his hands were under my skirt. Finally, something else overtook my nervousness—a pulse of heat between my legs as his fingers lingered there.

"Hold onto me if you feel weak," he said, a hint of teasing in his voice.

Nobody around us even flinched, either unsurprised or keeping their heads down. I tried to push his hands out from under my skirt. "I don't have anything on me, not even my phone."

"Is that wise?" he asked.

"I had nowhere to put it."

He paused but didn't remove his hands.

"And I'm not going anywhere alone with you," I added.

"We won't be alone." His lifted his eyes to look directly into mine. "My men are everywhere."

A threat. Perhaps Diego had my back, but he was one man against who knew how many savages. I couldn't go anywhere with Cristiano. Either I'd be leaving myself vulnerable or Diego would try to stop it and put himself in Calavera crosshairs.

Cristiano's gentle touch didn't distract me from the fact that it was still callused, or that his hands, as they moved to my other thigh, had taken many lives. His fingertips started high and then slid down to my ankle, which he squeezed almost tenderly before standing again.

Kicking some glass aside, he gestured toward an elevator I hadn't noticed before. "After you."

"I'm expected to trust that *you* aren't armed?"

He opened his arms. "Frisk me."

My heart skipped at the thought of touching him. The sprawling shoulders and flat pecs under a crisp white shirt. His wide, powerful torso. *He* was the weapon, big everywhere that I could see. What about where I couldn't? My gaze started to drift down, but I stopped it and turned my reddening cheek to him.

"I'll save you the trouble," he said, lowering his arms back to his sides. "Not only am I armed, but one signal from me could light this place up with fireworks."

I flashed back to the barrel of his gun under my chin. Diego couldn't stop his brother then—how could he take on the devil now? I crossed my arms. "I'm not leaving the dancefloor."

White light reflected off the disco ball and flashed over the hard angles of his face. "Then you'll have to come closer so I don't miss a word you say."

That was better than the alternative, so I closed the gap between us with a step. We were nearly toe to toe, but he still had to lean down to speak in a normal tone. "Of course I knew who you were at the party. I wouldn't whisper my wishes to just any butterfly."

I tried to force my muscles to relax. We were out in the open, and he was willing to talk. "Why me?" I asked.

"Perhaps to see if you'd cower. To test whether I'd scared that little girl well enough. The fact that you're standing here tells me I didn't."

"I do cower. You can't expect me not to in front of my mother's murderer."

He started to jut his chin but stopped. "I'm only dangerous to those who cross me or have a right to be afraid," he said. "Do you?"

My instinct was to look up for Diego, but I schooled it. "Did my mother?"

His jaw ticked. "No."

I dropped my eyes. I couldn't think of her now. Even as I questioned what I knew, it felt like a betrayal to even be in the same room as Cristiano without attempting to burn it down. This was for a greater cause, though. The sooner I had what I needed, the sooner I could be free of this place and of him.

I looked up again. "Why are you here?" I asked.

"It's my nightclub."

Words escaped me. If Diego had known that, he'd neglected to clue me in. "That's not what I meant. Why are you *back*?"

"To dance." Cristiano took my hips and pulled me flush against him. With a slow roll of his body, I felt every bump and ridge of what *had* to be a gun. If it wasn't . . .

"I warned you I was armed," he said.

A flush crept its way up my neck. He held me still and

moved his hips to the smooth, sultry beat of Donna Summer's "Love to Love You Baby." My body undulated on its own as my hands slid up his chest. He squeezed my backside, moving me against him faster, harder, until we were so synced, he could've picked up one of my legs and slipped right inside me.

I gasped at the thought and shoved his chest. "Stop."

He didn't budge, but loosened his grip on me, giving me space. "No need for violence, Lourdes. All you had to do was ask."

I inhaled a sharp breath. My second name had been my mother's first choice, but she'd deferred to Papá's love of *Natalia*. "Nobody calls me that."

"I call you what I want—Lourdes. Or maybe Natasha. How do you like that?"

"Years away, and you've forgotten me completely. It's Nat*alia*."

"Forgotten you? No. Not after the way you helped me escape." His eyes drifted to my mouth, then along my neck and chest. "Natasha is what you'd be called in Russia." He moved his hand to my upper back and pushed gently. "Let's go. Our drinks are ready."

"What? Where?"

"Come with me." He guided me through the dance-floor, which was emptier than it'd been before his arrival.

It was slightly quieter at the bar, where he handed me a tall, chilled shot glass of clear liquid. I put my nose to the rim, but it was odorless. "Vodka?"

"Straight from the heart of Siberia. I brought it myself. Have you eaten?"

"I had dinner. Why?"

"Good." He took a second shot from the bar, raised it, and said something in what sounded like Russian, followed by, "*Salud.*"

I followed his lead and tasted the cool liquid, holding it on my tongue a moment before swallowing. It was definitely smoother than the drugstore vodka my friends and I drank at school. "You've been to Russia?" I asked, hoping for a clue as to what he'd been doing during the years he'd disappeared.

"*Da.* That means *yes.* I've been many places, but like you, I've returned where I belong. I've come home."

I tucked the information away for later. "This isn't my home."

"Why not?"

"I don't want this life."

"Ah." He clicked his tongue like a wink. "But it lives in you, Natalia, and its roots never stop growing."

It was one of my greatest fears—that I'd seen and learned too much to ever lead a normal life. That no matter what, I'd always be the nine-year-old girl who could trip over the dead body of a loved one at any moment— and then be forced to get right back up and defend my life. "Like a cancer," I said into my shot glass.

"No." He tilted up my chin with his knuckle. "Like a heart. Like blood in your veins. Like bones."

"You're wrong." I tried to focus on anything but his skin on mine, but it only made me more aware of his touch. "Every day I cut more and more of this cancer from my body, and I'm still standing."

"You can't remove it completely. Pretend it's gone if it helps you sleep, but the poison's already in you. You grew up feeding on it, and any predator who comes after you will get a bitter taste. Because you're a survivor. Like the monarch. Like me."

Taken aback, I blurted, "I'm not like you."

He finished his shot and signaled for another. "Let's hope you're never forced to find out."

"With a bounty on your head, you strolled back into our lives. That sounds more like a death wish than a will to survive."

"I'm here, aren't I?" he asked. "I was driven from the only life I knew with nothing but what was on my body. Now, I'm back with the world at my fingertips."

"But it's not enough."

He tilted his head at me almost imperceptibly. "Meaning?"

"You want more than you have. I know that's why you're here." I rested my elbow on the bar. "Give me another reason that makes sense. There is none."

"What about history? A sense of home?" He raised his glass to someone across the room and drank. "I've found myself a family who'd die for me and I for them, but I've discovered a man can travel the world and never find home, Natalia. And *you* will never escape it."

Cristiano was more machine than man, always calculating, always locked and loaded to kill. Perhaps he couldn't help what he'd been taught, but it didn't make it any less true. "Maybe my father trusts you," I said, "but I don't. I know what I saw that day. I believe what I've heard, both when you worked for us and after. You're not here out of nostalgia."

"Why am I here then?" he asked. "Tell me, Lourdes."

"Power. Revenge. If you take out my father and steal his business, you get both." I hadn't meant to say so much, but with Cristiano, candor was best. It was becoming clear he and I could talk each other in circles—I needed answers, though. "And don't call me Lourdes."

"Why not? Because your mother did?"

My heart palpitated once. That was exactly why. It surprised me he remembered. "Yes," I said. "It reminds me of her, and for you to use it is a slap in the face."

"It suits you, though," he mused after another sip. "Natalia is a girl's name."

He thought he had me pegged, but he'd been gone a long time. I wouldn't try to change his perception of me. Any misconceptions could only hurt him—and help me.

"What if you're right about my plans?" he asked, setting his glass on the bar. "Will you stop me?"

I couldn't. He had an army and the means to fund it. All *I* had was a sliver of hope that somewhere in his body, a heart still beat. That maybe he'd cared for my parents and me once. "Don't hurt my family any more than you already have," I said. "That includes Diego."

A smirk ghosted over his hard, chiseled features. "No, I never forgot little Talia, fiercely loyal to someone who doesn't deserve it. Where is my snake of a brother anyway?"

Cristiano calling Diego a snake was like my nine-year-old self stumbling across my mother's body and taunting her murderer for being scared. "You have that one backward."

"Do you still believe after all this time that Diego would stick out his own neck to save yours?" Cristiano asked.

"He already did," I said. "He took a bullet for me. You'll remember—you were the one who shot him."

Cristiano scanned my face a moment, then laughed. It was a foreign sound that caught me off guard, a rumble both dark and delighted. As he reached up, I flinched, but it didn't deter him from pinching my chin between his thumb and forefinger. "You have no idea what it means to be willing to die for someone. Diego took a bullet, I'll give you that. But *for you*? No, *mamacita*. When someone does that, you'll know."

That was bullshit. Diego had been brave. There was nothing else he could've done. And if there was, I didn't blame him. We'd both been in shock—scared and worried for each other. Once he'd been shot, he'd passed out. What did Cristiano expect, that Diego would magically heal his leg, regain consciousness, and throw himself down the tunnel after us?

Why was I even questioning it? Diego had warned me Cristiano would try to manipulate the truth. "You're wrong," I said. "He'll always have my back."

"And yet, the evidence of his cowardice stands in front of me. Diego has sent a woman to do a man's job." He swept his thumb over my bottom lip and released my face. "Where is he?"

I refrained from touching my tingling mouth to erase his uninvited, overly intimate caress. "I don't know," I answered.

"I believe you don't know his exact location, but he sent you."

My heart began to hammer against my breastbone. Cristiano didn't believe I was alone, and I suspected he never had. "You're the one who came to me," I pointed out.

"Diego knew I would." Cristiano turned his head slightly over one shoulder. "Perhaps he's right at my back. Or above us. Or in the shadows of the dancefloor. He's not far, is he?"

If I thought I could fool Cristiano one moment longer, I might've tried, but he was too shrewd for that. I couldn't risk him catching me in a lie and walking away before I got any information. Honesty was likely the best way to get the same in return. "He's here."

Cristiano drew back a little, his eyebrows rising. "Maybe your loyalty isn't as strong as I thought."

"I'm loyal to Diego, but I'm not stupid. Neither are you."

"You may be if you thought you could deceive me." He cocked his head. "I should be mad, shouldn't I?" He cleared some of my hair away, lighting goose bumps over my neck and shoulders. "But I'm more intrigued to know that my brother is watching us now."

I stilled so I wouldn't betray how he was affecting me. "If you touch me, you'll be dead," I warned him.

"Ah, but I already have. Not once, not twice, not even three times," he said, grazing my hip with one hand as he brushed his knuckle under my chin once more. "And now, I'm touching you again." He placed his hands on my jaw, cupping my face as carefully as he might cradle a baby bird. He tilted my head up until I could look nowhere but into his eyes. "I put my hands up your skirt earlier. And where was your Diego?"

Chills made an icy trail down my spine as I tensed, waiting for some kind of consequence to befall Cristiano. And yet, he didn't even look back. His eyes remained unwary.

He turned my head to one side and whispered in my ear, "Understand me. The next time my hands are that close to heaven, they will enter whether Diego is watching or not."

Blood rushed to my head as the tender warmth of his breath warred with such an offensive suggestion. I couldn't respond, my throat suddenly dry, my tongue numb. *Gracias a Dios* I hadn't gone anywhere alone with him—I didn't question his hands would do as they pleased. And to make Diego *watch*? I shivered. How indecent. How obscene and filthy.

And yet, heaven throbbed between my legs. That was the devil's manipulation, making me think I *liked* the idea.

"You're here to do Diego's bidding," Cristiano said.

"To get answers for questions you don't even know to ask. But how far would you go to get them?"

He let me jerk my head away. "I have morals."

"You don't even know the game he plays with you—you never did."

"For some of us," I said, "life is more than a game to play, a prize to hold tight, a lesson to be taught. There's more to it than money and power."

"Such as?"

"Love. Ethics." I raised my chin. "*Justice*. You understood that once."

He narrowed his eyes. "You remember that?"

"What you said to me about justice? *Sí*. That there is none."

"There is in my world. I live by my own code, and you may not see it, but it's both fair and ethical." He inclined his head. "For those who are deserving, I ask before I take. I feed those who feed me. I can't control how others interpret things, but I give honesty where I get it. You'll find me dead before you find me a liar."

My chest rose and fell faster as I held his gaze despite the fact that I was stupidly pushing his buttons. "A liar would be an improvement for a murderer like you."

One corner of his mouth twitched. "I'm only deadly to those who've taken risks knowing the consequences. They traded a life of safety for money and power. They deserved it, as do I." He crossed himself in a gross display of blasphemy. What right did a depraved criminal like him have to ask anything of the Holy Trinity? A hint of a smile touched his lips. "If I died tomorrow, I would not say the assassin had no right to do it. Though I'd commend him for accomplishing a nearly impossible task."

"You say you're honest as you lie. You're not fair or ethical; you've executed people who didn't deserve it."

"Deep down, you know I didn't kill your mother, Natalia." Any suggestion of humor left his tone, replaced by graveness. "And that there's more to her death than you're willing to admit."

His acknowledgement of her murder made me step back. I'd heard the denial from my father, but not yet directly from Cristiano since his return. The conviction in his voice angered me. He had no right to dismiss her death. To question what I knew in the depths of my soul. "I saw you," I said. "The gun, the blood, the duffel bag—I . . ." I didn't want to believe there could be anything else to it. A hired hitman made her death even more confusing. More senseless. "You were a *sicario for a living*," I said. I slammed the rest of my shot, and my throat burned with its spicy aftertaste. "You took as many lives as my father and grandfather commanded you to. Maybe one of their rivals paid you handsomely for this order, or maybe it was retribution for what my dad did to yours, but either way, I caught you red-handed."

"You were naïve back then, but you're old enough to know better now. Nothing is black and white." He slid my glass toward a bartender, who refilled the vodka and replaced it in front of me.

I resisted my temptation to drink more. The liquor was dangerously good, and I needed my wits about me. "No, thank you," I said.

Cristiano leaned in. "This *is* a game, Natalia, and you *have* to play—or you'll lose. Learn your lesson should someone care enough to teach you. And never doubt that you *are* a prize to hold tight." He slipped an arm around my waist like we were going to tango again, and advanced until I was backed up against the lip of the bar. When our bodies were flush, he spoke firmly. "Believe me when I say, if Diego's and my roles were reversed, I would hold you so tight, you would forget what it was to breathe. And I would not, for neither money nor power, ever send you into the fire just to see my enemy burn as he has done."

My breathing sped. He was close, his spicy scent as smooth and dangerous as Russian vodka. And he was talking shit about the man I loved. Diego would never put me at risk. He'd fought me on coming here in the first place. There was no way Cristiano could know I'd walked into the blaze on my own, but let him distract himself into thinking Diego had orchestrated this. "Why do you care *how* Diego holds me?" I asked.

"Because *I* held you as a baby," he said intently. "I was responsible for your *life* once." Cristiano's hand tensed over my lower back. "My brother's using you to light the fire, but don't forget—a match also burns."

I resisted the mental image of Cristiano cradling me as an infant. That was what I'd hoped to tap into, but he also knew exactly how to soften me. I wanted to believe he'd cared for my family at some point during the eight years he'd been with us.

"Now, it's *my* turn for questions," he said, easing back. He fixed the roll of one shirtsleeve so it exposed a little more of his dark, brawny forearm. "That night at the costume party when I found you with my brother in the garden—was he forceful with you?"

Unprepared for the topic change, I didn't answer right away. What did Cristiano think he'd seen that night by the fountain? Diego'd had one hand nearly between my legs with his other holding my jaw. From behind, it could've looked as if he'd been covering my mouth as he'd made demands.

"Tell me how much you love me. I won't ask again."

"No," I said. "Diego's not like you."

"And how am I?"

"I've heard things. I've seen things. I know what you do to women."

He pressed his lips together, assessing me coolly. "And yet you still tested me by coming here. Some part of you must not believe the rumors."

"I believe them," I said without hesitation so he wouldn't guess the truth—where Cristiano was concerned, I was beginning to question anything I knew.

"You didn't answer my question." He took his cell from his shirt pocket as it vibrated but kept his eyes on me. "Has he ever so much as laid a finger on you without your permission?"

"*No*," I said. "We were playing a game." It was the most plausible excuse—and yet it also held truth.

One of Cristiano's dark, thick brows lifted. Without removing his eyes from me, he answered his phone. "*Sí.*" His eyes roamed over the alcohol bottles lining the back wall of the bar. After a pause, he said, "*Adelante*" and ended the call. While typing out a message, he said to me, "Tell Diego to take you straight home. It's not safe after dark right now."

After dark, when the creatures of the night played. "I suppose you would know."

"You're looking for a monster, and you found one in me." He tucked his phone back in his pocket. "But I'm not the one you should fear. Just remember—no monster thinks of himself that way. He's just living by a different code than yours." He nodded once at me and turned to leave. "Goodnight, Natalia."

Goodnight? I hadn't gotten nearly what I'd wanted from him. If anything, I only had more questions. This was my last shot. I had to demand his attention. "What's your involvement with the Maldonados?"

He froze. His large frame expanded with a breath, his

muscles pulling gracefully under his white dress shirt. Even from behind, he was beautiful—and menacing.

Had I gone too far? I slid a couple steps back along the edge of the bar.

Getting him to talk in hopes that something useful might slip was one thing. But legitimate information was dangerous. If he thought I actually knew anything, that could make me a liability. Or worse—a threat.

After a moment, he turned back. "I have no deal with them. You should be asking Diego this."

"I have, and I know everything he does." I was in too deep to turn back, and I realized I didn't want to, even if I was scared. Finally, I was getting what I came for. "Now I want to know what *you* know."

He returned to standing in front of me. "What I know? My brother's in serious trouble, and if he minimized the danger he's in at all, then he lied to you. He's putting everyone at risk, including you."

"*He* isn't, but someone is. *Someone* doesn't want this deal to happen. Is it you? Are you the one stealing from him?"

His jaw sharpened as it ticked. "Be careful, Natalia. You're out of your depth."

It was the first crack in his composure I'd gotten tonight, and it sent a thrill through me. I wanted more. "I'll come upstairs with you," I said.

He glanced at the glass wall behind the DJ booth. It wasn't a wall at all, I realized, but a one-way window that most likely looked from his office onto the dancefloor. I wondered if he'd been watching me before I'd even noticed him.

"*Nyet*, Natasha."

I turned back to him. "*No*, in Russian," I guessed.

"Correct. I have business now. Maybe another time."

I tilted my head. "Is it easier to think of me differently as a Natasha?"

"Why would I want to think of you differently?"

"So you don't have to see me as the little girl you once promised to protect."

He tilted his head. The pulse at the base of his neck jumped as he let his eyes wander down my dress. "Believe me, I see you just fine as you are. I happen to like the name. I knew a Natasha once." His eyes leapt back to mine. "She sucked my dick like it would end with a mouthful of gold."

My throat constricted. Nobody had ever said anything like that to me. "That's not why I wanted to come up. I won't do that willingly. Not ever. But maybe Natasha said the same thing."

He stilled completely. The lights and music seemed to dim along with his demeanor. "You're accusing me of rape?"

My mom's dress was ripped. It was perhaps the one thing I couldn't bring myself to ask about. The answer might be too painful. "You expect me to believe your men do it, but you don't?"

"You insult me. If I want a woman, I can get her without force," he said sharply. "That includes *you*."

I drew back with an audible swallow. He didn't treat me the way others did, yet despite his steely expression and cool gaze, my gut told me he didn't mean it. He only wanted a reaction. Could I trust that instinct, though? In my experience, cartel bosses didn't tease.

And they didn't invite women in skimpy dresses anywhere private to talk.

The dark cloud that'd just fallen over him seemed to lift. "With me, you always have a choice. You're not beholden to my wishes, but I hope you'll still carry them on your wings and deliver them for me." He brushed hair from my cheek, trailing a fingertip over my skin in a way that I had to fight to keep my eyes from falling shut. "Just know that I don't rely on anyone, not even the heavens, to grant my wishes. I make them come true on my own."

He retreated a few steps, holding my gaze, before he turned and walked away.

I hung on his words. What *were* his wishes? What did they have to do with me? I stayed where I was despite my urge to call him back and ask the questions forming in my head.

Because nothing good could come from chasing after *el anticristo*.

Especially if he was saying what I thought he was.

If you're what I want, then I'll find a way to have you.

12

NATALIA

Diego's hand slipped higher up my dress as the glowing red hand of his speedometer rose. He sped away from the club through deserted roads as if he also knew of the after-dark danger Cristiano had warned me of.

Only the warm lights of the dashboard glowed against its all-black interior. Silence stretched over the smooth hum of his Mercedes once I'd finished relaying most of my conversation with Cristiano. All in all, there wasn't much to tell.

"Are you okay?" Diego asked for the second time.

"I'm fine." *Because you're a survivor. Like the monarch. Like me.* Cristiano's words echoed in my mind.

"He kept touching you because he knew I was there." He released my leg to grip the steering wheel. "I assumed he'd frisk you, but that's all."

I wouldn't even call what he'd done *frisking*. Cristiano had tested my boundaries as he'd taunted Diego. He'd had his hands everywhere from my ankles to my thighs, my neck and face. He'd touched me in ways only Diego should.

And Diego had let him—or had he not seen well enough the liberties Cristiano had taken with my body? "Cristiano said next time he frisks me, he won't stop his hands at the gates of heaven, even if you're watching."

"Heaven?" Diego's nostrils flared as he hit the steering wheel. "Let him try. I'll cut off his devil hands." He snorted not unlike a Pamplona bull. "Not that you'll ever be in that position again."

I wasn't sure what aroused me more—Diego's possessiveness or the idea of Cristiano boldly taking what didn't belong to him. I only knew that what aroused me, also horrified me. What was wrong with me for getting excited Cristiano might want me when his brother already had me? The same Cristiano who, the last decade, I'd vehemently hated? I shifted in the leather seat. "He only said it to scare me," I said. "It didn't mean anything."

"I know. Still . . . I should knock his teeth out." Diego massaged around his nose. "It wasn't easy to watch. He knows you're mine and that you're the quickest way to get under my skin."

"He only thinks of me as a weapon against you." And if anyone knew how to wield a weapon, it was Cristiano. "I'm sorry I didn't get more information."

"You were perfect." He glanced over at me, running a hand through his hair to get it out of his eyes. "Cristiano *didn't* scare you, did he?"

He'd tried. But had he succeeded? With his comments about Natasha and about how he could have me if he wanted, what unnerved me most was that I *wasn't* scared. "No."

A dog darted into the street. Diego hit the brakes, and I

outstretched my arms to catch myself against the glove compartment.

"Shit. Sorry," he said as he decelerated for a yellow light. "You all right?"

I glanced behind us for the dog, but it was gone. "Yes."

Diego stopped the car at an intersection and slid his hand in mine. "You look so beautiful tonight. I can't say I blame him for being so forward. As angry as it makes me, I feel lucky to be the one who gets to take you home."

"Always," I said.

"It's good you didn't go anywhere with him." Diego's phone rang. He released my hand to get it from his pocket as he reiterated, "I would've beaten him half to death if he'd tried to get you alone." He swiped his thumb across the screen and held it to his ear. "*Bueno.*"

As Diego listened to the line, I turned my head toward the faint strains of buoyant violin and guitarrón coming from a corner market. Mariachi music didn't always remind me of the moments before I'd skipped down the hall to hurry my mother for the parade, but in that moment, I saw Cristiano standing in the bedroom, dressed in all black, rising from the ashes. Out front of the *mercado*, a few men smoked, drank, and blared a boombox. Despite opaque, bulletproof windows, I got a chill when one of the men opened his jacket and flashed a gun in our direction. I'd never liked riding around in showy cars when poverty permeated our state.

"I'm not far, but I have Natalia," Diego said into the phone. "I'll drop her off and come." The stoplight changed to green, but he didn't move. "No. I want everyone on site."

"What's wrong?" I asked.

"Some issue at the *fucking* warehouse," he whispered to me. He paused, listening. "No, don't send one of them. I

don't trust them around Natalia. Can you break into it?"
He snorted. "*Claro que no*. I'll be there in an hour. Just move
on to something else until I'm back." He hung up, dropped
the phone into a cup holder, and stepped on the gas.

"Is that the warehouse with all the Maldonados'
stock?" I asked.

"*Sí*. We moved it all to one spot since none of our
regular houses are safe right now. Then it's all going *al otro
lado*—into the U.S.—at once." He rested an elbow on the
door panel and bit his thumbnail, steering with one hand.
"Every call I get, I worry something else has gone wrong."

"Who was on the phone?"

"Jojo. We transported everything to the new location in
armored vehicles," he said. "I have the only set of keys to
the truck they need to get into right now—and of course,
it's impenetrable, so they can't break in, *puta madre*."

I glanced through the windshield. "You said we're
close?"

"We just passed the turnoff."

"When does everything need to go?"

"Tomorrow afternoon." He shook his head out the
window. "They're loading everything tonight."

I reached over to knead the back of his neck with one
hand. "Go to the warehouse. Drop off the keys."

He shook his head. "It's too dangerous."

"Isn't *everyone* in the cartel there guarding it?" I argued.

"Not everyone. In case the hits were due to a leak—which
I don't believe—I only have my most trustworthy men there."

"Then what's the danger?"

"No matter how many precautions we have in place,"
he said, slowing for another red light, "with all the product
consolidated in one location, all the risk is there too."

"We're still twenty minutes from the house, which

means it would take you forty round trip to get back. This is a priority."

The stoplight changed to green, but he just scratched his chin. "Which won't matter if Costa kills me for taking you to the warehouse."

"He thinks I'm still at the movie theater for a *Star Wars* triple-feature." I checked the clock on the dash—half past nine. "Right about now, Pilar and I are finishing *Attack of the Clones*. The next episode is almost two-and-a-half hours."

"*Dios mío*. You know the runtime and everything?" He reached over to squeeze my knee in the exact spot I was ticklish. I laughed as I squirmed. "Are you this devious in the States?" he asked.

I leaned over the console, batting my lashes up at him. "You'll soon find out."

Someone honked behind us for sitting at a green light before swerving past. Diego barely noticed.

"Mmm." He nuzzled my nose with his, then kissed me softly, sweetly. "You make a good argument, my little C-3PO, but I don't want to risk it." He brushed my hair from my face and tucked it behind my ear. "Even if nothing happens, I don't want anyone to see you there. If it gets back to Costa, or if the wrong person sees you unguarded—"

"I just faced off with Cristiano by myself," I pointed out. "I'll be *fine*. I'll wait in the car. Just go. It'll take five minutes."

"Not even. I'll have Jojo come out and get the keys." Diego sighed, resigned. "You're tough."

"This is good practice for when we're married and I win all our arguments."

He scoffed, seizing my leg again. I squealed, grabbing

his wrist as I backed against the door. "Tickling is off-limits."

"I don't think so, *princesa*," he said but smiled and released me. He checked his rearview mirror and swerved into the next lane. Ignoring the red arrow, he flipped the car around to zoom back the way we'd come. The men loitering outside the *tienda* were gone, but as we whizzed by, I could've sworn I heard the echo of mariachi music.

In under ten minutes, we were at the edge of town and approaching a sprawling concrete block. Surrounded by desert, it seemed to have risen from the ground.

"I'm going to park in back so nobody sees you," Diego said, slowing to turn down a dark road. "Do you see a black fob in the center console?"

I opened it and sorted through several sets of keys until I found the one he needed. He rolled down his window and stuck it out as we pulled up to an industrial looking metal gate. As it slid open, Diego killed the headlights and parked in an unlit backlot. He quickly sent off a text, then reclined the driver's seat a little and rubbed the bridge of his nose.

It was the second time I'd noticed him do it since we'd gotten in the car. "Do you have a headache?"

"Yeah. I'm just tired and feeling queasy." He squinted through the windshield. "I've barely slept in days. Every time I close my eyes, I think of what'll happen if tomorrow doesn't go well."

"Come here." I unfastened my seatbelt to give him the best sideways hug I could and kissed his cheek. "You're almost there. By this time tomorrow, the shipment will be on its way and you'll be *that* much closer to pulling off the most impressive deal the Cruz cartel has ever seen."

He turned his head to graze the tips of our noses. "And then?" he asked.

"And then it's you and me with nothing ahead of us but our future."

He tilted his head and kissed me gently. "I love the sound of that. I love *you*."

"I love you too," I said. *Enough to die for you*, a voice in my head said. The fortune teller. Why did she still haunt me when I knew her words held no truth?

A knock at the driver's side made me jump back with a gasp. I clutched my throat, my heart pounding.

"It's just Jojo," Diego said, patting my thigh. I could barely make out a figure until Diego rolled the window down.

Jojo, one of Diego's foremen, nodded at me. "*¿Qué tal*, Talia?"

Even though my heart pounded from the scare, I nodded. "*Todo bien*. All good."

"How's it going in there?" Diego asked, passing Jojo the keys.

Jojo wiped his hairline, leaving a grease mark on his forehead. "One of the semi engines is fucked. We're working on it."

"Where's the mechanic?" Diego asked.

"Not picking up his phone, but don't worry, *jefe*. We'll get him here."

"You checked the fuel and oil levels? The battery?" Diego asked, his brows cinched.

"Yeah, *I* didn't, but Tomás knows all that shit and I think he—"

"Did he disengage the lock?"

Jojo showed us his grimy palms. "I dunno."

"Tell him to try that," Diego said. "If it doesn't work, check the ECM ground wire."

"What the fuck is that?" Jojo asked, wetting his finger to rub grease off his wrist.

"Come on, *cabrón*. Like I don't have enough on my plate?" Diego blew out a sigh. "I'll text Tomás."

Seeing the veins pop in Diego's hands and neck as he gripped the steering wheel, I caressed his right forearm. "Go look at it," I said. "I'll be fine here for a few minutes."

"Maybe if I didn't hire such dumb motherfuckers," Diego muttered.

Diego didn't mean it—he cared a great deal for his men—and Jojo knew it. Jojo smiled with a shrug. "Sorry I couldn't afford to go to college for engines."

Diego rolled his eyes. "Wait there," he said and raised the window before turning to me. "Are you sure? It's dark out here, and you can't turn on the lights or someone might see you. I know that scares you."

Nothing happened in the dark. That was part of why it frightened me—not knowing whose footsteps were coming or going, or who might be at my back, or whether the right or wrong person had found me until it was too late to do anything about it. When Barto had come rushing down the tunnel ladder for me, I hadn't known who he was until he'd held the flashlight under his chin. The shadows had created a ghoulish, haunting mask that hadn't looked at all like the Barto I'd grown up around. I'd gone with him willingly, relieved to have been found, but part of me had questioned him—and everything—until we'd emerged from the tunnel into the closet. Doors had been broken down, my mother's body had been covered, and Papá had crushed me to him for a breathless hug.

I wished there were at least lamps in the lot, but if I said that, Diego would stay when he was clearly needed inside. "I'm not nine anymore," I told him. "I'll be fine."

"I'll just go talk to Tomás and come right back." He leaned over to peck me once more. "Okay?"

"Go."

The dome light came on as he switched off the engine and handed me the keys. "If you see anything—anything *at all*—get the fuck out of here."

"Without you?" I asked.

"Yes." He shut off the light and the car went pitch dark. Not even a sliver of moonlight touched the area. He passed me the keys with the fob. "These are for the gate and the warehouse. Nothing will happen, but I don't care if a jackrabbit hops by and looks at you funny. Just go."

I nodded, gripping the keys. "Got it."

"Lock the door after me and keep the lights off." When he ducked out, I hit a button on the roof to plunge the car back into darkness. I barely made out his shadow as he met Jojo at the back door and disappeared inside the warehouse.

With desert all around me, it might've *felt* as if I was in the middle of nowhere, but I had to remember there were many people here. Specifically, men with guns who'd been hired by my father. They wouldn't let anything bad happen. They were on our side.

Then again, Cristiano had been too when he'd left me in the dark.

Even though it was hard to see, nothing would ever be as pitch-black as the underground tunnel. At least now, I wasn't covered in blood and on the precipice of a future that'd been dimmed significantly. I'd hugged my knees to my chest and tried to stop picturing all the vibrant colors of my mom's dress darkened with blood. What if I'd been ten minutes earlier? Or had heard the shot? Would it have changed anything?

The only thing I'd actually seen in that tunnel had been Barto's shadowed face. All I'd heard was his voice, oddly as cajoling as Cristiano's hours earlier, my own sobs, and the pests scampering around me.

As my chest tightened with panic, I coaxed myself to breathe through it. But no matter how many times I told myself I was too old to be afraid of the dark, fears as deeply rooted as mine knew no age.

With a piercing screech of metal scraping metal, I spun in my seat to look out the back window but saw nothing. My heartbeat echoed in my ears. I turned forward again. The time on the dash changed. In an alternate universe, Pilar and I were starting *Revenge of the Sith*. I closed my eyes and hummed the opening bars to *Star Wars*.

Like a clap of thunder, rumbling motorcycle engines jarred me back to reality. As two bikes pulled up to the driver's side, I ducked into a ball on the floorboard. It went silent again. A large shadow passed Diego's window. My heart pounded as the other biker approached. Keys jingled from somewhere. A silhouette peered into the car. On what looked like a beanie or hat, I made out the small but distinct glowing outline of a white sugar skull. A *calavera*.

They were Cristiano's men.

At Diego's warehouse.

Which held every last gram of the Maldonado product.

Diego had been right—Cristiano *did* have something to do with the robberies. And it looked like he was back for more.

Diego had told me to go if I saw anything suspicious, but he had to know I'd never leave him stranded. I had an opportunity to warn him, and I needed to take it.

13

NATALIA

The Maldonados wouldn't hesitate to kill Diego if he lost any more of their shipment. That was why this deal had been haunting Diego's nights since the first theft. I had no idea how the Calaveras had found the top-secret warehouse, but I knew why they were here—for the drugs.

As soon as the skull-adorned bikers stepped away from Diego's car, I opened the glovebox to get my cell. I sent Diego a hurried text that some Calaveras were out back. The keys to the Mercedes dug into my palm, but I wouldn't leave him here.

I stared at my screen, praying for a response. I couldn't take the chance that these men would ambush Diego and turn the situation with the Maldonados critical. Or worse —hurt him. When a minute had passed without a response, I stuck my phone in the neckline of my dress and sat up. I didn't see the men anywhere, but I couldn't see much to begin with.

I could help. I had to. I knew what it was to feel help-

less during and after a tragedy, and it was a form of
torture, especially paired with grief. Tonight, I could move
soundlessly and use the element of surprise to my advantage to hopefully reach Diego before they did.

I fumbled for the fob to make sure I had the right set of
keys, then quietly opened the car door. I ducked behind the
side panel, listening as my eyes adjusted. The area seemed
clear, so I tiptoed toward the back door, where I deftly tried
each key until the lock finally gave.

The door opened to a wide, dark hallway with a light
at the end of it. I tugged down the hem of my dress and
felt my way along one wall, stepping carefully over boxes. I
almost rolled my heel on some screws but managed to
steady myself against a crate. As I got closer, men's voices
and the *clink* of what sounded like metal tools carried
through the doorway. I listened for yelling, threats, or
arguing but heard nothing of the sort.

When I'd reached the end of the hall, I inhaled a deep
breath and peeked in. It was a garage with two eighteen-
wheeler trucks parked side by side. The one closest to me
had its hood popped. Diego worked underneath it,
standing on a stepladder with a tool belt around his waist
and his sleeves rolled.

I scanned the room for the men I'd seen. I recognized
my father's soldiers as they unloaded cartons from an
armored vehicle, but others didn't look familiar at all.
Hadn't Diego said only their most trusted men were here?

When I returned my eyes to the semi, Diego had his
phone out. After reading the screen, he looked toward the
doorway, and his eyes widened when he saw me. Wiping
his hands on a rag, he nodded for me to get back in the
hall. I hid as he said something about the engine to the
other men. Moments later, he came around the corner and
nearly knocked me over.

He grasped my shoulders. "You okay?" he whispered.

"I saw men in Calavera clothing outside," I rushed out. "I think they were sneaking in the back door."

"Yeah, I know. They're with us."

I blinked twice as my mouth fell open. "*What?*"

"This is Cristiano's warehouse." Diego took his suit jacket from over his elbow, put it around my shoulders, and moved me farther from the doorway. "We decided to store everything here after our locations were compromised."

I leaned in and spoke softly. "But what if Cristiano is behind the attacks?"

"It wasn't my decision, believe me, but we're in a crunch." Diego frowned. "I had no other option. I just hope Cristiano has enough of a reason not to sabotage us."

I eased back. "You mean because he might be planning to take it all over."

"Right." Diego glanced over his shoulder. "Jojo says everything's been quiet. They're even getting along with Cristiano's guys. But you still shouldn't be in here."

"I don't want to go back to the car," I said. "The dark . . . it just takes me back to being down there."

"I get it." He pulled the jacket closed and kissed my forehead. "I actually feel safer with you inside. The engine isn't fixed yet, but I see the problem. Tomás can probably take it from here."

"I have two hours before I have to be home. I'd feel better if you guys just fixed the problem," I said. "Because if you can't get the truck to start . . . then what?"

"Then I can't make half the delivery tomorrow," he said. "And all our plans go to shit."

"Then you should handle it. I'll just stay hidden."

"Not here. People are coming and going." He glanced toward the ceiling. "We take breaks on the roof. You could go up there, because I assure you, no one's taking a fucking break tonight. There are lights too. You still have those keys?"

I held up the set. He picked through them until he found the one he was looking for, then walked by me to open the door to the expansive warehouse. He flipped some switches and fluorescent lights flickered on as I entered.

My heels echoed through the building that stored stacks of massive wooden crates and heavy-duty machinery. Attached to one wall was an office with storage lockers. "What is all this?" I asked.

"Calavera contraband. Artillery. Semi-automatics, grenades, drones, IEDs—that kind of thing."

I turned in a circle. No wonder this place was so dangerous. "Where's it all going?"

"Most of it is coming. Smuggled from up north so criminals like us can organize and protect our product. From each other and from law enforcement." He pointed across the warehouse to a staircase. "Just take that up to the access door on the roof. Up there, you'll see lounge chairs and stuff."

"What if someone comes up?"

"Nobody else has keys to this side of the warehouse except me and Cristiano's right-hand man, who's not here tonight. But the door locks automatically behind you, so just in case, take the keys." He kissed me quickly. "I'll be up shortly."

I held Diego's jacket closed as I crossed the room, climbed the stairs to the second level, and continued up a short access hall. At the end stood a single door with a long glass window big enough for me to glimpse the sky.

I stepped out onto the roof. Outdoor LED lights guided me through rows of solar panels and across a helipad.

I found an area of loungers and camping chairs where the men must've taken their breaks, picked up a *sarape* blanket, and sat underneath it near a portable grill. Clusters of stars were the only light in the black, horizonless desert. Behind me, the town twinkled. In that direction, light and life thrived in the dark while the desert had killed the most resilient of men. Why had I chosen to face the direction that was nothing but desert? Why confront Cristiano when being on his radar could only lead to trouble?

Darkness called to me.

That didn't mean I had to answer.

It'd been too easy to enmesh myself in Cristiano's game. Too natural to succumb to the shadows that swarmed my nightmares. Cristiano had said this life lived in me like a heart. Maybe that was true, but hearts could be replaced. A brain couldn't. I wasn't going to walk toward darkness like my mother had.

I leaned my head back. As adrenaline from my emotional and mental warfare with Cristiano wore off, I drifted in and out of consciousness until my phone dinged with a text from Diego that he was on his way up.

I went to meet him at the door. He slipped his arms inside my jacket and scooped me up by my waist, walking us backward. "Nice up here, isn't it? You wouldn't expect it to be."

"I can count every star."

"Funny, I'm seeing stars too . . ." He captured my mouth for a kiss. "Put your legs around me."

He lifted me by my ass, and I locked my ankles at his lower back. "Did you fix the engine?" I asked.

"It's all good." He pecked me. "Everything's on schedule to leave late-morning." His lips brushed the underside of my jaw. "Border patrol is expecting us. Law enforcement is standing by to escort us." He moved his mouth down my neck, warming me with his breath. "We're closer and closer to freedom."

That explained his sudden good mood. I raised my eyes to the sky as he sucked and nibbled the tender skin along my throat. "We're so close," I said, nearly moaning.

"We are."

"And we've been *so* good."

I felt his smile against my skin. "We have."

"Almost saintly."

He laughed hotly into the curve of my neck. "I didn't know saints kissed this way."

My dress inched up the backs of my thighs. He helped it along until my thong was almost exposed. I lifted up to readjust, and the length of him pressed solid between my legs, eliciting my gasp and his pained groan. He wanted me. He was ready for me.

Maybe it was being out in the open, but I was hit with the uneasy question of what my mother would think if she was looking down now. Would she understand Diego and I were meant to be as she and my father had been? They were younger than me when they married. And Diego's optimism was contagious. Finally, I felt as if he wanted to start over in California more than he needed the constant threat of danger that made cartel life both treacherous and exhilarating.

He lowered me onto the cushion of a chaise lounge and kneeled at my feet to remove my shoes. He kissed the inside of my ankle, and I shivered as he grazed his five o'clock shadow up the inside of my leg. He climbed over me, and fixed his mouth on mine, his kiss becoming hungry as our tongues met fast and slippery. "I want you so bad, Tali," he said, panting. "I can't wait any longer to bury myself inside you."

His bold words thrilled me, and as he kissed his way

down my collarbone and chest, I doubted my decision to wait. Diego and I were destined. Tomorrow would go well, and he'd come to California.

If it didn't, then I'd have bigger worries than my virginity.

If anything went wrong, wouldn't I wish I'd had this night with him?

We were as good as committed to each other. Why wait for a ceremony?

Diego paused, lifting his head. "Where'd you go, *princesa?*"

"I'm here. I was just trying to remember why we're waiting."

"How much of that vodka did you drink?" he asked with a haphazard smile.

"It's not that. I feel fine. I'm just . . ."

"Horny?"

I laughed. "That goes without saying."

"You have no idea how much it turns me on to know that *you're* turned on." He sat back on his calves. "But if you have to think about whether you're ready, then we shouldn't go any further."

I sat up on my elbows, awed by his restraint. By his *gallantry*. "Really?" I asked.

"Our first time isn't going to be on top of a warehouse. Or any piece of property that belongs to my fucking brother." He stretched out next to me, and I lifted my head to settle into the crook of his arm. "Damn," he said. "It feels good to lie down."

"Do you have to come back here after you drop me off?"

"Yeah I will, even though Jojo told me to go home and sleep since I need to be alert during the delivery."

I glanced up at him. "You're going with them tomorrow?"

"I have to." With his eyes on the sky, his jaw squared as he swallowed. "It's too important for me not to be there."

My heart sank. The last shipment to attempt to cross the border had been blown up, killing two men. "Aren't you more valuable here?" I asked. "Like those people in the movies who stay in the control center during a shuttle launch?"

Diego kissed my temple when I shuddered. "I'll be all right. Don't worry. I'm more resilient than you think, and I'm not planning to meet God any time soon."

I let his resolve soothe me. Because it was that same determination in his voice that told me I wouldn't be able to talk him out of going. A sense of duty ran almost as deeply as loyalty within the cartel. Diego would see this through to the end.

I wanted to be content to sit in peace with Diego and take in these rare moments we had alone, but because the past had crept up on me in the car, my mind kept flashing there. The nebulous shape of my mother's blood on the cold tile. The black, cold-as-steel Glock engulfed by Cristiano's hand. I smelled gunpowder and expensive perfume and heard my father's sobs, as subdued as thunder, the night he'd returned home from his trip. My mother had struggled to warn me about Cristiano. If he hadn't shot her, why had she looked so scared as she'd pleaded with him for my life?

I'd locked these memories away, but Cristiano's presence dredged up more each day. His cryptic words earlier had wormed their way into my consciousness. I'd gotten good at pushing the darkness away, but tonight, it pushed back.

Were there other things about that day I hadn't noticed? Could someone else have gotten into the house somehow? I'd spent almost half of my life seeing Cristiano as a protector—but I'd spent more of it thinking of him as my mother's murderer. Diego, too, had believed the worst in his brother for a long time.

Diego squeezed me closer. "You got quiet. You all right?"

"Are *you*?" I asked.

His eyebrows drew together. "Why?"

"We've talked a lot about how I'm dealing with everything, but I haven't really asked what it's like for you to have Cristiano back—and to consider he might not have done this."

He scratched the bridge of his nose. "I . . . I'm not sure it matters. Whether Cristiano murdered Bianca or not, too much damage has been done." His chest expanded with a deep inhale. "There's no chance Cristiano and I could repair our relationship."

"Even if he's proven innocent?" I asked. "I've spent a long time blaming him for this too, but as much as I don't trust him, I *do* trust my father."

"Cristiano's not innocent," Diego said without an ounce of doubt. "But neither am I."

I cocked my head into the nook of his shoulder. "What?"

"It's beginning to hit me that Cristiano and I . . ." He shifted in the chair. "We're more similar than I'd like to admit."

Diego and Cristiano—*similar*? Aside from sharing some physical attributes, they were night and day to me. "You're not like him," I said, tracing my index finger over the stubble shading his chin. "Not in a million years."

I lifted my head when Diego repositioned his arm under me, as if he couldn't get comfortable. "He betrayed our family," Diego said, "and I betrayed him."

"You mean Cristiano betrayed my father . . .?"

"No. Mine." He paused, lowering his eyes from the sky to the desert. "When Costa killed my parents, I didn't fully grasp the business they were in. I do now. I understand why they couldn't continue down that path." His face screwed up as if he'd bitten into something sour. "But they didn't need to die for it."

Diego didn't talk about his parents much, but when he did, he got pensive. Still, I'd never questioned that he understood why their death had to happen.

"Our families had a pact not to get into human trafficking. Your parents broke it," I reminded him, flattening my hand over his chest. His heart beat strong against my palm. "But the real reason Papá did what he did was because they plotted against him."

"I know. I get it. But they're my blood, Natalia."

"That doesn't excuse everything under the sun. It *can't*."

"I thought it did. Cristiano went against my parents because he didn't agree with how they ran their business. At the time, I thought him a traitor—and I still do." He wiped his forehead with his shirtsleeve and blew out a breath. "I didn't think anything should ever break the bonds of family. But then I did that exact thing to Cristiano."

"It takes courage to resist blind loyalty," I said soothingly, trying to comfort him.

"Or does it take courage to stick by family no matter what?" he asked. I heard the struggle in his voice and wondered how long he'd been thinking all this. "As Cristiano couldn't excuse my parents for getting involved in things like forced labor or sex slavery, I couldn't excuse him for taking your mother's life—and I turned on him. My own blood."

"You had no other choice, Diego." When he didn't respond, I added, "There has to be a line somewhere, even for family."

"I'm not sure I agree. Sometimes, I get overwhelmed by helplessness wondering if I betrayed my family by joining yours. I hate Cristiano for what he did to Bianca, but perhaps doing nothing was just as bad."

Doing *something* would've meant retaliation. "Did you ever think of taking vengeance for their death?"

He didn't answer right away. As seconds ticked by, I grew uneasy. There was only one person Diego would take revenge on. My father.

"In my darkest moments, yes," he admitted.

My heart thumped once. I'd never heard Diego mention a desire for retribution, but I supposed that was human nature. It wasn't as if *I'd* never wondered how things might've turned out differently if I'd actually known how to operate the gun I'd pulled on Cristiano all those years ago.

"But that's how you and Cristiano are different," I said, balling his shirt in my fist. "*You* are good. You never would've acted on those feelings."

"At the core of it, though, Tali—we've each committed the highest sin in this world. We turned against family, and that's how we're alike." His body depressed into the chair with a long exhale. "It's why we can never repair what's left between us. Even if we're forced to do business together as Costa wants, even if we find a way to make things right again—the distrust between us will never go away."

"You keep saying Cristiano turned against family," I said, trying to decipher what exactly he meant. Did he mean because Cristiano had joined our cartel? "When he hurt my mom, he was close enough to my parents to be *like* family, but they weren't blood as you continue to point out."

"I'm not talking about what he did to your family. I'm talking about what he did to *mine*."

What? I furrowed my eyebrows. I didn't understand what he meant, but as Cristiano had warned me hours earlier—I was starting to believe there *was* more to my mother's murder than I knew.

I sat up on one elbow to look down at him. "What are you saying?" I asked.

"You asked if I ever think of vengeance," he said slowly. "I do. But not against your father. He may have pulled the trigger, but Cristiano is the one who told Costa what my parents were doing, and what they were planning."

It took a moment for his words to sink in. I'd never questioned how my father had learned that the de la Rosas were conspiring against him. I wouldn't have guessed the information that would get them killed would come from within their own family. "Cristiano had your parents killed?"

"Yes. That's the betrayal I mean." Diego glanced away. "My brother has no loyalty. He never has. It's what I've been trying to tell Costa. I can't trust him . . . but I *can* trust a man's motivations."

"What are his motivations?" I asked. My mind raced as this new door opened. Could this help reconcile any holes in my past? "Why is he back? I thought it was to avenge his parents' death, but if he caused it, then Papá was right. He's not here for revenge. So what does he want?"

Diego searched the night sky as if it might hold the answers we needed. "By this time tomorrow, the Maldonado deal will either be done or it won't," he said. "I don't know why Cristiano is here. But I suspect we'll find out soon enough."

14

NATALIA

My mother would sometimes braid her hair into a thick, black arrow she wore over one shoulder. It was that way now, but tonight was the first time it twinkled with stars. They winked at me as she held my hand and led me to my bed.

"It's time to sleep, Natasha," she said.

"*Natalia*," I corrected as I got under the covers.

She kneeled next to me. Heavy bracelets *clinked* on her wrists as she touched my forehead, chest, and each shoulder. "You're old enough to know better now," she said.

"I'm only nine."

"The truth is in you like a heart. Like blood in your veins. Like bones." She smiled. "Kiss me goodnight."

I sat up and hugged her neck, resting my head on her shoulder. Somewhere on the compound a shot rang out.

"*Mami?*"

"It's okay, *mariposita*." She laid me back on the bed. When she drew back, blood covered my nightgown. With another shot, she fell over me.

I couldn't breathe. From somewhere in the house, my

father screamed at me to get down, but I was stuck under her body. I curled up under the bedspread and hid from the next round of shots. This time, they kept coming, an endless *rat-a-tat-tat*.

"Natalia!"

Jolted out of my dream, I launched forward, gasping for breath, as if someone had been sitting on my chest.

The sky was lightening from black to indigo. Sweat trickled down my temple. I was still in Diego's jacket . . . on the roof. We'd fallen asleep. My father would be looking for us, and—

"Get *down*." Diego shoved me over the side of the chaise, and I landed on my shoulder on the concrete.

I hadn't dreamed the shots. With another round, I covered my ears and moved my head under the chair. Most everyone I'd known had heard the echoes of a turf war at some point, but this wasn't happening *somewhere*. These shots were being fired right underneath us.

"Stay here." Diego crawled to the side of the roof, rose to his knees, and looked over. "Fuck." He ran both hands through his hair and made two fists. "*Fuck*."

"What?" I cried just as the shots stopped.

"Shh." He motioned for me to be quiet before slinking back. "The warehouse is under attack. Stay up here."

"*What?*" My heart beat hard enough to shake my whole body. I reached under the chair to grab his elbow. "Don't leave me."

"They're trying to steal what's left, Tali. You know I can't let them. I can't, or else—" He inhaled a breath. "That product down there is the difference between life or death for me."

"They could *shoot* you."

"I won't let that happen." He dragged himself close enough to kiss me. "It'll be okay."

"Diego," I said shakily. "Let me come with you."

"Talia, you *must* hide under here. Give me the keys. Listen. Are you listening?" He took the keys from my shaky hands. "Do you have your phone?"

I nodded quickly. "Yes."

"If I don't make it back, stay hidden." His words were soothing, but I heard the crack in his voice. When more shots sounded, he flinched. "Don't come looking for me. Text Barto—he'll find you. I'll be back for you in no time."

I clung to his arm, tears blurring my vision. Was this what I'd been warned of? *I see pain. I see betrayal and violence. And much death.* What were the chances Diego would go downstairs and never return? They weren't odds I wanted to take. I choked back a sob. "Don't go."

"I have to, *princesa.*"

My hair fell over my right eye, but I refused to release him. "I'll come with you."

"It's too dangerous. It's for your own protection, and those are my men down there. I can't leave them stranded."

"But I need you." My heart had already been irreparably damaged losing one person—I couldn't say good-bye to another. I wouldn't abandon Diego. "You can't die. You can't."

"I'm not dying today, Talia. No way in hell." He lifted the black veil of my hair and settled it over my shoulder. "When I go, you'll be by my side, okay? I'm with you, life or death."

With a thick throat, I nodded. "Life or death," I rasped.

"Good girl." He kissed my forehead. "I love you."

He angled to get his 9mm from its holster, maneuvered out from under the chair, and sprinted across the roof.

"I love you," I whispered back.

Night's cloak lifted as the sun peeked over the distant mountains. With the whir of a helicopter, I curled all the way under the chaise and clutched Diego's jacket closed around myself. A spotlight flashed over the roof. With a whistle from above, an explosion on the ground shook the building. The helicopter circled one more time, dropping grenades that rattled every bone in my body. I covered my mouth. Tires screeched, and the helicopter flew off.

With unsteady fingers, I shot Barto a quick text. After what could've been thirty seconds or five minutes of silence, I crawled out. The helicopter was nowhere in sight, so I peeked above the concrete ledge. The rising sun cast rich purple shadows over a vast desert. Behind me, the town woke up, cars honking and people screaming. Men yelled below me. The blasts had stopped, so I risked getting to my feet to look all the way over the side of the roof.

Flames raged below, licking the side of the building, jumping from one wood container to the next as black smoke billowed from the windows. I had to get off the roof now, or I'd be trapped. I needed to get to Diego. I snatched my shoes off the ground, ran for the door, and grabbed the handle, but it was locked.

I slammed my fists against the industrial metal door, then my stiletto against the sliver of glass. I traded it for a discarded lead pipe and smashed the window. It shattered, leaving a space just big enough for me to get an arm through. Smoke wafted out, curling around me before it disintegrated in the wind. My eyes watered, and my nostrils burned. I whipped off Diego's jacket to cover my mouth, knotting the sleeves at the back of my head.

I rose onto the tips of my toes, feeling around. My skin heated fast while glass sliced into my forearm, but finally, I managed to grab the handle. I cranked it, opened the door, and ran down the stairs holding the jacket in place. I tried to blink away the burn blurring my vision as plumes of smoke surrounded me. I leaned over the railing and jumped back as heat scorched my hand. Movement below caught my eye. It looked as if men were running in and out. I waved the jacket and screamed for help. Flames engulfed almost everything on the ground floor, consuming the base of the stairs. If I didn't get through, I'd have to jump over the side of the roof.

I started down the steps when someone caught my waist from behind, picked me up, and carried me back up the stairwell. "Diego?" I cried.

Strong, sinewy forearms pinned me to a hard body, easily wrapping around my torso. A voice rumbled against my back, deep and full of grit. "Try again."

Cristiano.

I struggled to turn, and when we were back on the roof, I kicked his shin. He released me, and I stumbled back, spinning to face him.

"What are you doing here?" I choked out.

"Ladder," he said, coming toward me. "*Now.*"

"What ladder?" I backed away. With my eyes watering, he almost seemed like an apparition from the night before, still in his open-collar white dress shirt and wrinkled suit pants. It didn't take long for me to connect the pieces. "You did this."

"We have to get out of here."

"I'm not going *anywhere* with you." I snarled. "Your brother's inside."

"You have no other choice." He grabbed me by the arm. I wrestled with him, my chest tightening in panic as he easily yanked me toward the ladder. Suddenly, I was nine years old again and his puppet, pulled along like I weighed nothing, forced to the edge of nothingness.

I coughed as smoke suffocated my lungs. "Let *go.*"

He took my shoulders and shook me. "*Wake up*, Natalia. This warehouse could blow any second."

It hit me then what was inside—gunpowder. Artillery. Explosives. Fear gripped me as easily now as it had the last time Cristiano had torn me away from my loved ones when they needed me most. But this time, I wasn't afraid of what Cristiano would do to me. I feared for Diego. I didn't think I could survive the crumbling of my future if he was taken from me. I tried to wriggle free. "I have to tell him."

"He knows. Diego can take care of himself, and if he can't, it's already too late."

I pushed him away. "Fuck you. I'm not leaving him."

"What are you going to do? If you run back in there, you'll burn alive. Down is the only way out." He didn't give me a chance to answer. In one mighty swoop, he had me off my feet and over his shoulder.

"What are you doing?" I screeched.

He strode toward the edge with no signs of stopping. For a split second, I believed he was going to launch me over the side until we reached an access ladder I hadn't noticed before. "What the fuck were you doing up here?" he growled, descending down the side of the building swiftly, as if he didn't have an adult female hanging over his back. "I told you to go straight home."

"He's your *brother*."

Upside down, I spotted Diego's Mercedes. We were at the back gate. The fire roared on all sides but hadn't reached the lot yet. On the ground, Cristiano set me on my feet and scanned my legs and dress. In the cold light of breaking dawn, he seared me with a different kind of heat than he had the night before. He didn't seem to like what he saw anymore. "Get on the horse," he said.

Near the open gate, a man on a horse held the reins of a rearing black stallion. I wasn't going anywhere without Diego. I turned to run around front where the semis were parked, but Cristiano snatched my elbow, pulled me back, and hoisted me up. I struggled, trying to kick him as he carried me toward the exit. He put a hand to the horse's nose, and when it'd calmed, Cristiano dropped me on its back.

"You can't do this," I said, my throat thick. "We can't leave Diego here."

He grabbed the horn and butt of the saddle, trapping me. "Your misguided loyalty is going to get you killed, but not today." He pulled himself up, took the reins in one hand, and wrapped an arm around my waist to secure my back to his front. "Hold on," he said and spurred the horse with a "*Hyah!*"

The stallion jerked into motion, and we exited into the desert. I squirmed against Cristiano, fighting to look back. The other rider took off in the opposite direction to catch up with a group of men on horses. I braced myself for a bone-rattling explosion, and another irrevocable shift in my life. "He's going to *die*," I said.

"Cockroaches survive fire. Butterflies, on the other hand . . ." He tightened his hold on me. "They go up in smoke. You'll see your Romeo again, I guarantee it."

"Let me go." My imagination jumped ahead to Diego's funeral. The only black dress I had was the one on my body. The last one I'd seen him in. A scrap of fabric. I'd have to buy one. Or dye something black. Another dress for another funeral . . .

"Please." My voice cracked, but I clawed at the solid bar of his forearm, trying to free myself, prepared to fall off if I had to. I didn't expect him to release me, so when he did, I braced to hit the ground. He grabbed me again, capturing my upper arms and pinning them to my sides. "I can't leave Diego there."

"You're not," he said. "I'm forcing you away."

"Take me back."

"Have you learned nothing from your mother's death?" Cristiano held me in a grip so tight, his fingertips dug into my bicep. "If you're drawn to this life, fine—but you can't be so fucking reckless."

My vocal cords protested, but I continued to fight. "I'm not drawn to it. I want no part of this."

"You're lying to yourself, but if you want me to make that true, say the word. I'll put the fear of God into you and send you sprinting back to California for good." He put his mouth to my ear. "I thought I'd scared you straight years ago, but I'm happy to try again."

In that moment, any thoughts of Diego vanished. I remembered who I was with—the devil himself. "Where are you taking me?" I asked, twisting my torso against him.

Riding one-handed, he slid his coarse palm higher up my bare shoulder. "I suppose I could take you anywhere, couldn't I? Imagine if I showed up at the gates of hell with an angel like you."

Where young women were trapped and used, bought and sold. Dread spread through my body to my toes and fingers. There were worse things than death in this world, and Cristiano wanted to teach me a lesson. My heart hammered as his suit pants scraped my bare outer thighs. "But—why w-would you . . . you can't—"

"Mmm, there it is, the fear," he said as I struggled to beat back my panic. "Don't worry. You get used to the underworld's fire." He put his scratchy cheek to mine. "And I suppose, in exchange, *I* could be persuaded to give heaven a try."

We'd left the warehouse behind and were galloping along the edge of town, toward the thick of trees that surrounded the compound. Even when I recognized we were on our way home, my shivering didn't subside. The power in Cristiano's every touch, in his words, reminded me that despite the time that had passed, and despite the fact that I was no longer a child—I still held no chance against him. His grip on me never relented. He was in control of my fate.

I couldn't fight Cristiano. I was in both God's and the devil's hands now. Wherever he chose to take me, I had to go.

"That's it," Cristiano said when I sank against him, his voice suddenly hoarse. "I suspect you'll even like the feeling of surrender."

For possibly the first time since it'd happened, I recalled crying into Cristiano's neck as he'd taken me down the ladder into the tunnel. I'd had a strange albeit fleeting sense of safety. Despite all the things he'd done and the rumors I'd heard, I'd been programmed as a girl to see him as a protector no matter what he was, and somehow, a piece of that trust in him still remained.

The sun rose between two mountains as we steered away from endless desert. Wind whipped my hair the way it hadn't in years—not since the last time my mother and I had ridden the Cruz property, cataloguing different types of vegetation, a project for my science class that'd turned into a regular weekend activity for us. The fresh morning air felt good—reinvigorating even. The thought came with a wave of guilt. How could I think that when there was a possibility Diego had taken his last breath?

Cristiano rode up the long drive toward the house. A team of men in black scurried around trucks and tanks like ants on a hill. They stopped to look as we approached, some of them raising their rifles, only lowering them once they saw me.

Cristiano halted the stallion, hopped down, and reached for me. I slid off the other side and gasped as I landed on my bare feet. Pain shot through my soles, but I ran into Barto's open arms.

"We were looking for you all night," he hissed.

"There was an attack," I rushed out. "And a fire at the w—"

"I got your text." Barto frowned as he rubbed between my eyebrows and showed me his soot-darkened thumb. "Diego took you there?"

"Is he alive?"

"I just spoke to him."

Barto clutched me to him as my knees gave out in relief. With gritted teeth, I turned my glare on Cristiano, who stared daggers right back at us, his eyes narrowing on Barto. "He did this," I told Barto.

"Who, Cristiano?" he asked. "Did he hurt you?"

"No, but—"

I jumped with a *bang* behind me. My father stormed down the front steps, the door swinging in his wake. "Natalia Lourdes King Cruz. Where the fuck have you been?" He stopped abruptly when he saw Cristiano. "You brought her back?"

"I called him about the warehouse fire," Barto said.

"I was already on my way, so I said I'd look for her," Cristiano said.

"*And?*" Papá demanded. In a rumpled button-down and jeans, he looked as if he'd gotten dressed in the dark. "You have as much in that warehouse as we do."

"More," Cristiano said.

"Yet you bring my daughter back to me yourself? The

warehouse could explode. You should be there putting out the fire."

Cristiano pushed back some of his jet-black hair that had fallen over his forehead. "She was stuck on the roof," he said. "Everything else can be replaced. Protecting your family has always been my priority."

My father's ashen face stilled. He charged forward and shook Cristiano's hand with vigor. "Your courage will be rewarded. What the devil was she doing there?"

Cristiano glanced over. "Ask her."

Papá turned on me. Shadows marked his face like bruises. "What happened? Why were you there?"

As my immediate fears of losing Diego and being kidnapped by Cristiano subsided, I was left with my father's fury. "*Lo siento, Papá.*"

"You're *sorry?*" His voice rose as he stepped toward me. "Answer me when I question you. *¿Qué la chingada* were you doing there?"

I tried to stand tall in nothing more than a skimpy dress as my father, all his men, and Cristiano stared at me. "I—I . . ."

"She spent the night there," Cristiano supplied. "With Diego."

Father took one look at my outfit, hair, and makeup, and he grabbed me by the arm. "He better pray he burns alive. I will kill him for this."

"No," I cried. I'd managed to keep my emotions in check since I'd been torn from my dream earlier, but now, they overcame me. "It's not what you think," I said as my voice broke. "We were talking and we fell asleep—"

"Get inside." He shoved me up the stairs to the house. "Indecent *brat.*"

"Papi—"

"Do you think this is a game?" he bellowed, throwing

me into the foyer so I landed on my behind. Standing over me, he seethed, "It wasn't enough I lost my wife and the love of my life? I should lose you too? You want me to spend the rest of my days mourning my entire family?"

While anger reddened his face, pain was clear in his eyes. My chest stuttered as I tried to hold in my breaking sobs. "No. I'm s-sorry."

"I have *enemies*, Natalia. Do you know what they do to daughters like you? Kidnap, rape, and beat you half to death as—"

"Enough," Cristiano said.

"As they videotape it all for me. Then they cut your neck. Is that the memory you want to leave me with?"

My throat closed hearing him talk more candidly than he ever had around me. "But I was with Diego—"

"You will never—*ever*—see him again. You're forbidden."

I closed my fist against the tile. "You can't do that," I said.

"Do not talk back to me." He raised his hand, and I ducked to cover my head. "My father would've belted me a hundred times by your age for all the ways you've defied me."

"Enough," Cristiano repeated. It was the calmest, most controlled threat I'd ever heard. I peeked out from under my arms. Cristiano filled the doorway but said no more.

Papá started as if broken from a trance. He began to shake and lowered his arm before limping forward to steady himself on the foyer table. "I can't lose you too," he said shakily as tears filled his eyes. "Nothing scares me more than that possibility, *Lourdesita*."

He hadn't called me "Little Lourdes" since before I'd left for school. And he'd never even come close to laying a finger on me. He was in pain. I scrambled to my feet and hugged his waist. "I love you. I never want to hurt you."

His heart pounded against my cheek. "I'm—I'm sorry, *mija*. You're not the one I'm angry with, and you know I would never . . ."

"*Yo sé*, Papi. I know." I buried my face in his chest and cried until he kissed the top of my head.

"All right, Talia. I have to deal with this fire. Go upstairs and get cleaned up." He pulled away and said over my head, "Ride with me."

"I have transportation," Cristiano answered.

I'd almost forgotten he was there.

"I'll see you at the warehouse then," my father said on his way out the front door. He disappeared into a black car. Trucks rumbled and shuddered with power. The first in a line of cars tore down the winding road, and the rest followed, kicking up clouds of dust.

The house became eerily and unusually quiet. For everyone except a couple guards out front to leave, it had to be serious. For them to leave me alone with a killer, it had to be life or death.

And it was. Reality dawned. The warehouse . . . the goods inside. The damage done was enough to seal Diego's fate. There was no escaping a loss of this magnitude.

"You're responsible for this," I said. Had Cristiano's talk of games the night before been a warning? If so, he'd made a move that would put us all in the crosshairs of the Maldonados. "My father trusted you. *Diego* trusted you, and you tried to kill him."

"If I had, he'd be dead."

"Like your parents?"

He took a step toward me. "Meaning?"

"Diego told me everything. If you'd have your own

parents killed, you wouldn't hesitate to do the same to anyone else."

As he advanced, I retreated until I was up against a wall. "And you think I'd destroy my own livelihood to do it?" he asked.

If it meant getting what he wanted, I wouldn't put it past him. Which suggested he'd go to great lengths to grant his own wishes. To position himself at my father's side and strike when Papá least expected it. To see Diego gone.

To take back what he thought he was owed.

What did loyalty mean to a man who'd betrayed and been betrayed by those he'd trusted? Even if he hadn't committed the murder, what loyalty remained after eleven years on the run? A feral cat could be domesticated, but it would never stop looking over its shoulder.

If Diego's suspicions were right, then Cristiano wouldn't stop until he got what he'd come for.

The question was—did I fit into this somehow?

The answer, I feared, I was about to learn.

"My father's expecting you at the warehouse," I reminded him.

"I'm not going to the warehouse." Cristiano wore no expression. He spoke with the ease and confidence of a predator who'd cornered its prey and had the time and proclivity to savor picking it apart. "I'm staying right where I am. Now, come here."

15

NATALIA

Was this how my mother had felt? Cornered by Cristiano with nobody in the house to protect her? *No.* It was worse for her. Cristiano wasn't breaking my trust like he had hers. And he couldn't destroy my sense of safety in my own home. He'd already done that years ago. It wasn't the first time Cristiano and I had squared off under this roof.

His eyes lingered over my dress. "Did my brother do that?"

I followed his gaze to the blood and dirt smeared on my legs. As soon as I noticed the bruises on my forearm and wrists, and the cuts on my ankles and feet, they began to throb. "I already told you, he isn't like that."

Cristiano came toward me, and I backed away, suddenly aware of the glass wedged in my feet. When he was close enough that I could inhale his smoky mix of sweat and burnt wood, he said, "You can limp to your bedroom, or I can carry you there."

My breath caught in my throat. "My bedroom? Why?"

"Use your imagination."

I could think of no reason Cristiano would want to take me upstairs except for the obvious one. What chance did I stand against him? He might as well have been made of marble for all his muscle. Resisting him would be like fighting a statue. He knew that. Maybe he wanted my struggle. If it was he who'd tried this with my mother, her fight had cost her her life.

But if he touched me, he'd lose any shot at uniting our families. I had to believe that was reason enough to stop him from hurting me.

"My father would murder you in cold blood," I warned.

"Understood." He moved aside to let me pass.

With Cristiano at my back, I crossed the foyer to the dining room and made my way to the stairs. On the second floor, I stopped at my closed door, remembering how I'd skipped down the hall to my mother's room. He reached past me, turned the handle, and pushed it open. "Inside," he said.

I took a breath and stepped over the threshold. With the curtains drawn, my room was dark. He shut the door behind himself, stood at my back, and moved my hair over my shoulder before lowering the zipper of my dress.

"Strip," he said.

Fear and curiosity warred inside me. Was Cristiano so weak that he'd risk his chance at an empire just to have me? If he raped me, killed me, or both, there'd be no question as to his guilt for doing the same to my mother. He'd be back on the run.

My trust in him was buried somewhere deep, and I drew from it now. I was hit hard with a memory I hadn't thought of in over a decade—my mother and I encountering a young Cristiano while gathering flowers in the garden for one of Mamá's parties. I had to have been five or six, which would've made him almost twenty. He'd never picked flowers, he'd told us, and we'd giggled as Mamá had made him carry our baskets of bouquets around for the afternoon. It was one of the only instances I could remember him without a scowl. Even when he'd promised me he was a monster far worse than any that dared hide under my bed, he'd spoken gravely.

"My mother is watching," I said into the dark. If any part of him regretted what'd happened to her, maybe he'd soften.

"I'm not going to hurt you," he said.

I supposed that was the best I could ask for. To come out of this no more wounded than I already was. I pulled down my dress and stood in my thong and strapless bra.

He placed his palm on my upper back. "Walk," he said.

I raised my eyes to the bed in front of me. He could have me any way he wanted, and nobody would stop him. Everything I'd saved for Diego would be taken in a flash. Was there anything left of that man who'd been so devoted to our family that he'd carried baskets of flowers for us? There had to be. I wasn't sure how I knew, but like the way he'd nonchalantly referred to Natasha, my gut told me Cristiano only wanted to see how far he could push me.

I straightened my shoulders and stepped toward the bed. When I neared the footboard, he applied pressure to my back, guiding me away from it and toward the en suite bathroom instead.

Inside, he flipped on a dim overhead light. I watched in the reflection of the mirror over the sink as he circled me, his eyes roaming over my back. He set his jaw, inspecting my body almost clinically. Just another Natasha.

He stopped at the counter to empty his pockets. With his attention diverted, I studied him back. His stark white dress shirt had been marred by smoke, ash, and what looked like blood. My blood, I realized, from when he'd carried me down the access ladder. Without thinking, I dropped my gaze and sucked in a breath at the bulge in his pants.

He glanced up at me, his watch *clinking* as he set it on the Italian marble countertop. He tightened the roll of one sleeve, securing it at his elbow, then the other. The mere sight of his powerful, sinewy forearms made me light-headed. They were weapons in their own right. Every part of him was, it seemed, down to the beast straining against his zipper. Most of the men I knew couldn't match his strength. What chance did *I* stand against him if he tried to overpower me?

He stepped forward, towering over me, soot smudged on his admittedly handsome face—he looked the way I imagined the Grim Reaper might if he shopped in the finest apparel stores and possessed the chiseled features of a god. "Wash the cuts," he said.

I tensed. "What?"

He moved around me and turned on the faucet to the bathtub. "The cuts on your arms and legs. I told you to watch out for glass, did I not?" He grunted. "I can't help but think you ran through it just to spite me."

"I did it for Diego," I said, although it was only half-true. "And I'd do it again."

He looked over his shoulder at me, his gaze shadowed. "So you continue to remind me, even though I was there. I watched you run into the fire for him."

I limped to the tub. "You were wrong earlier. Butterflies aren't delicate."

We switched places. He pulled open my top drawer and started pushing products around. "No?"

"During a wildfire, they don't go up in smoke. They bury themselves in soil."

He moved to the next drawer, shoving aside my hair dryer. "Another way they're survivors."

I perched on the inside edge of the tub so I wouldn't have my back to him. He kept his to me as he rifled in my drawers, his muscled back rippling under his dress shirt. He dumped my makeup bag into the sink, picking through items while I gently soaped my right arm and hand.

He went through every basket, drawer and cabinet, including the medicine one over the sink, gathering things and placing them by the side of the toilet.

I moved on to cleaning my feet. Eventually, Cristiano sat on the outside lip of the tub and held out his hand for the soap. I gave it to him, and he reached in to clean my other foot. He alternated between lathering the soap over my cuts and massaging my ankles. "What happened to your shoulder?" he asked.

I hadn't realized I was holding it. Or the throb of pain when I raised my arm. "I fell."

When he seemed satisfied with my feet, he stood and lowered the lid of the toilet. "Sit," he said to me before disappearing into my bedroom.

I moved from the bath, dried myself off, and slipped on my purple satin robe. Seated on the toilet, I swayed a little, recalling the sensation of riding for the first time in over a decade. For some time, I'd craved that feeling of driving a horse again the way I had with my mother on one side, but the longer I put it off, the harder it was to get back on.

Cristiano returned with my desk chair. He sat in front of me and handed me a towel of ice. "For your shoulder."

I inspected it as if it might be hiding mini daggers before deciding to take my chances. I held it to my arm. "Thank you."

He took tweezers from the counter and grasped my wrist. "This is a deep one, but it'll be the worst one."

I'd sooner faint than show him my pain. I made a fist with my opposite hand as he squeezed my skin.

"Why were you at the warehouse?" he asked quietly as he inspected the cut. Somehow, he was more menacing when he was calm and collected than when yelling.

"Diego stopped to check on a problem."

"And he decided *that* was the right place to fuck you? You're a foolish girl."

"*Foolish?*" I bit out, my temper flaring. "For your information, we barely touched."

"I don't believe you."

I set my jaw. "You don't know a single *thing* about him, me, or our relationship—"

One corner of his mouth crooked. "There it is."

"What?"

Belatedly, dull pain radiated from a spot on my palm. He held up the tweezers to show me a thin but substantial shard of glass. "If you can take that, the rest should be easy."

I shut my mouth. I hadn't even felt it. He'd tricked me to distract me.

His expression defaulted to a scowl as he turned over my hand to inspect my knuckles. "You should never have gone anywhere without your guards," he scolded. "Not the club, and especially not the warehouse."

"I don't need to be looked after," I said firmly, but my heart skipped. Perhaps what scared me most wasn't Cristiano's reputation, but the fact that he was unreadable. Unpredictable. That he had not only the strength to shove me down a dark tunnel but that he might do it for no other reason than to amuse himself. *How* could Father trust him?

"You'd feel differently if there wasn't anybody to look

after you." He tweezed a few small pieces from my fore-arm. "You've never had to survive in the wild. You're just the kind of prey some predators are looking for—one with a false sense of bravery."

He had no right to accuse me of that. We'd faced off when I'd been weaponless and small enough that I'd only come up to his waist. I'd held my own for a kid. "I *have* survived," I said. "Not all danger is physical. I've navigated through a different kind of wild, one you know nothing about."

He worked silently a few moments. "You forget I've lost parents too—and a brother as far as I'm concerned. I was thrown out of the only life I knew and forced to fend for myself."

"You have only yourself to blame for the consequences of your actions."

He glanced up at me. "You still think I'm guilty?"

"Yes," I said. No matter what questions I had, he'd latch onto any weakness I showed, so I kept my mounting doubts to myself.

"Nah," he said. "I'm innocent. You know I am. Yet my brother chose not to believe me, even though it would end my life. So what do you suggest I do about that?"

I tried not to let his twisted truths worm their way into my consciousness. He was only trying to manipulate me against Diego, that was all. "*Nothing.*"

Like Diego, Cristiano had long, full lashes. But behind them, his dark, calculating eyes betrayed the differences between them. "You know I can't let something like that slide."

Goose bumps spread over my skin, prickling my hair under my silky robe. "So you are here for revenge."

He returned to the task in front of him. "I reached out to him once, about four years after Bianca's death. Did he tell you? I wanted to come home. To tell Costa the truth and pledge my loyalty to him."

I shifted on the seat. I'd only been thirteen and already away at school. I hadn't heard anything about Cristiano reaching out then or since. "What happened?"

"He said he'd broker a meeting between your father and me, but it was a setup. He tried to have me killed." Holding my wrist in one hand, he ripped open a bandage with his teeth and stuck it on one of my cuts. "There's no trust amongst us, and there never will be."

It wasn't as if my father or Diego told me much to begin with, but that seemed like an important detail to keep from me. And if they'd hide that, what else didn't I know? Could I even believe Cristiano?

"What about me?" I asked quietly. "I said you were guilty too. You must think I also betrayed you."

I swallowed when he didn't respond. If Cristiano had anything to do with the fall of the Maldonado deal, he must've known they'd come after Diego—and the people he cared about. "I guess that was your plan all along. We didn't give you a chance to prove your innocence. My father and Diego hunted you for years. Now, the Maldonados can take us all out in one fell swoop and you command both cartels."

"If you believe that, why aren't you running for your life?"

"I wouldn't leave my father or Diego behind."

"You don't know what you're toying with, *mamacita*," he said, shaking his head. "Where was Diego when you were on the roof alone? *He* left *you* behind."

"He had to salvage what he could of the product. When he ran downstairs, the fire hadn't started yet. He couldn't have known that would happen." I adjusted the ice pack. "He was coming back for me."

"It only matters that you believe he would've."

He released my arm, and I pulled it back, cradling it to my body. "That's not fair. Diego has been there for me my whole life."

"It must be coincidence that staying by your side also serves his best interests."

I wanted to ask Cristiano what he meant, but giving him the chance to spin more lies felt like a betrayal to Diego.

I bent my knee as Cristiano picked up my foot and placed it in his lap. He held my ankle in one hand and ran his fingers along my arch. I jerked but tried to hide that I was ticklish. His touch firmed and my reflex to squirm disappeared. A sharp, pleasant thrill traveled up the inside of my thigh. My instinct should've been to pull away, but warmth coursed through me instead. Satisfaction bloomed like surrendering to a protective embrace as arousal tightened my insides.

Cristiano had a face made to lure prey, a voice as powerful as the sensation of skin on skin, a presence that demanded my attention. But I knew the danger he presented—how could I possibly harbor any attraction to him? What had given me the confidence that he hadn't brought me up here to hurt me? My body and mind betrayed me.

As he dug the tweezers into a particularly sensitive spot, I clenched my fist around the towel of ice and sucked in a breath. He raised his eyes to mine. "Mmm," he said. "*Qué interesante.*"

"What's interesting?" I breathed.

"You're excited by a little pinch."

"I am not. I'm in pain."

"And a part of you likes it." He blinked lazily at me. "A part of *me* likes it."

I inhaled. *Please tell the heavens it is my dying wish to hear you scream.* The warmth he'd awakened in me simmered to a tingle between my legs. Why did things that should intimidate me arouse me instead? So far, his threats had been hollow, but just because Cristiano was handling me gently now didn't mean I was in the clear.

"I'll bet you wish your guards were here now," he said with an almost imperceptible smile.

"I want my gun back," I said.

He paused, then glanced up at me. "Will you learn how to use her?"

"Yes."

He extracted more shards and wiped them on a towel before setting aside the tweezers to spread antibiotic ointment onto the wounds. "Better?" he asked when I put down the ice pack and rolled my numb shoulder.

I mumbled my agreement as he applied bandages to the deepest cuts. He smoothed his thumb back and forth over the final one to make it stick but didn't stop there. The pad of his finger slid to my ankle, and he turned my foot over to inspect it. It tickled slightly, but resisting the urge to squirm only made me more aware of his palm as it grazed upward. His breath shallowed as he looked over my leg, then glanced at me. His pupils dilated, and his eyes grew darker.

My heart pounded, not just because his hand kept going but also with surprise for the effect I had on someone as taciturn as Cristiano. He wanted me and wasn't hiding it. My traitorous body came alive under his firm but deliberate examination. I shouldn't notice how good his touch felt. I *should* have cared that we were alone and nobody could hear me scream.

As Cristiano moved the hem of my robe aside, I slapped my hand over his, stopping him in his tracks. "I'm waiting until marriage," I blurted. I wasn't sure why I said it, or why I thought that might deter him.

His lip curled in a way I could only interpret as angry. "A virgin?"

I swallowed as an electric current passed between us.

His fingertips dug into my thigh. "You've saved yourself," he said slowly, half statement, half question. "And you think using that as an argument won't have the opposite effect you want it to?"

My brain scrambled to keep up. It sounded as if he meant my virginity was something he'd want, but I couldn't fathom why. I wouldn't know what to do with a man as experienced as he was.

But I could learn.

I forced the thought away. "I've saved myself for Diego," I said. "You'd be taking that away from him. From *me*."

His nostrils flared. "You think I'd go as far as to rape you in your father's home?"

My thigh pulsated with warmth where his hand had stopped, my skin sensitive under his rough palm. "I think back then, whatever plans you had were interrupted by my mother or by me. And I think you're too smart to make that same mistake twice."

His gaze drifted down between my legs, where only a silky piece of fabric hid what he so clearly wanted. "Plans? Regretfully, I have none for *you*, Natalia."

He stood and returned to the sink to replace his watch and the contents of his pockets. I waited, tense as a bowstring, until he left the room. And I didn't breathe again until I heard the front door close.

Once the immediate fear of what Cristiano might do subsided, a violent tremble overtook me. I waited for relief to come, but adrenaline coursed through me. Now that I was alone, I felt as if I should do something. I was safe, but would it last? How long until he returned? Until he struck again?

I hugged my shoulders, dropped to my knees on the bathroom floor, and crossed myself. I thanked *La Virgen de Guadalupe* for sparing myself and Diego.

Then I prayed I'd never see Cristiano again.

16

CRISTIANO

I n my office overlooking *La Madrina*, I fixed a drink. Mid-afternoon, the nightclub was quiet as the cleaning crew scrubbed the downstairs floors and walls. In a few hours, the bar staff would prepare for all the sinners who'd spend their Good Friday night celebrating tonight's theme—*la iglesia roja*. Red church. Sturdy construction would mute the thump of bass, and the dancefloor's crimson glow would make my office look like an opium den.

I'd been up most of the night, but I felt invigorated. Serving justice could do that to a man. With a third direct attack on his deal, Diego would've worked everything out by now—but he'd be missing the final piece. "You can expect my brother any minute," I said to Maksim, who stood straight-backed by the door to my office.

"I figured."

I held up a bottle of *Rey Sol Añejo*. "Drink?" I asked.

"Nah." Max chewed on a toothpick. "Guess I should have my wits about me. His claws will be out."

"He'll fight, but not physically. He can't win. Instead, he'll try to manipulate the game board."

Diego had run out of moves, though. After over a decade of being hunted by my brother, our day of reckoning had come. Only, I wasn't the one caught in a trap. For a third of my life, I'd been mislabeled a traitor, had been forced from friends, family, and a life I'd valued, and I'd done whatever I'd had to in order to survive. And in mere moments, Diego would pay the price for it.

I swirled my drink, breathing in caramel and tobacco. "Try not to kill him if you can help it."

Max's two-way radio beeped and Alejo's voice came through. "We've got a visitor."

"Bring him in," I said.

Max removed his assault rifle from across his body and held it with one hand. "You got it, *jefe*."

"*Oye. Muy bien.* Your Spanish is coming along."

With barely a chuckle, Max went downstairs to meet Diego and his other escorts. I shrugged into my suit jacket and stood at the one-sided glass wall. I wasn't in the habit of spending so much time at the club, but it'd been easier to conduct business here than drive back and forth from the Badlands. The evening before, I'd been on a call to Turkey when my men had alerted me of Natalia's presence. I could still see her now, all bronze legs and arms, the ends of her black hair brushing her waist as she'd moved her hips to disco. Her wide, nervous eyes as she'd turned to face me on the dancefloor.

I shouldn't have been surprised to return home and find Natalia so enchanting—she'd always fascinated me, but not just with her beauty. She tested boundaries, even when fearful. *Especially* when fearful. She'd manipulated her parents in childish but effective ways. She held unwavering devotion to my brother. Her sheltered childhood had given her a false sense of safety as an adult, but I'd hoped her mother's death, and our encounter that day, would scare her into obedience. I didn't know if it was more frustrating or charming that it hadn't.

She'd still dangled herself as bait in front of me, a man she knew to be dangerous. A man she believed was her mother's murderer. Every time I tried to scare her, she returned for more. Even hours earlier, when I'd stood at her back in her bedroom and had practically watched her imagination run wild with all the possible things I could to do to her while we were alone, she hadn't cowered long.

She should cower, though. Testing boundaries got her into trouble. Case in point—she'd stupidly spent last night in the most dangerous place possible.

With Diego. *For* Diego.

It hadn't occurred to me they might be there. None of my men had seen her. I gripped my glass at the thought of Diego alone with her all night. It was like the unnerving feeling I'd gotten when I'd come across them in the courtyard at the costume party. Jealousy had warred with my fury. Any other time, I would've been delighted to catch Diego in a vulnerable moment, but Bianca Cruz's dying words had been for me. A plea. And no matter how far I'd run, or how hard I'd worked, I'd never forgotten them. And that tied me to Natalia in ways she didn't understand.

Maybe Natalia Lourdes was no longer my responsibility, but that instinct to protect her remained. Seeing her again had reawakened an unwelcome fondness for her, but my fascination wasn't nearly as innocent as it'd once been. But who could blame me?

She had mesmerizing violet eyes that could charm a man to walk into a burning building.

Long legs that could wrap around him for days.

And I hadn't stopped thinking about that virgin pussy since this morning.

Diego wouldn't know what the fuck to do with a *panocha* like that. I knew exactly what I'd do with it, though. And it would start with my tongue buried so deep inside her, I'd be tasting her for weeks.

With a knock at the door, I took a moment to collect myself. This was why I didn't fuck with sirens like Natalia King Cruz. I was thinking about *her* when I'd spent years anticipating this final standoff with my brother. Costa had cleared my name, and I was back where I belonged—but I still had one more loose end to tie up. I couldn't let Diego's faithlessness in me go unpunished.

And I was going to revel in every moment of what was to come.

I turned from the window. "*Pasen.*"

Maksim entered first, followed by two of my men as they restrained Diego. Max tossed a semi-automatic pistol next to the bottle of tequila on my desk. "He's clean."

"My brother shouldn't cause you any trouble," I said, picking up a second glass from the drink tray to pour a fresh one. "He's smart enough to know he's cornered."

"Your head of security has a glass eye and your bouncer a severe limp," Diego said. "They'd be lucky to get a shot anywhere near a target."

"I'd think twice about insulting anyone in this room." I gestured at a club chair. "Have a seat."

"I'm not staying," Diego said. Covered in ash and soot, with cuts along his face and hands, my brother looked as if he'd been up all night fighting for his life. Which, I supposed he had.

"*Siéntate,*" Eduardo ordered.

"You were expecting me." Diego sat on the edge of the

chair. "Why not show up at the warehouse like a man to face those you ruined?"

"I had something to attend to at Costa's." I held out the tequila to him. "Here."

He waved off the drink. "Costa was with me."

"*¿Seguro?* Are you sure?" I asked, offering it again. "It's top-shelf. A special edition sent especially from a tequila bar in Guadalajara."

"I'm sure what's 'special' about it is a dram of poison," Diego said.

I gave Eduardo the glass. "Enjoy, *compadre*," I said.

Ed nodded as he accepted it. "*Gracias, señor.*"

I returned in front of Diego, picked up my drink, and sat back against the edge of my desk. "Costa left his poor, trembling daughter alone in that big house this morning. And during such a dangerous time." I frowned into my drink. "I took it upon myself to offer her my protection. And my comfort."

Diego narrowed his eyes on me. "What'd you do to Natalia?"

"Nothing she didn't enjoy—don't worry."

"*Vete a la chingada,*" he said, jumping out of his chair. "Fuck you, *pinche puto pendejo.*"

As Diego released a string of curses, I held up a hand to stop my men from drawing their weapons. Had I hit a nerve? When it came to Costa and his family, Diego put on an admirable performance, but today, we had no audience. Could it be that his feelings for Natalia were *genuine*? I smiled. That would make this even more interesting. Diego was about to lose more than I could've even planned for.

"You almost *killed* her this morning," Diego said.

She wasn't supposed to have been at the warehouse, nor was he. It was a fuck-up on my part, but I wouldn't let him see that. "*Tranquilo,*" I said, keeping my tone light to calm him. "I simply bandaged her up." Bandaged her up and resisted my every urge to fuck her until she forgot my brother's name. If waiting years for this moment with Diego wasn't evidence of my unrivaled self-control, removing my hands from Natalia's smooth, firm thigh was.

A round with me and she'd question everything she knew—including her devotion to Diego. It hadn't occurred to me until now that she might actually mean something to him.

"She was trapped on the roof of the warehouse with no way out," I said. "Luckily, I was there, or she'd have been burned alive."

"You say that like it was a coincidence," he said. "You planned it that way."

"Planned it? No. I was supposed to watch from a distance as your hopes, dreams, and livelihood went up in smoke." I took a sip. "I hadn't intended to risk my own life for your Natalia." Despite the silky vanilla-almond flavor the tequila had left, *'your Natalia'* tasted bitter on my tongue. *My Natalia* sounded better, but I couldn't entertain that thought.

After this, she'd never forgive me.

"You did this, Cristiano," Diego said evenly, taking a step toward me. "The hits on the safe houses. The tunnel explosion. The warehouse fire. You're responsible for all of it. And now, I have nothing to offer the Maldonados but ashes."

I stood to meet him. "I warned you one shot was all you'd get it," I said. "You missed. That was your mistake."

"I've never taken a shot at family. That was you."

"You put me in front of the firing squad, which is worse," I said, holding his stare. "First, by accusing me of Bianca's murder, then years later when I reached out to you for help. You sent men to kill me as soon as you knew where I was, and they came home empty-handed. Never take aim if you can't hit the bullseye. You missed both times."

"You went to Costa, our family's enemy, with information that you knew would get our parents killed," he said, balling his fists. "I tried turning you over to Costa, yes, but that's no different than what you did to our mother and father."

"It's completely different. The victims of my crimes are never victims—they know exactly the risks of the life they lead." I picked up the tequila bottle in the likeness of a smiling golden sun and pulled off the top. "Our parents were getting deeper and deeper into trafficking innocent children and women," I said. "I went to Costa for help because you and I were too young to do anything, and they had to be stopped."

"Nothing breaks the bond of family," Diego said. "Costa might've pulled the trigger, but you murdered them. Their blood is on your hands."

I made a show of checking my knuckles. They were calloused and scarred from years of defense, offense, and survival. But there wasn't a spot of blood on them. "You're one to talk about breaking family bonds." I refilled my drink. "Do you know what tomorrow is, Diego?"

Diego took my drink off the desk and gulped from it. "Holy Saturday."

"The burning of Judas." I filled another glass on the tray for myself. "We'll be celebrating here at the club in case you know any traitors. There's still time to make an effigy."

"Then make it in your likeness." His nostrils flared. He thrust the glass in my direction, and tequila sloshed over the side as he pointed. "You killed *our parents*."

"Costa did."

"And he has paid half the price," Diego bit out. "His debt will be settled once his daughter chooses me over him. Once he realizes I can take her away from him if I choose. But *you* haven't been made to pay at all."

"I've paid, believe me. The Cruzes were my family, and they turned on me for a crime I didn't commit."

"They are not your family!" He shoved a hand in his hair and turned around, pacing to the glass. "They never were. You don't deserve one after what you did to ours."

The Cruzes *had* been family to me once, especially Bianca. Costa's wife could've easily cast me off or ignored me as she had Diego—who, I was certain, she'd seen through from the start.

But she hadn't. She'd cared for me the way a mother should when she had no reason to. But she'd never get to speak her truth—so I would do it for her.

"Bianca *was* family," I said. "You didn't know her like I did."

"No, I never got the privilege," Diego said, turning back to level me with a glare. "We all know how *well* you knew her. Despite Costa's pardon, the state they found her in speaks for itself."

I dropped my glass and charged at him, seizing him by his shirt. "I never touched her, and you know it. You talk of loyalty but reek of betrayal, and that's why she kept you at arm's length. It's why Costa will *never* let you near his daughter. They only trust you so far."

Diego grabbed my lapels to try to push me off, but Max drew his gun in a split second. Glass eye or not, my right-hand man had as unshakeable an allegiance to me as I did to him, and that made him a killer of the deadliest sort. Diego clenched his teeth but let go of my jacket.

"You've planted some bullshit ideas in Natalia's head,"

I said, "but don't think I don't know where they came from. You're the one with plans to take over, not me."

Diego laughed grimly. "I'll do it the noble way. I don't have to force a woman like you. My plans are to marry Natalia, who loves me, and stand by Costa's side until he's ready to hand over the reins."

I released him with a shove. It was uncanny, my ability to sniff out when my brother was lying. Why other certain people couldn't see it, I had no idea. "You fused yourself to Natalia when she was most vulnerable. Bianca would never have allowed you to get so close to her. You saw an opportunity and you took it. And if Costa wasn't going to give you what you wanted, you were going to use Natalia's love for you against him."

"You'd have done the same," Diego said. "The difference is, Natalia fell for me, not you."

I had traveled the world in search of the kind of loyalty she gave Diego. I'd lost any family bonds I'd had or formed. My parents were dead. Bianca was dead. The only man I'd ever looked up to had thought I'd violated and murdered his wife. I'd gone through great pains to surround myself with men and women I trusted my life to every day—ones I'd give mine for in return.

Yet I remained haunted by the day Natalia had risked her life for my *brother*. A man who didn't deserve her. To have what I'd built was one thing. To have the unflinching devotion of a woman like her, to be loved the way Bianca had loved Costa, was surely nirvana.

But devotion to the wrong man could get you killed; my mother was evidence of that.

Diego made Natalia weak—I was doing her a favor.

Because Natalia had proved a woman who couldn't be moved with words or reason. It had to be with action and force.

"Natalia didn't fall for you. She was manipulated." I stalked closer to him, enjoying the way he pulled back his shoulders, as if he thought he stood a chance against me. "You slowly secured her loyalty to you over anyone else, so when you were ready to make demands of Costa, he'd have no choice but to give in or lose her."

"That doesn't mean I don't love her or see him as a father," Diego said. "I know what's best for all of us."

A monster didn't always perceive himself that way. But I saw right through my brother. "It was an admirable grab at power, not unlike something our father would've done, but it didn't work. And in the end, it doesn't matter, because it won't change your fate."

"Once the Maldonados hear about the fire, they'll come looking for me." A vein in his forehead appeared as he tensed his jaw. "I can't recover from this."

"No, you can't."

He swallowed, his hands twitching as if he had to resist throwing a punch. "So, here I am. You have me where you want me. What do you want, Cristiano?"

"Nobody gives me what I want. I take it."

He ran a hand through his hair and made a fist. "I've cost them over a hundred million dollars. They'll crucify me. And Costa. And everyone who ever spoke a word to me."

I undid my jacket as I rounded my desk to make a fresh drink. "You knew the risk of writing a check you might not be able to cash."

"I would've been able to—if not for you."

"There is no use in *if*, Diego." I sat in my leather chair and leaned back. Diego continued to stand tall, though I read the agitation in his eyes and hands. "What's done is done."

"So that's it. You'll ruin the Cruzes too? Stand back

and watch as the cartel takes revenge on everyone involved —me, my men . . . Natalia?"

I didn't respond at first, letting that sink in for Diego. He had fucked with me, and now I had the power to destroy him and everyone he loved. His precious Natalia too, who'd be especially devastated since she'd been lying to herself for years that she wanted nothing to do with this life. Now his sins would be hers.

When recognition of my reach began to cross his features, I spoke again.

"Ángel Maldonado and I happen to have an amicable relationship," I said, crossing an ankle over one knee. "For his mercy, I will pay a hefty price, but it can be arranged— for those I find deserving, at least."

His shoulders loosened just a little. "I figured as much. So what do you want in exchange for that 'hefty price'?"

"From you? Nothing. I'll pay the toll to spare Costa and his family—who have acted as *my* family."

"And me?" he asked, drawing back. "Your own brother?"

"You've been in my shoes." I opened the top drawer of my desk and took out a box of Cubans. "You had the chance to save my life by speaking to my innocence, but you didn't."

"I was trying to protect the family you claim to love. I had no reason to believe you weren't guilty."

I cut the tip of one cigar and glanced up at Diego to scrutinize his reaction to what I said next. "I'm not sure I believe that."

His jaw set as the pulse at the base of his neck quickened. He flattened his hands on my desk. "Whatever lies you've convinced yourself of, you can't hide from the truth. You'd murder your own brother."

"No. The Maldonados will do it for me." I flicked my

lighter and held the flame to the end of the cigar. "You left me at the mercy of another—now I'll do the same for you."

"Why not just shoot me here?" he asked. "Don't you have the guts?"

"I hope for a long, prosperous relationship with Costa if he wants one."

"And killing me might jeopardize that."

"I'm not killing you. You got yourself into this mess. I'm simply not going to help you." I puffed on the cigar, feeling gratified, then offered it to him. "Eye for an eye, Diego. It's more than you deserve after everything you've done."

He ignored my gift and straightened up, regaining composure as if he'd grasped an answer that could earn his freedom. There was none, but I'd play along until I got bored. I'd waited for this moment too long to rush it.

"You want to see me stripped of everything? My family, my money, my woman?" he asked. "You hold the cards, Cristiano. *Tienes todo el control.* I'm at your mercy—but you cannot let the Maldonados go through with this. They won't just kill me . . . they will make an example of me—"

"As they should." I traded the cigar for my drink. With a celebratory sip of tequila, I ran my tongue over my teeth, pleased to find revenge had hints of peach and sweet agave. "There has been a snake in the grass far too long, and it's only fair somebody separate its deceitful mind from its body."

He began to pace in front of my desk. "Name your price, then."

"There's none."

"There's always a price. Whatever it is, however high, tell me now."

I watched him quietly, reveling in the way his eyebrows knitted together when the truth dawned on him. *This* was the final puzzle piece he'd come looking for today, the one thing he couldn't figure out. What did I want in exchange for taking mercy on him?

Nothing.

I hadn't manipulated him into this position to extract anything. Because of him, I'd suffered. For years, I'd been on the run, looking over my shoulder for a *sicario* in the dark. I'd lived with the knowledge that the people I'd cared for most had thought me a traitor. I had pulled myself from nothing and built an empire. I was wealthier than God and surrounded by a steadfast army. I'd made peace with Costa. All that remained was to see my brother pay for his sins, which I suspected ran deeper than he was willing to admit.

And now I would.

And now he knew the truth.

Betrayal had a price, and even family had to pay.

"Confess your sins and pray for mercy," I said. "But you'll get none from me."

Diego had plans to take over Costa's cartel and drag down Natalia as he followed in my father's footsteps, but I wouldn't allow it. The world would be a better place devoid of any de la Rosa men, but especially without the two of them.

Diego shut his eyes, his chest expanding with each deep breath. When he looked at me again, his gaze burned with hatred. "You can't do this," he said.

"It is done." I looked to Maksim, Eduardo, and Alejo —my friends and my *compadres*—as I spoke to Diego. "You can run. I did for years. But I expect you won't make it months." I returned my eyes to my brother. "Then again, perhaps you'll surprise me."

"Or *perhaps* I'll spend my final days in California. Natalia is headed back soon. She'd like to have me with her."

I flattened a hand on my desk. I could order the Maldonados not to kill Natalia, but there was no guarantee they wouldn't if she purposely got in the way. I hadn't been able to stop my mother from supporting and defending my father's decision to get into the sex trade industry.

"You'd be putting Natalia at risk. You know what they'd do to her. It would be selfish. Are you a selfish man, Diego?"

He glanced away.

I didn't need an answer. I'd convince Costa to keep Natalia close in the coming days. With his help, no harm would befall her. I took a final pull from my cigar and stood, cracking my knuckles. "Do as you please with your final days. We're finished here." From my pocket, I took a silver coin and flipped it at him.

He caught it and turned it over in his palm. "What's this?"

"The ferryman demands a toll to take passengers to the underworld," I said. "This one's on me. Safe travels to hell, *hermano*."

Diego stood his ground, raising cold, bitter eyes to mine. "I'll beg if that's what it takes. Whatever you want, it's yours."

"You have nothing to offer me. What've you got that I can't buy for myself?"

"Besides my loyalty—information," he said. "I know everything there is to know about Costa's business. I can give you inside access. Together, we can take over his cartel and you can rule them both with me as an advisor."

"I have no need for Costa's business, but if I did, I'd

manage to secure it fine without you." I signaled for my men to remove Diego.

"Help me leave town," Diego said, growing louder as he rushed out his final pleas. "This will be the last you ever see or hear of me. You can tell everyone, including the Maldonados, I attacked you and died as a traitor. Tell them anything."

I rose from my chair, buttoning my jacket as I strolled around the side of my desk to face him. "You've plotted against Costa; why should I believe you wouldn't do the same to me? I can already see the wheels turning in your mind as a plan forms. I won't spend my life looking over my shoulder anymore."

"I will, you have my word," he rushed out. "I'll disappear completely."

"Your word means nothing. A parasite doesn't change its ways." I nodded to Maksim. "Remove him."

Eduardo and Alejo rushed forward like a stampede and took Diego's arms, forcing him toward the door.

"*Suéltame*," Diego said, struggling against them. "Get off!"

As they dragged him backward, I turned back for my cigar.

"You're wrong, Cristiano," Diego said. "About one thing, you're wrong."

Despite the desperation that remained in his voice, something about it had turned chilling, almost satisfied. He wasn't entirely defeated as he should be. Nor was he filtering himself anymore or hiding behind a persona he'd crafted.

It was enough to get me to look back and raise a hand to stop my men. I smiled. "Tell me what I'm wrong about."

His breathing evened out as smug certainty tainted his

words. "You say you have everything you want—but that isn't true. Some things can't be taken. Some things must be *given*."

I narrowed my eyes on him as red light flickered and faded downstairs. "There's nothing in this world you have that I can't take for myself."

"Then you're no different from our father."

I drew back. He was right—because my father had taken *people*. If Diego was saying what I thought he was, then even *I* had underestimated the lengths he would go to to save himself. Something stirred deep inside me, a desire I tried not to acknowledge for fear of where it could lead.

"Don't think I don't know your weak spot, brother," Diego said. "Because it is mine too."

I raised my chin. I couldn't protest. I should've stopped him by now, but I hadn't—because in this area, I wasn't sure I wanted to be strong. "That's not yours to give."

"It is. Call off the Maldonados." He bowed his head and spoke ardently. "Spare my life, and I will deliver it to you."

I should've had Max finish him off there for trying to tempt me. I had a plan. More importantly, I had a code, especially when it came to human lives. I hadn't encountered many reasons in my life to break it.

But this possession wasn't only something I wanted. It was something *Diego* wanted.

And that made it all the more precious.

17

NATALIA

I sat at my dresser in a daze, unsure of how long I'd been brushing my hair and willing my phone to ring. I hadn't heard from Diego since the warehouse had burned, and my father was making arrangements to get me out of Mexico. Diego had to know how worried I was. And how that anxiety ruled my imagination. If the Maldonados knew about the warehouse, Diego could very well be dead by now.

Until I spoke to him, there was nothing I could do but pray for his safe return. I traded my brush for a match. When I struck it, fire flamed. I held it to the wick of my Virgin Mary candle, lit a few others on my dresser, and closed my eyes.

But I didn't think of Our Lady or God or even Diego.

Instead, the devil came to mind.

Cristiano had fooled everyone around him—except me. I still hadn't completely processed Cristiano's involvement in the death of his own parents. At only fifteen, he'd come to my father, the head of their rival cartel, with information that he knew would seal their fate. How could my father have trusted someone who'd committed that kind of betrayal against his blood?

And now, Diego would pay the price.

No, I couldn't think like that. Diego would pull himself out of this, and I had to hold on to that hope for both of us. Whatever it took, I wasn't going to let him go. I couldn't. Having Mamá ripped from my arms was enough heartbreak for one lifetime. Diego wasn't just the love of my life—he was my past and future. He anchored me. We had a long life ahead of us—a cliffside California wedding, children that would resemble each of us, safety and security that had been earned over a lifetime.

Saying good-bye to all of that would be too difficult to bear.

I'd protect it however I needed to.

Diego had already shaken hands with one devil. Whether it was the Maldonados or Cristiano who held his fate, we'd take it back—even if it meant making a new deal.

No matter what my father said, I wasn't leaving Mexico until I knew Diego was safe.

I paid no attention to the first couple taps at my window, but when the third came, I jumped up. Barely noticing how my feet smarted, I ran onto the balcony, tying my robe closed, and leaned over the side. On the dark lawn, a shadowed figure looked up at me from under a black hoodie.

My heart leapt. "*Diego*," I said. "I've been trying to reach you."

He held a finger to his lips. After glancing left and right, he scaled the trellis along one wall he'd used before to sneak into my room.

I scanned the yard as he climbed, making sure nobody saw. As he reached the top, the wood lattice under his foot snapped. He jerked, cursing as he almost lost his footing. I reached for him, and a vision flashed—his fingertips centimeters from mine before he lost his grip and fell to his death.

I shook the harrowing thought from my mind. "Careful," I whispered.

He grasped my hand and heaved himself up the rest of the way. I grabbed his cheeks and pulled his mouth to mine. He thrust one hand in my hair, holding me as he devoured me for a kiss that tasted of soot, smoke, and death. My fingers traveled his face, brushing over cuts and bumps. I drew back to take in the bloodied bruises on his cheekbones, nose, and forehead.

Seeing the evidence of his fight against that morning's attack made my chin wobble.

"Oh, no, *princesa*. Don't cry," Diego said softly. "Let me in. After the last twenty-four hours, it'd be a waste for me to get shot here."

I moved so he could climb over the concrete balustrade. Once inside, I hugged his neck. "I'm so scared."

"Shh." He rubbed my back. "Come. I need you to be strong for me."

I swallowed down the urge to cry and reluctantly released him. "What's happening?"

Diego sat on the edge of the bed, put his elbows on his knees, and ran both hands through his hair. "Please forgive me for last night. Please. I need you to know that I came back for you, but you were gone."

"Against my will," I said. "I would never have left you, either."

"Cristiano." As he cupped a hand over his other fist and squeezed it, the tendons of his forearms went taut. "Did he hurt you?"

The fear and concern in his eyes made me go to him. He pulled me onto his lap and wrapped his arms around me. "No," I said. "He forced me to leave and brought me home."

His fingertips dug into my hip. "I want to curse him and thank him all at once. He may have saved your life, but it was only so he could flaunt that in my face."

"You've spoken to him?"

"Yes." Diego looked up at me, his expression pained as he caressed my back. "First, just promise me he didn't lay a finger on you."

I nearly shivered remembering Cristiano's threatening presence behind me in my bedroom. My thoughts as they'd strayed to the possibility that he'd unapologetically take what I'd saved for Diego. The way he'd held my wrist and provoked me with words to distract me from the pinch of the tweezers. His fingertips trailing up my leg, his grip on my upper thigh, his unusual reaction to hearing about my virginity.

I smoothed Diego's brown hair from his forehead. It was no less silky for whatever trauma he'd been through. "He dropped me off," I said. "That's all."

"Really?" Diego's expression eased. "He never touched you?"

"Really." I was surprised at the lie, but relief crossed Diego's face for the first time since he'd arrived.

"I never should've taken you to the warehouse," he said. "Being around me puts you in danger."

Because my father had said the same to me many times, hearing that from Diego almost felt like a betrayal. I drew back. "That's *my* choice to make," I said. "Papá wants to send me home early, but I'm not leaving you."

"When?"

"Sunday. He says we'll go to Easter Mass, but the helicopter leaves before nightfall."

"I'm doing everything in my power to get us out of this," Diego said. "I need you now more than ever—you are my strength." He glanced out my window, setting his jaw as if he were fighting himself. "But Costa is right. You shouldn't be here. I'd never be able to live with myself if anything happened to you."

"But you just said you need me." I gritted my teeth to stem a fresh wave of tears, but not because I was sad. I hated that Diego and my father wanted me gone when this was the only place I should be. "I won't abandon either of you."

"This isn't a game, Tali," he said, looking back. "When the Maldonados come for me, they'll come for us all." He lowered his voice. "We owe them a lot of money."

I would've had to have been a fool not to know that, but hearing it sent chills down my spine. "How much?"

"Millions and millions," he said quietly. "More than we can ever repay."

I covered my mouth. "There has to be a way out. Can you borrow it from somewhere? Ask for more time?"

"Years wouldn't be enough. Retribution is taken with a long arm and a firm grip. Not even Costa can protect us."

"Then we have to leave," I said, standing, ready to run the second he agreed. "Fuck this life! Just come with me."

"I can't." He reached for me. "You know there's nowhere I can run they won't follow."

I went to my closet. "Well, we can't stay here," I said, wrestling my suitcase from the top shelf. "Since when are we sitting ducks? Why not at least try to disappear? We can get passports and start over—"

"Please, Talia," he said, rising from the bed. "Don't pull away from me."

He caught my elbow and drew me into his embrace. Cupping my face, he kissed the tears that'd escaped down my cheeks. "Forgive me," he whispered, sliding his hands everywhere on my body. "I'm desperate."

His hungry lips found mine, and I grasped his hair as he took my mouth. I arched into him, letting him walk me backward toward the bed. He untied my robe and slipped his hands inside to grab my ass. His kiss grew more feverish. This time, he didn't stop it, as if sensing this might be the last time.

As that reality hit me, I choked back a sob but tried to hide my despair with a moan.

Diego wrenched himself away and strode to the other side of the room. "We can't do this." His hair fell forward, and he tucked it behind both ears. "My God, Natalia. You are so beautiful . . . but we can't. I'm weak."

"Then let us be weak together."

He paced the room. "It was a mistake to let myself fall in love with you, but I could no more help it than I could growing older each day."

My gut smarted as if his words had delivered a punch to my stomach. "You don't mean that."

"How can I not?" His anguished eyes met mine. "I'm a dead man. I'll never have you. Not now."

"Don't talk like that." My throat thickened again. "You'll find a way out of this, and then my father will understand—"

"Your father? He's the least of our worries." Diego unzipped his hoodie, balled it up, and tossed it on my reading chair. It slipped over the arm onto the floor. "It's *over*, Tali—don't you see?" He strode back and forth, his muscles straining his black t-shirt each time he thrust his hands in his hair. "Even if I found a way out of this, Costa would never forgive a failure of this magnitude."

"Then there's nothing keeping us here," I said, reaching for him. "We have to go."

He avoided my eyes as if it was easier to pretend I wasn't here. "They'll find us, and when they do, they'll kill us both. I can't put you in that position." Finally, he stopped moving and pinched the inside corners of his eyes. "I'm as good as dead. The only peace I can have now is knowing you're safe."

My chest stuttered with a panicked breath. Fear crept into every part of my body. I had known it was bad, but seeing Diego come apart in front of me made everything even more real. He'd never expressed anything close to this level of anguish. "We'll elope," I said. "Papá will understand how much I love you, and he'll find a way to stop the Maldonados. He has that power."

"He doesn't," Diego said. "If he did, he would've stopped them already because he . . ." His jaw squared as if he were checking his emotions. "He's in just as much danger as I am."

No. My heart fell to my feet. I'd lose the two people who meant the most to me in the world. I put my hands over my face. "They'll kill him too."

"I'm sorry." His voice came out strangled. "I'm so sorry, Tali."

I wanted to sink into a ball on the floor, but that wouldn't help. As despair weighed on me, I forced myself to hold it together. I picked up his hoodie to fold it over the arm of my chair. "There has to be another way. There must be."

"There . . ." He hesitated. "There is."

I glanced up at him, unsure I'd heard him correctly. "What is it?"

"It's not on the table," he said. "I won't involve you in any way."

Me? I could do something? I didn't care what it was. I hurried over to take his hands. "If I can help, let me. *Please.*"

He brought the backs of my hands to his lips. "I don't deserve you. You should walk away now."

"You must know I'd die for you if it came to that," I said firmly.

He swallowed, his eyebrows cinching. "Tali."

"I would," I said. "Now tell me what can be done."

With obvious trepidation, he paused for a breath, seeming to struggle to get the words out. "The Maldonados are too powerful. Nobody who would help us can match them. They don't fear us—but they could."

Hope surged in me. There was a way—that was all that mattered. Not all was lost. I would take a sliver of hope over nothing. "How?"

"Neither your family nor mine is strong enough to stand against them alone. But together . . ."

Together. Two families standing as one. Unified.

"You've been part of our cartel longer than you haven't," I said. "We *already* stand together."

"Not officially."

To bind our families in a legal sense meant . . .

Marriage.

My heart soared. Relief and joy—and a sense of rebellion—spread through me. They thought they could destroy us, but we'd fight back. My father thought he knew better, but he'd see that keeping us apart wasn't the answer. Taking Diego's name was not only a privilege, but now it was my destiny. I could save us—and I'd be getting exactly what I'd always wanted.

"We'd stay in the shipping business but bring on a weapons and narcotics division," Diego explained. "Each cartel would benefit from the others' infrastructure. Pooling our resources, network, and cash, we'd become a formidable front."

"Father would forbid it," I cautioned. "He'd never let us go through with it."

"Once it was done, he'd be forced to see it was the only way. Our houses, united, expands his empire. He'd control the movement of his own drugs and guns—we'd be untouchable."

"But where do the drugs and guns come from?" I asked.

"Cristiano."

My stomach dropped. So it had come to that—making a deal with Hades to get another devil off our back. "But he set all of this in motion. Why would he help us?"

"Because it gives him power. Even more than our parents had. More than your father has. More than the Maldonados." He closed his hands over mine, pressing my palms together as if we were both in prayer. "That was his goal all along, and this is the fastest way to get it. He gains more than he did as Costa's partner—the protection of family. He knows what it means to bear the Cruz-de la Rosa name."

I got a silent thrill hearing our names together that way, even if it meant tying us to Cristiano. For once, I didn't feel so helpless. I could act. Wanting to marry Diego—to take his name and give myself to him in every sense—no longer felt small, selfish, or disobedient. With our promise to each other before God, I'd be saving us all. There was no holier union than that.

"But *would* Cristiano help us?" I said. "Have you asked?"

"It came up when we spoke earlier, but I'd decided not to ask this of you."

"I'm glad you did," I said.

"If you go, Tali, you at least have a chance of survival. Your safety can be arranged, and you can continue your schooling. Agreeing to this means—"

"I stay. I know." None of that mattered now. I could figure out my school situation later. "Did Cristiano agree when you spoke to him?"

"He's greedy and calculating. For once, it works in our favor. But a warning—I'd have to be willing to promise him anything to get him on our side. Even if I don't mean to keep those promises. Once we're safe and can regroup, we'll strategize a way to separate from him." Diego gently took my face, thumbing the corners of my mouth. "I wish it had never come to this, Tali, but it's where we are. Would you do this for me?"

My heart skipped. I didn't need a proposal or pretty words or a grand gesture. I just needed Diego. "Life or death. I belong to you in either."

He swooped down to wrap his arms around my waist and lift me off my feet. "What have I done to deserve your love and loyalty?"

"*Everything.*"

He brushed kisses along my neck and jaw, eliciting a shiver from my body. I had no idea how it was possible that moments ago, everything had felt hopeless, and now I couldn't stop smiling. "How do we do it?" I asked.

He caressed my cheek with his stubble, a scrape that soothed me with its familiarity. "On Sunday, pack your bags before Mass. Bring them. Don't breathe a word to your father, or he'll try to stop us." Finally, his eyes danced as his posture straightened once again. It felt good to be able to take away his worries. "When we were kids, you wanted to go to Antarctica."

I laughed. "Are we going on a trip?"

"No, but is the coldest place on Earth still on your bucket list?"

"I thought it sounded exotic—it was always so hot here. The grass was greener and all that."

He smiled. "I'm not even sure they have grass there. So where do you want to go?"

Fleetingly, I thought of my life in California, and all the dreams I'd had for us there. Was that over? Or on hold? I couldn't think of that now. Nothing mattered more than the man standing in front of me. "Why?" I asked. "Will we have to leave for a while?"

"No, *mi amor*." He lowered me onto my feet. "Just indulge me."

Ah. A honeymoon? He kept me in his arms as I kept mine around his neck. I lifted one shoulder, trying not to seem too giddy. "I've been many places with Papá. New York, Buenos Aires, São Paulo . . . and I've seen even more with my school friends." I ran my palm down his wide, muscular chest. "But I've not yet been to Southern Europe. I'd like to see Tuscany."

"Make me a promise," he said, absentmindedly twirling the ends of my hair around his finger. "If things get hard, if you miss me and we can't connect, promise me you'll dream of us under the warmth of the Italian sun. When it's dark, and you're worried the light won't come again, dream up ideas for us to do once we can get there."

As tempting as it was to fall into that fantasy, all I heard was what he wasn't saying. Was there a chance we'd be separated? "Diego . . ."

He kissed the tip of my nose. "Just know that it may not be right away, but we'll make it to Europe one day. When the time is right."

I balled his t-shirt in my fist. "You're making me nervous."

"*I'm* the one who's nervous." He raised his eyebrows. "See the sweat on my temple?"

I blew gently on his hairline to cool him. "What is it?"

He took my hands, kissed each of my palms, and held them between us as if we were standing at the altar. "I can't ask what I want to ask. It wouldn't be right. But . . ."

I blinked up at him. What could possibly make him nervous when his life had just been on the line—and still was?

Oh. With the realization, I involuntarily rose onto my toes with excitement. We were promising our lives to each other. I didn't need a proposal—but now that I was getting one, I couldn't keep my grin at bay. "Yes?"

"Natalia." He smiled down on me, gently squeezing my hands. "Make an unworthy man happy. Meet me at the church this Sunday."

18

NATALIA

I t was a question that had only one answer.

There wasn't a sliver of doubt in my mind that I'd marry Diego. He'd been my best friend and my love for a long time, but now, he'd finally be my husband. "Yes," I whispered. "I will meet you at the church on Sunday."

He lifted my hand to kiss my ring finger. His lips lingered there until he pressed his forehead against the back of my hand. "*Por favor*," he whispered. "Holy Virgin Mary."

"What's wrong?" I asked at the overwhelming sadness in his appeal. "Why don't you look happy?"

"I am, but I fear what lies ahead."

The gauzy curtains of my balcony fluttered, causing the candles on my dresser to flicker. I pulled him by his hand toward the bed. "Then lie with me and forget."

"Tali . . ."

"It's not a request." Diego and I had waited long enough. I had no more doubts about making this union. My heart hammered as I slipped my robe over my shoulders. "I almost lost you today," I said, tugging on the sash to open the bow. My robe fell to my feet, revealing my negligee. "And I'll be damned if either of us leaves this world without having spent a night together."

"You *may* be damned, Tali."

"I won't, because I know what's true in my heart." Sunday, we'd commit ourselves to each other before God, but tonight, we'd make love as husband and wife in our souls.

"And what's true?" he asked.

I put my hand to his cheek. "That I love you."

"And I you." His eyes roamed over my short, strappy nightgown. "You are so lovely in indigo silk that matches your eyes."

"*Mi madre* said a lady never wore anything less than the best to bed."

He smiled crookedly at his basic black tee and chinos. "I'm underdressed."

"You're *over*dressed. If you want to see more, you have to show more."

He arched an eyebrow. "A motto I can stand by." Bathed in candlelight, he grimaced as he slowly pulled his shirt over his head.

"Are you hurt?" I asked.

"A couple bruised ribs, nothing more."

I gently pressed my lips to a purple mark blooming on his chest and then a small gash on his right bicep. "I'm sorry."

"I'm not. I'm still standing. And here with you, no less."

I touched the button of his pants, pausing to ask for permission. It came in the form of his low-lidded stare as he wet his lips. I undid his pants and pushed them down.

He cast them aside, took my chin, and tilted my eyes

up to meet his. After a tender kiss to my forehead, then the bridge of my nose, he gathered up the hem of my negligee. I raised my arms so he could slip it over my head.

He stepped back, gripping the purple silk as his eyes drifted down my bare breasts and stomach to my lacy underwear. I kept my shoulders back even as nerves tickled my tummy. He'd never seen me this way. I knew he'd been with other girls—and that I actually meant something to him. But as he stared, doubt took over. Had he been expecting more? Was he worried about my inexperience? Or was it simply too strange to see his best friend naked?

He wore only boxer briefs, but it wasn't much different than seeing him in a bathing suit.

"Well?" I asked finally.

"My life is on the line," he said, swallowing, "and yet, I don't believe I've ever experienced such happiness."

My heart fluttered, pumping relief throughout me. "I've heard it only gets better from here."

He grinned, then swooped down to hug my waist and litter kisses on my neck until I laughed.

"You were never *this* ticklish when we were younger," he said, lifting me so my legs wrapped around him.

"Well, you never tickled my neck, did you?" I arched into him as he lowered me to the mattress and climbed over me. I bent and opened my knees to make a home for his hips.

"Would you like to hear my ode to you now?" he asked when we were mouth to mouth.

I nodded breathlessly.

He cupped my cheek, thumbing the apple of it. "She is a heavenly creature cut from the finest cloth with which God had to work. A fabric *so* fine, that to be dressed in it is to be a king, and to forget anything that came before it." He paused as candlelight flickered over his face. I ran a fingertip along a cut near his hairline. "Her love is all-consuming and more addictive than any high. It can twist fantasy to truth and make honest men lie—without blame. Those hopeless to receive it turn mad."

I didn't know any other man who felt so deeply, much less possessed the gift of expressing it so beautifully. A tear of love and joy slid down my cheek. "Diego."

"There is no greater pleasure than to be in the presence of your love," he finished.

I put my arms around his neck and pulled him down to me. He kissed me, running a hand along my waist and under my backside, then drew me against him.

I gasped softly as the length of him slid over my thigh. I was both eager and tentative to finally touch him. I wanted to do it right, to know that I could make him feel good.

He brushed his lips along my neck, and I quivered as he kissed my collarbone, then down my chest. "I can't believe we've held off this long," he said.

"Our patience has been admirable."

"Our patience has been *foreplay*," he said, running his tongue along the skin under my nipple, "and it will be rewarded."

In that moment, the sensation of his breath cooling my tender skin was the best thing I'd ever felt—until he pulled my nipple into his mouth and sucked, sending ripple after ripple of pleasure down my stomach.

"*Oh.*" I moaned, inadvertently drawing my shoulder blades together to give him more access.

"I'm trying not to rush, my love—but I can't wait much longer to be inside you," he said before lavishing the same diligent attention on my other breast.

My heart skipped at the thought of unleashing a fire between us that had been simmering for years. I wanted to tear through our patience, but I was grateful for Diego's slow, careful movements that forced me to savor this.

He took the elastic band of my underwear between his teeth and tugged it down, murmuring, "*Jesucristo.*"

Calling for Jesus between my legs inspired thoughts of heaven and hell. As Diego discarded my panties, parted my thighs, and slid his tongue over my core, I was reminded of his brother's hands threatening to trespass. No, I didn't think of Jesus, or my Diego and his tender promises, but of the antichrist's violent passion.

I thought of Diego's brother.

I jerked my head to the other side as if it would rid him from my mind, and my eyes landed on the framed Virgin Mary over my dresser.

"Diego," I said, shoving away thoughts that could only be blamed on the stressful events of the past few days.

"Hmm?" His response vibrated before he plunged his tongue inside me.

I gripped his hair with the unnerving sensation. It felt neither good nor bad, just new. A friend of mine in California liked to brag that her boyfriend ate pussy like he was trying to get all the meat off a chicken bone, and ever since, I'd been scared just at the thought of it—but Diego's gentle tonguing wasn't anything like that.

"Talia?" he asked.

"Hmm?"

"You shouldn't be this . . . quiet."

"I'm not—I think I hear something," I said.

He stilled, glancing up at me. "Really?"

I shook my head, putting a finger over my mouth to quiet him. Footsteps echoed in the hallway. Papá was unlikely to be anywhere but his bedroom or study this late, and since my mother, he'd never had overnight visitors.

Nobody wandered the halls of the second floor except the housekeepers, Barto, or the security team.

"I don't hear anything," he whispered.

Neither did I.

Perhaps they'd been phantom footsteps, sleek dress shoes that'd followed me to the foot of my bed earlier that day. Cristiano had cleaned me, bandaged me—tended to me without my explicit permission. He hadn't violated me, but if he had, he wouldn't take care like Diego did. Cristiano would eat pussy like a wild animal feasting on its kill, fending off any other predator foolish enough to approach. *I'm scarier than any monster*. Twin threads of revulsion and desire pulled sharply in my tummy, and I sucked in a breath at a visual that should've appalled me.

"There she is," Diego said. He slipped his arms under my hips and gripped them as he pulled me hard onto his mouth.

"*Ay*," I breathed on a moan.

"*¿Te gusta?*" he asked and then dove back in. He went from licking and sucking my most intimate spot to making love to it with his mouth. His tongue plunged deep and flicked over my clit. When he added one finger, and then another, my back bowed as I cried out.

"This is just the warm-up," he said, smiling at me from between my legs. "But no matter how wet I get you, or how careful I am, you might bleed."

"I know. The maids will think it's my period."

He climbed up my body and kissed my breasts again, sending spasms of pleasure through me with each pull of my nipple into his mouth. He took one between his teeth and pinched, and I bucked my hips into him.

"I think you might be ready for me, Tali."

"I'm ready," I said, nearly panting. A flush had worked its way up my chest; I was burning up for him.

I threaded my fingers through his hair, focusing on the way he dragged the tip of his tongue up my breastbone to the base of my neck. His fingers trailed down my side and over the curve of my hip. Just his presence made my head swim and my toes curl—what could lay ahead except more bliss as we fed a hunger we'd been forced to conceal for so long?

I lowered my hand between us, cupping my palm over his hardness. With just that simple touch, he was already pleading me with his eyes. "Don't stop there," he whispered. "Give me more."

He pushed his underwear down and kicked it off the bed. Finally, I held him, skin on skin, the full remarkable length of him in my hand. He was bigger than I'd imagined—not that I'd known what to expect or had anything to compare it with.

He would be my one and only. My forever.

The perfect first time with my perfect man.

Diego smiled down at me as if we shared the thought. "You're glowing."

His hair fell in a dark curtain around his face. I pushed some strands of it behind his ear. "I'm happy. I'm ready."

He nudged my legs apart. "You'll tell me if it's too much?" he asked.

I nodded and glanced between us, taking him in for the first time. Pink, long, hard—and all mine. Perfect. And naked. There would be nothing between us, and as much as I wanted to feel every inch of him, seeing him prepare to enter me also forced me from my fantasy into reality.

"Wait," I said.

He lifted up on one arm. "What is it?"

"We should get a condom," I said.

He took himself in his hand, sliding the head over me

in a way that made me bite my lip. "You have no idea how fucking good it feels without one."

I moved onto my elbows. "I'm not ready for . . . you know. I'm not taking the chance that I could—get pregnant . . ."

"I want our first time to be pure." He grazed his fingertips over my cheek and lowered his mouth to my ear. "Let me empty myself in you, just this time. Mark you as mine, first and always."

A primal desire for the same rose inside me. I wanted that too, but with such uncertain days ahead of us, we couldn't take the risk. "Then we'll have to wait," I said, and started to close my legs. "Once our future is more—"

"Wait." He grabbed one of my thighs, staying it.

Was he forceful with you?

I hated that Cristiano's unfounded accusation popped into my head. Maybe violence ran in their bloodline, but Diego wasn't his brother or his father. He'd never pressure me as Cristiano had implied.

"I'm sorry," he said after a second, releasing my leg to get up from the bed. "You're right."

Though he tried to hide it, I sensed his frustration. I was disappointed as well. I drew a throw from the end of my bed over myself as he picked up his pants from the floor. "You're leaving?"

"*Leaving?*" He gaped at me. "Not unless you toss me over the balcony, and even then, I can't promise I won't climb back in." He took something from his pocket, made claws, and crawled with exaggerated movements over the bed to me. "I won't be deterred," he said, snatching the blanket and tossing it away. He tickled my sides until I squirmed. "I'll keep coming back for more."

I laughed, relived that he wasn't angry. "I'm sorry, Diego," I said. "I don't want to stop, but—"

"Stop? Are you mad?" He flicked up two fingers. Between them, he held a foil packet. "*Nothing* will ruin our first time."

I flopped back onto my pillow as my anticipation returned. "Thank God."

"Thank *me* for being prepared. *El Señor* has *nada* to do with it." With a sexy grin, he used his teeth to tear open the packaging. "Still ready for me?"

I sighed happily up at the ceiling. "I've been ready."

"Get under the covers," he said, drawing back the comforter.

I slipped between the sheets. He rolled on the condom and climbed in after me. "Kiss me," he said from above.

I lifted my head to meet his lips. We each took a breath, and then he opened my mouth with his, running his tongue over mine, nipping my bottom lip. He grasped the side of my neck, his thumb caressing my throat as he deepened the kiss.

"Are you still wet?" he murmured, lowering a hand to touch me. I spread my legs for him, and he found his answer there. "Good, my love. Very good. I love you, Natalia."

I nodded, struggling to speak as I prepared my mind and body for what was to come. "I love you too."

I held my breath as he lined himself up between my hips, then fisted the sheets as he began to press inside me. "Good?" he asked.

My body resisted at first, but with a push, he slid in partway, and I exhaled with relief. Any pain I might've experienced was non-existent under Diego's care. "Yes, weird."

His eyebrows rose. "Weird?"

I covered my mouth. I'd meant to agree with him. It *was* good, of course. I was exactly where I wanted to be.

But in a way, it was also strange. I had dreamed of this moment, worried it might never come. Diego had always been around, watching over me, protecting and shielding me. I remembered looking up to him as a girl, too young to recognize I was falling in love with my best friend.

And then realizing he was more than a best friend.

He was a man, and I was head over heels for him. I hadn't come down to Earth since; I was still floating on cloud nine.

In his green eyes, I saw everything—a *past* that consisted of pain and support and unconditional love. A *present* that added to the framework of our promising *future*. He'd looked upon me this same way many times, with hope and tenderness.

"We've known each other so long. We've talked about this and now we're doing it—what I'm trying to say is . . ." I glanced away. *Weird*? I felt silly I'd picked the wrong word to describe this.

He turned my face back to his and pecked me. "Keep going. Tell me every thought you have in that beautiful brain."

I smiled a little as my muscles loosened, and I relaxed deeper into the mattress. "The weird part is that being with you now *isn't* as strange as my friends said the first time would be. I'm . . . I'm happy."

"I know you are," he said. "I recognize my own feelings in your eyes."

He slipped his arms under me to cradle my shoulders as he nuzzled my cheek. He pressed his lips there, then to the corner of my mouth.

I wrapped my legs around him and urged him deeper.

"You've been one of the only constants in my life," he said. "There were times even Costa overlooked me. But you, well . . . your love continues to anchor me."

"And me," I said.

He relaxed on top of me, giving me more of his body weight—he finally let go. I wrapped my arms around his neck as he entered me completely. He stayed rooted there a moment as our breath synced, then drew back and drove inside me. I bit my bottom lip, expecting some kind of pain, but it only felt right. And his first plunge only made me crave the next.

As I picked up the rhythm of his lovemaking, I met his thrusts with my hips. Each move he made came with a tender caress or a look of askance, making sure I was comfortable. He was every inch the gentleman, but I sensed there was also a hunger for me he kept bridled so as not to hurt me. I looked forward to unleashing that passion in him.

His drives became hungrier, faster, harder. His hand slipped between us and he knew just the right place to touch me to bring me to the edge. He looked down on me, arresting my gaze. Any time I got shy or my lids started to fall shut with pleasure, he called me back. The electricity between us crackled, pulling me out of this world and into a deeper state of love with him. It was just us, nothing else existed, and suddenly my body was spasming, drawing him deeper, contracting around him as he shuddered and came along with me.

Neither of us moved for a while, and I didn't want it any other way. My only desire was to stay in Diego's embrace and receive the love he showered on me.

To be with him for as long as time would allow.

And to bask in the glow of knowing that in only two nights, I'd officially be a de la Rosa.

B ells pealed overhead as Pilar and I navigated our way to the church. We opened the gate, passed the garden, and found an unlocked door in back.

How Diego had secured the church so quickly, and on Easter, I had no idea, but he'd sent word that someone would come for me when it was time.

Inside, I found us an empty room with some chairs and a full-length mirror. I set down a garment bag and tote, disturbing a cloud of dust motes that sparkled in the light coming from gothic-style windows.

"Can you get out my dress?" I asked Pilar, unpinning my hair since I'd put it up to set.

"Why are we here?" She unzipped the bag.

My hair fell to my waist in large shiny black curls. I looked at Pilar in the mirror. "Because I'm getting married today."

She froze, her hand in the bag. Slowly, she withdrew a cream lace dress. "*What?*"

I turned and unzipped my Easter dress to shimmy out of it. "It's a long story, but Diego's in danger."

"And?"

"And a wedding will get him out of it." I reached for the bridal gown. "Hand me that."

"Get *him* out?" she asked, handing me the slinky lace. "Or bring *you* in?"

I waved a hand. "We have a plan."

"Natalia . . ." She made a noise akin to a whimper. "It's just, I know how important marriage is to you, and that you've dreamed of having a beautiful ceremony with all of your family there. You can't do it as part of a *plan*."

I stepped into the long dress and slipped my arms into its full sleeves. "I *want* to marry him," I said, walking over to take her hands. "It's not just a plan. If it works, I'll save Diego. If it doesn't . . ."

Pilar paled. "What?"

Then at least Diego and I would have this day together.

Heaviness weighed on my chest. I didn't want today to be anything other than perfect, though. I took a cleansing breath and forced the thought away with a smile. "I'll be Diego's wife, Pila, and our two families combined will be too powerful to challenge."

She frowned. "Exactly what kind of danger is he in?"

My body tightened, but I focused on survival. I needed to keep positive thoughts and prayers for all of us. I drew my hair over one shoulder and turned, then frowned at the black strappy heels on my feet. "Damn. I forgot to bring my silver shoes. Will you do me up?"

"Where'd you even find a gown this late?" she asked, moving behind me to start with the bottom button.

"It was my mother's." I admired the dress in the mirror. The high-necked ivory bodice was fitted but not tight, and the lace around my neck was intricately crafted.

The dress had buttons all the way from my lower back to my nape.

"Costa doesn't mind that you're wearing this?"

"He doesn't know. I had to sneak the dress out."

Pilar touched her forehead. "*Dios mío*, if Costa finds out I helped, he'll put me in the grave."

"Don't worry. You'll be the last thing on his mind. He'll be either too relieved to care, or he'll kill Diego—which I hope he doesn't, because we're going through a lot of trouble to keep him safe from the Maldonados."

"The *Maldonados?*" She muttered something and made the sign of the cross. "*That's* who he's in trouble with?"

"*Sí.* It's scary, I know. That's why we have to go to extreme lengths."

"Hopefully they involve *una bruja*. He'll need black magic to immortalize himself if he has upset them. Or to resurrect him from the grave."

When she'd done the last button, I turned in the mirror. The dress just grazed the tops of my heels. I frowned. "It's too short."

Pilar squatted to inspect the hem. "I can let it out quickly. It won't be perfect, but because of the lace, you won't be able to tell much."

Pilar got a sewing kit from my bag, squatted at my feet with a seam ripper, and did her best to lengthen it. "You won't miss having Costa walk you down the aisle?" she asked.

I didn't have to consider my answer. I would, of course. The thought of it had been plaguing me for days. "Yes," I admitted. "But once Diego and I are safe and everything is as it should be, we'll have a real wedding and a huge celebration, hopefully in California." I could envision it perfectly, a cliffside resort where we could have an outdoor ceremony in late summer as the sun set on the water, then a reception on a dancefloor strung with lights. "You can be my maid of honor. I'll throw you the bouquet so I can set you up with a handsome American."

"A *gringo*?" she asked, incredulous.

"*Bueno, un chicano.*"

She smiled a little. "What about Manu?"

"You're too good for him," I said, but I knew there was slim chance of getting Pilar out of the marriage her parents were hell-bent on arranging.

She waggled her dark eyebrows as she tugged on the lace. "Are you ready for your wedding night?"

I failed to suppress my smile. I shouldn't tell Pilar what Diego and I had done, but I was too giddy. "We already had it."

Her mouth fell open. "*¿En serio?* Really?"

I nodded hard. "Friday night, he stayed with me."

Her eyes widened. She lowered her voice. "At your dad's house? How was it?"

"Magical. He was such a gentleman, and made sure I enjoyed every second." I searched her face for judgment. When she didn't respond, I continued, "People say your first time is bad, but it didn't hurt at all."

"Well, that's the most you can ask for."

I agreed. There was a great deal of passion between Diego and me that we hadn't even explored because he'd been holding back so as not to hurt me. I could only imagine that next time, we'd be tearing off each other's clothes like animals. "It was perfect."

Pilar sat back on her heels. "How's that?"

The dress swung at the bottoms of my heels. "Better. What am I missing?"

"A bouquet."

I gasped, covering my mouth. "I completely forgot."

"Just take something from the garden," she said.

I glanced out the window. "Do you think Father Rios will mind?"

"Without the money your family has donated, there'd be no garden at all."

"There's a flowerbed out there in my mother's name."

Pilar came up behind me and rubbed my back. "She's here now. I'm sure of it. Anyway, without a bouquet, you'd be offending the Virgin of Guadalupe."

"Ah, *verdad*. I need an offering in exchange for her blessing." I removed my shoes, gathered up my dress, and walked across the lawn behind the church. Sparrows chirped in the trees as I entered the garden that bore roses, lilies, marigolds, dahlias . . .

I closed my eyes and breathed in their fragrance, curling my toes in the springy, freshly cut grass before I picked red roses and white lilies and arranged them into a small bouquet.

I glanced up at a hovering monarch butterfly. I'd never seen a rare, elusive white one, and likely never would, but nonetheless, I stopped to appreciate this one in all its colorful beauty. It passed over the roses and landed in a ray of sunshine atop a lone group of marigolds.

I smiled to myself until it hit me—marigolds were the flower of the dead. "Mami?" I whispered.

It wasn't the season for monarchs, not like autumn. They'd been everywhere during my mother's funeral, so close to *Día de los Muertos*. As a girl, I remembered each year when they'd migrate south from the States and Canada in awe-inspiring kaleidoscopes through town— especially dazzling in our yard where Mamá had planted milkweed. I regretted how she and I had captured them just to feel their wings flutter against our palms. How must it have felt to be trapped?

The same as my mother had in her final moments?

"*Lo siento mucho*, Mamá," I said, my throat thick. "I'm sorry."

I hated to admit that I understood what Diego had meant when he'd spoken of a deeply buried desire to avenge his parents' deaths. It was the kind of thing I never poked at for fear of awakening a thirst for revenge only the life of my mother's murderer could quench. And that was why I'd tried to leave this life behind. Family bonds, wealth, vengeance, and violence—it was a vicious cycle of sins and pain. I was still leaving, I told myself. Not now, not yet, but when things had settled, Diego and I would have our fresh start anywhere but here.

The butterfly fluttered her wings. "What is it?" I asked.

What wish was she trying to deliver? Or was it a message? A breeze passed through the garden, ruffling leaves. I realized I was gripping the stems of my bouquet, and a thorn had pricked me. I sucked my fingertip and tasted metallic just as I got the sudden sensation I was being watched. I glanced around, but nobody was there.

Thoughts of my mother, and hope that she was looking down on me, should've brought happiness, but suddenly, a sense of dread permeated the fragrant air.

The wind picked up, blowing my hair into my face as the monarch flew off through the trees. I watched until she was out of sight. In the distance, the sky had darkened to a deep blue-gray, the way it only did in the desert when a storm approached.

I wished my mother was here to see me exchange vows today, but since she wasn't, I would carry her with me into the church. I squatted down to add the marigold the butterfly had landed on, the most brilliant of the bunch, to my bouquet.

I didn't doubt she'd bless my union with Diego or that she'd be at the church today in whichever form she took.

She would have understood my urgency, my passion. She had loved deeply too and had given up a family to gain one.

She had known Diego was worth saving as a child and had taken him in. She would approve, I knew it.

The bird above my head stopped chirping and flew away the same instant a shadow moved over me. Two dirt-sodden boots stopped beside me, inciting a memory from eleven years earlier I often tried to forget. Blood-splattered boots and a Glock in the devil's grip. I raised my eyes, hoping to finally meet Diego, but half-expecting Cristiano. I dropped my bouquet with a gasp.

A man with pockmarked skin, scraggly, graying hair, and an angry, diagonal scar across his face looked back at me. "They're ready for you in the church, Miss Natalia."

He was hard to look at, ugly as sin, scowling even as he smiled—the stuff of nightmares. I swallowed dryly. "Who are you?"

In one hand, he held a gun at his hip. With the other, he ran a fingernail between two of his teeth and then inspected it. "I'm just s'posed to take you in."

He leaned down, and I flinched, shooting out my hand to catch myself before I fell back in the dirt. He picked up my bouquet, dusted soil from the lilies, and held it out to me. "Don't wanna forget this."

I brushed off my hands, clutched the bouquet to my breast, and hurried back to the church. Pilar waited out front with my shoes and a lace *mantilla* veil, looking uneasy.

"Who is that?" she asked, helping me back into my heels. "He came looking for you."

"I don't know," I answered.

She held up the veil and draped the ivory Spanish lace over just my hair and shoulders. "I've never seen him before," she whispered.

I glanced over my shoulder to where he waited by the door. "Diego sent you?" I asked.

"*Da.*"

Da. Yes.

Did my father have any Russians on his payroll? It could've been, though I didn't recall one.

The man stepped forward and held out a small black box with a white satin bow. "From your intended."

I exchanged a look with Pilar, and the pit in my stomach dissolved. What was Diego up to? With renewed excitement, I took the present, slid off the ribbon, removed the top—and inhaled a sharp breath at the familiar rosary inside.

"What is it?" Pilar asked.

My eyes watered as I handed her the box and held up the gold chain of rubies and pearls. I ran my fingers over the Sacred Heart center and intricate gilt crucifix. "It's an exact replica of my mother's." I shook my head as a tear threatened to fall. "How did he remember it so well?"

"And when did he have time to make it?" Pilar pointed out.

That was an equally impressive feat. Perhaps he'd known for some time he would give it to me on our wedding day. I held it to my heart. "Thank you," I said to the man, who just shrugged his wide shoulders.

I looked over myself once more in the mirror. The beads spilled from my hand, and for the first time, I glimpsed the grace Barto had said I'd inherited from my mother. I could think of no better way to meet my groom.

We hurried to the front of the church, me with my head bowed, Pilar on one side and the Russian on the other. When we climbed the steps and reached the carved wooden doors, he pulled one open for us.

Bells began to chime. I had only an hour before Barto

was supposed to pick me up to meet the helicopter. One hour to meet my fiancé, return with my husband, and break the news to my father.

"Are you coming in?" the man asked Pilar behind me.

"*Sí.*"

"If you insist." He grinned. There was something funny about the eye with a scar over it. He closed the door behind us as we entered a small antechamber that opened to the grand, high-ceilinged church.

Light spilled through the stained-glass windows, and candles lit the aisle to the altar, which was surrounded by fresh flowers, including the red roses and white lilies of my bouquet. I passed into the nave slowly, taking it all in. I would've never thought Diego could pull this together so quickly.

My heels echoed off the empty pews as I walked deeper into the church. Father Rios stood at the altar, his head bent as he murmured to himself, reading from the book in front of him. I would have to remember to thank him later for ending his services early to perform this without notice.

Three men in suits stood around the priest with their backs to me. My stomach dropped. I flattened my hand against it to quell my nerves, welcoming the coarse lace under my palm as I picked up my pace. I looked for Diego but stopped after only a few steps. My betrothed wasn't amongst them. Two of the men had rifles strapped across their suit jackets. And the third, even from behind, was unmistakable. A constant presence in my nightmares, a monster even to monsters—the devil himself.

What was *he* doing here? I took a step back.

Cristiano turned his head over his shoulder, giving me his profile. His jaw sharpened as he paused there. I didn't realize I was holding my breath until I began to feel faint.

Finally, he turned and faced me. "What a beautiful bride you make, Natalia," he said, meeting my eyes. "Not that I expected anything less."

He had no reason to expect me *at all*. How dare he show his face on my wedding day? The beads of my mother's rosary dug into my palm. He looked wrong next to the elderly, homely priest—and at the altar, where Diego should've been.

The heavy door to the nave closed behind me with a *click*, causing candle flames to flicker and sigh. The distinct, pungent smell of marigolds invaded my nostrils.

Perhaps the monarch hadn't come to deliver a wish or a message—but a warning.

Run.

20

NATALIA

Sunshine streamed through the archways on both sides of the church, but it didn't touch me in the center. The aisle that would lead a bride to her groom remained dim and candlelit.

The aisle that ended with Cristiano de la Rosa.

He stood in Diego's spot wearing a perfectly cut suit and a satin tie as sleek and jet-black as his styled hair. His eyes trailed from my lace-adorned neck, to the rosary and bouquet in my hands, to my ankles. Even in such a modest dress, his perusal stripped me bare. Heat warmed my cheeks. He acted as if he had every right to linger his gaze on the curves of my breasts and hips. As if he was deciding where to start. As if he owned me.

The room had gone still, not even a breath exhaled.

A pit formed in my stomach. There was a chance Cristiano had come to stand for his brother, but with the way he looked at me—possessively, but with more satisfaction than longing—I knew he wasn't here just to show support for the joining of our families.

"What have you done with Diego?" The panic in my voice reverberated off the pews around us.

Cristiano's eyes shifted over my shoulder. I turned. Diego stood at the door, sagging under the weight of something I couldn't name. It didn't matter. He was here. I ran to him and threw my arms around his neck, breathing in the heady fragrance of my bouquet and Diego's soapy scent.

He hugged me back until Cristiano barked a single warning that echoed off the high ceilings. "Diego."

Diego moved his hands to my shoulders and peeled me off, separating us. He seemed to have aged years since I'd last seen him. "My dearest Talia," he whispered, his green eyes searching mine. "My love. You know you are, don't you? My only love?"

It felt like a good-bye. Since I'd stepped into the garden, dread had been slowly gathering in me like the dark clouds on the horizon—and a storm was about to hit. I moved back and stepped on the bouquet I hadn't even realized I'd dropped. I held the rosary with both hands, as if in prayer. "Please tell me Cristiano is only here to see this merger through."

Diego scrubbed both hands over his face, then smoothed back his hair. "Everything is gone, Talia. I can't replace it, and I can't pay for it. If the Maldonados aren't already on their way, they will be soon, and they'll come after *all* of us."

"I know," I said. "I *know*, but you said you had a plan—you said . . ."

"Cristiano has admitted to the attacks. He sabotaged my deal with them."

I knew it. It should've come as no great shock, but heat rose up my neck and cheeks as anger brewed inside me. I gritted my teeth. "Then let *him* pay for it."

"I can't prove it. I have no credibility or influence with them. But *he* does." Diego nodded over my shoulder. "There's only one way out, and it's through him."

The only way out was to form an alliance and stand against the Maldonados. We'd already figured that out, so what did Cristiano have to do with it? "What do you mean?" I asked.

"Cristiano will settle our debts and smooth things over with the Maldonados, but only if . . ." He trailed off as if he couldn't bear to say more.

"Only if *what*?" I asked. "What about our plan? By marrying and uniting our families, we'll—"

I froze.

Make an unworthy man happy.

Meet me at the church this Sunday.

Diego had never actually proposed.

He went to touch my face but stopped himself at the last second. "I swear to you, Natalia," he said so softly, I almost didn't hear him, "I will fix this. Trust me. *Please*."

I reached out for something to steady myself as I became light-headed, but there was nothing. "This . . . you . . ."

Cristiano cleared his throat. "My patience grows thin, *hermano*."

Diego glanced over my shoulder and wiped sweat from his forehead with the butt of his palm. "I told you there'd be a union of families today—"

"No." I was shaking my head—slowly at first and then harder. I ripped off my veil as it loosened. "*No*."

Diego gripped my shoulders. "It's the only option. Cristiano will throw us at the mercy of the Maldonados unless you agree."

I breathed out a shuddering gasp, and a laugh of disbelief escaped. The space around us sharpened into a distortion of reality, as if I'd been hit with *déjà vu*. "Unless I agree to . . . to what?"

Diego nodded once. "To marry Cristiano today."

My heart thudded painfully. I dropped the veil and my rosary clattered on the wood floor. Marry *Cristiano*? I couldn't. I *wouldn't*. I shifted my gaze over Diego's shoulder to Pilar, whose eyes flitted from the men at the altar to us to the armed Russian next to her—guarding the door. Had this been planned? When? How long had Diego known?

My limbs weakened. The church's grim atmosphere said it all. I wasn't here for my wedding but for something much graver. "I can't," I whispered. "You can't ask this of me."

"That's his condition to help us." Diego glanced at the ground, and his brown hair eased around his cheeks. "I can't save us. But you can."

"*Why*?" I asked.

He squatted to pick up my rosary, clutching the beads in a fist as he spoke through his teeth. "He covets you, but he knows he cannot command you, or it would make him like my father." He lifted his eyes. "He has refused my money, servitude, power—everything." Diego stood and pressed the rosary back into my hand. "I offered to leave town so he'd never see me again, but he's determined to see me dead."

"He has refused power?" I asked, raising my voice. I couldn't look at Cristiano, but I'd make sure he heard me. "This *is* a power play. He unites two families, consolidating power for himself while stripping you of yours."

"The only thing he wants is you—and for you to willingly go to him."

I gaped at Diego, who wore a special-occasion gray suit as if he'd tried to look *nice*.

"This has *nothing* to do with me," I said evenly. "There has to be another way."

His jaw firmed as he swallowed. He pinched the inside corners of his eyes, and a tear escaped. "There *isn't*, Talia," he cried. "I'd never ask this of you if it wasn't my last resort."

"The Maldonados will come for us once they have their money," I said, trying to get him to see. "*You* said they don't forgive failure. That they'll make an example of you."

"They respect Cristiano. He can keep them at bay, and even if he couldn't, they cannot come against him and your father." His brows cinched. "Even they aren't that powerful."

I didn't want to believe it, but I knew I hadn't even begun to fathom the kind of havoc the Maldonados would wreak—not just on us, but those around us. I could almost sense them closing in now. I touched my throat as if *El Polvo* poured sand down it. *That's* who I was to marry? I had to choose between the lesser of two evils—to be married to a vicious murderer or face a mob of them.

I looked down and released my fist. The rosary beads had made indents in my palm. "The Maldonados . . ." I said. "They'll listen to Cristiano? You're sure?"

"Yes. But not until he's gotten what he wants."

Me.

No. I couldn't do it.

I took Diego's hands. "You and I can get married. Cristiano will still be united with my father. We'll leave. Let them have it all."

I started to turn, but Diego pulled me back. "I tried. It won't work. Walk down the aisle to him—or walk out. I'm desperate enough to beg you to do this for me"—his voice broke as his nose reddened—"but I will respect whatever you decide, Tali. I've always been willing to die for you. That hasn't changed."

"*Please*," I said, looking at our intertwined hands. I held one up, showing him my initials on his ring finger, knowing it would say more than I could. "Please. There *has* to be another way."

Diego didn't speak, but another tear slid down his cheek. "We wouldn't be standing here if there was an alternative," he said finally, pulling his hands away. "This is it. The last option. To deny him what he wants is to put a bullet in all our heads."

"Then let them kill us!" Frustration overwhelmed me, and a sob rose up my throat. If I left here with Cristiano, I'd be stripped of a future anyway. "What kind of life would I lead with him?"

Diego inclined toward me, speaking near my ear. "It's only until I can get to you," he whispered. "I'll do anything to free you. I'll build an army against him. He won't hurt you, Tali. If he wanted that, he would've done it by now."

"No. He wants to hurt *you*, and he'll use me to do it. What do you think he'll do with me once we leave here? We'll be *married*, Diego."

He turned his face away, swallowing. "I can't think of it. If I suspected he had any intention of hurting you, I'd die first. He won't. I'm asking you to do this and hang on for me, Talia. Can you?"

Pressure built in my chest. I'd declared not days ago that I'd save him any way possible. This was what I'd been called to do to prevent us from meeting a gruesome death. "I . . ."

"You must understand—you'll be safe with him while we settle things with the Maldonados. More than you'll be anywhere else."

My jaw tingled. I was safest in the grip of a devil.

Nobody was willing to budge, negotiate, or listen to reason. I pressed my hand to my chest as my anger gave way to fear for what Diego and Cristiano truly believed was about to happen. I wasn't sure Diego understood that once I belonged to Cristiano, he wasn't going to share. I would be his to do with as he pleased.

"Once he marries me," I said quietly, "he'll have only one use for me, if even that. I won't be able to escape him."

"That's enough," Cristiano said from the altar. I refused to turn and look at him. "Come to me now, Natalia, or I'm taking the deal off the table."

"Life or death, Diego," I begged. "I'm yours in either. Where you go, I will follow."

"And they will hunt us like dogs."

I swallowed through a painful lump in my throat. They would find us, but at least we'd be together. At least *I* wouldn't be left at the mercy of Cristiano. He'd restrained himself around me so far, and hadn't given me much reason to believe he'd hurt me—but I had no idea how he'd act once he thought he owned me like one of the women he kept behind Badlands' gates. Except *I* would belong to the master himself. "Then we'll face the Maldonados together," I said.

"And Costa?" Diego asked.

My heart stopped. *Papá.* They would come for all of us. Me, Diego, my father. Tepic, Jojo, Pilar. My father's family. Maybe even my mother's, who were the only ones wise enough to stay far away from this life. And it would touch them anyway. Unless I did this.

I would do this for Diego, but I *had* to do it for the man who'd given me life, who'd loved and protected me always. If I didn't, maybe I would find my father dead on the cold tile floor before they killed me too. Or took me. Was I better off enslaved to them or Cristiano? I hated that the answer was obvious.

My nose tingled, and I shut my eyes as resignation set in.

"The Cruz cartel will cease to exist," Diego said. "They'll execute those at the top to warn others, keep the ones they have use for, and discard the rest."

My core seemed to have frozen. I wrapped my arms around myself as the cold hit, inciting a shiver deep inside me. "You can't put their lives on me," I said. "Maybe I can save them, but *you* did this. Father did this. Cristiano did this. I'm innocent."

"Be that as it may," Cristiano said from behind me, "I've named my price. Turn around, Natalia."

No. No. I wouldn't. I grabbed the lapels of Diego's suit and pulled him close. "Please," I implored one final time. "Find a better way. Don't ask this of me."

Defeat. That was what I'd seen in the slump of his shoulders earlier. I could name it now because he drew up, lengthening his spine. His resignation morphed into resolution. "Okay," he said. He hesitated, then slowly enveloped me in a strong hug. He looked over my head to Cristiano. "I'm sorry. She won't do it."

I waited for relief, but it didn't come. In the following silence, my insides tangled. Cristiano's menacing presence pervaded the church. With the reality of how I'd just changed the course of things, my head filled with visions of what came next. A massacre. Bloodshed. News stories that would never be reported. Deaths that would stand for nothing and happen in vain.

"I never truly thought she'd go through with it," Cristiano said finally. "You've asked too much of her love."

Bastard. My teeth mashed together. My love wasn't weak as he implied. Perhaps he didn't know true love because he wasn't capable of it. He was wrong. *Life or death.* I repeated it to myself, trying to bring my courage up to meet my indignation. *Life or death.*

"Put Natalia on her plane out of the country," Cristiano continued. "Once Ángel Maldonado finds out, it's out of my hands. I can't protect even her, though I will try."

Diego's heart pounded against my cheek. "It's all right," he murmured in my ear. "I understand."

"My offer is off the table," Cristiano announced. "Max, pull the car around."

I pressed my face into Diego's chest as he smoothed my hair away and shushed my cries. I didn't want to leave this spot, but I heard the resolve in Cristiano's voice. In his footsteps down the aisle. These could be my last moments with Diego, and if I survived, I'd have to live with knowing I hadn't saved him. I would rather die by Diego's side than marry my enemy, but even death did not seem to be an option for me. Only for Diego.

Clutching the rosary, I lifted my head and asked in a watery whisper, "You'll come for me?"

He spoke into my hair, only for me. "As soon as I can. I just need time, and this is the only way to buy it."

What awaited me when I turned and faced Cristiano? What unspeakable things did he have planned once I left with him? At least with the Maldonados, there was a chance they'd kill me quickly. Cristiano and his bucket of sand wouldn't rush his torture.

Cristiano's footsteps neared.

"Wait," I said into Diego's neck. "*Espera.* Wait."

Diego tensed, then loosened, and he breathed a loud exhale near my ear. "My girl," he said, ghosting his lips over my temple. "My savior. Thank you." He rubbed my back briefly, then slid his hands to my upper arms. "Turn and go to him."

"I can't." I hiccupped. "I can't do it."

"Strength, *princesa.*" Diego squeezed my shoulders affectionately, then spun me around.

Cristiano stood halfway down the aisle, tall and imposing, not a hair out of place—and utterly lacking in any softness, understanding, or empathy for what he demanded of me.

I stared at him from under wet lashes heavy with mascara. What a farce, getting made up. And in my *mother's* dress. It was profane, a sin against her sacred day with my father. "Why?" I asked Cristiano.

"I believe the words you're looking for are 'thank you.'" Cristiano walked closer to us. "Diego would be halfway to the grave if not for me."

"His life is in danger *because of you*. And you don't need me to pardon him. Look inside yourself for forgiveness, Cristiano. You were human once—he is your *brother*."

"He ceased to be anything to me long ago—and now, he is nothing to you. He deserves to die. All I did was push fate along."

"You can stop it."

"My price is very, very steep, Natalia. I can't be expected to let him go unpunished, can I? So he can make an attempt on my life?"

By Diego's words pleading me to hold on just now, he did have plans. And Cristiano likely knew it.

Cristiano stuck his hands in his pockets, looking down on me. "Didn't I warn you about him? You should've listened. At least with me, you'll be safe."

"Safe? With you? You're forcing me into marriage."

Even as I straightened up, Cristiano seemed to grow

bigger. He filled the room, demanding everything of the space around him. "There's always a choice, Natalia. If there wasn't, I'd throw him to the wolves and take you anyway. Who'd stop me? Diego? He's giving you up. Your father? He isn't here. I can easily take you, but I'm offering a choice. Come with me willingly, or go and say your good-byes."

Without moving from his post, Max said, "The car is here, boss."

Cristiano checked his phone. "*Vámonos.*"

I shut my eyes and tears spilled down my cheeks. There was no more time, and no more I could say except my decision. "I'll do it," I said in darkness, then opened my eyes.

With slow, deliberate movements, Cristiano slid his phone in his jacket pocket and closed the space between us. "A lesser man would make you beg for another chance—I already took the deal off the table. But a simple 'please' would go a long way."

I dug my fingernails into my palms until they throbbed. "I won't beg."

"Oh, you will, *mariposita*. But I can be fair. I'll go first." Our gazes met, and for a moment, it was just the two of us. "Marry me, Natalia. Please."

"You're mocking me."

"I'm not." He stared into my eyes, seeming almost unsettled, as if battling something inside himself. "I've not made this arrangement lightly. I would like very much to call you my wife."

"Then you will. But I want to hear, from *your* mouth, what will happen if I don't. Diego has said it. You should have to as well."

He arched an eyebrow. "Now you're being smart. It's only good business to hear the terms of an agreement."

"This is my term—promise me you won't hurt my father."

"I have no quarrel with him."

"Swear it on my mother, who placed all of her faith in you."

He pressed his lips into a line. "You have my word."

Perhaps it was foolish to believe him, not that I had much choice, but I took him for his word.

One corner of his mouth rose into a crooked, sinister smile as he looked to Diego. "Now for the other terms you failed to mention to her."

I glanced back. Diego's shrewd green eyes were fixed on his brother. I could read the hatred in them. Cristiano wanted to torture him, and it was working.

Diego loosened his tie and turned his head out the window.

"At a loss for words? I'm happy to fill her in." Cristiano rubbed his jaw and took a few paces to one side, stopping at the end of one pew. He turned to me. "Diego has confirmed what you shared with me the other night—that you're waiting for marriage."

Diego put a hand to my back, spreading his fingers between my shoulder blades, a warning to keep my silence. Cristiano thought I was a virgin. "Why does that matter?" I asked.

"Because I want to be your first. Your last. Your only. And because denying him brings me pleasure," Cristiano said. "So there's no question—the deal is contingent on the consummation of our marriage."

My head filled with images of Cristiano's massive arms trapping me to the mattress. An ache formed between my legs as his beautiful but cruel face hovered above mine, his broken soul taking what he wanted. His broad shoulders blocking out everything else. Everyone else. *Your first. Your last. Your only.*

Had Diego come to my balcony knowing any of this? He said he'd spoken to Cristiano but had decided against bringing me into their deal. My heart said Diego wouldn't lie, but doubt formed in my mind, mingling with a tinge of humiliation over my complete faith in him. I hadn't breathed in so long that I gasped with an inhale. Had Diego taken my virginity after promising me to his brother?

Cristiano tilted his head at me, smoothing a hand over his jacket. "You *are* a virgin, aren't you, Natalia?"

To admit the truth would mean Diego's death. To lie, I feared, could mean my own—I would have to take the secret of my night with Diego to the grave. "Yes," I said. "I am."

He narrowed his eyes and took a step toward me that echoed around us. "You're sure?"

I dipped my head in a firm nod. "Yes."

"Then you, Natalia Lourdes King Cruz, and your virginity—are mine."

Surrounded by people who stood by and did nothing as Cristiano imposed his will on me, my face burned. As he declared me *his* and promised to defile and abuse me, his men stood back. And Diego—he had *arranged* this.

You will die for him, your love.

"What's your decision, Natalia?" Cristiano asked.

I inhaled a deep breath and exhaled the things I could not control. I had to trust that Diego wouldn't accept a life without me in it. He had to have a greater plan that would put Cristiano in the ground—this couldn't end any other way. Because I knew without being told that when Cristiano said till death do us part, he would mean that literally. Even when my use to him had run out, I wasn't naïve enough to believe he would release me.

To save Diego, I could hold on until he and my father came for me. I had known strength and poise in my mother. She'd fought back and lost, but her determination would live on—in me.

"*Que será, será*," I said. "My answer is yes."

Cristiano stilled, his eyes dark, bottomless pits that stewed with plans—the games he would play, and the violent delights he would take. "Then it is done," he said with a rumble. "I will make you a very good husband, Natalia. Come to me."

I glanced back at Diego.

"I'm not leaving," he said. "I'll be right outside, waiting."

"You'll watch every moment," Cristiano said to him, then turned to me. "And you will not look to him again. You're finished with him. Now, come."

21

NATALIA

Candles flickered along the aisle, burning a fiery path to the man watching me from the altar.

Cristiano de la Rosa—my future husband.

I picked up my bouquet and twined the rosary around the stems. As everyone around us looked on, I took one step toward him, then another, wobbling in my heels as the room tilted around me. I steadied myself on a pew. Cristiano tightened his shiny tie but didn't rush me.

Father Rios avoided my eyes, but when I reached him, I saw the tears in his. The suited men with guns flanked him—a bridal party from hell, hired to enforce Cristiano's will. To force fate's hand—and mine, in marriage.

I kneeled on the pillow before the priest. Organ music I hadn't noticed stopped.

"Pilar." Cristiano faced the back as his voice echoed around the room and vibrated in my chest. "*Trajiste un lazo?*"

"I-I . . ."

I didn't have to look back at my friend to know she was

scared—I heard the fear in her voice. "Yes," I answered for her. "There's a lasso in my bag."

"Bring it to me," Cristiano said.

Pilar's rapid but light footsteps sounded toward us. She handed him the shoulder bag.

"You can sit," he told her, pointing to a pew behind me and said to no one in particular, "I like this tradition, this unification of man and wife." He took out a black rope and inspected it, tossing the bag aside. "Where'd you get this?"

"It's the tie from my curtains," I murmured. "That was the best I could find on short notice."

"It will do fine. Someone else lassoes us, no?" he asked the priest. "I haven't been to many weddings."

"The priest or a family member," one of his men answered. "I can, *padrino*. I did it for my sister."

Cristiano hummed. "I'd like to do it myself, if it's acceptable to the reverend."

As if anyone would stop him. Cristiano came to stand in front of me, waiting until I looked up. Even when I wasn't on my knees, he towered. Now, he reached the sky. He ran the silken cord through his hands as if deciding the best use for it. He tied the ends of the lasso together to form a circle, then tugged to tighten the knot.

Cristiano squatted in front of me and looped the rope around my neck, letting his fingers brush my throat and collarbone.

My back ached from holding it so straight, but I couldn't loosen if I wanted to. I avoided his gaze by looking at his suit. I'd never seen such fine tailoring in all my life, even though my father had benefited from my mother's good taste.

Cristiano pulled the lasso taut enough that I could feel

it when I swallowed. He lifted my face by my chin. With a rough touch, he used his whole hand to palm away my tears. "I wish my bride not to cry on our wedding day." He kneeled beside me and handed me the remaining cord. "Now you."

Finally, something I could happily agree to. I twisted toward him and coiled the *lazo* around his neck to form an infinity between us. To leash me to him. I gave the rope a tug, and he arched a dark, scolding eyebrow at me.

If I'd had the guts, I would've asked why he'd bothered with this charade at all. As "willing" as Cristiano demanded I be, summoning tradition didn't make this anything more than an extravagant kidnapping.

As fresh flowers perfumed the space around us, and tall candles warmed it, the priest recited a prayer with a shaky voice and obvious trepidation. I had to keep myself from looking back at Diego.

Cristiano's shoulder touched mine, and only then did I realize I'd been shivering. Despite the way he bullied and intimidated, he had that kind of soothing touch, one that would still you, if not with serenity, then out of dread. It confused me now the way it had when he'd frisked me at the club, or when he'd bandaged me up after the warehouse fire.

The way he'd slid his hands up under my dress and then robe . . . and I hadn't run away either time.

And his touch wouldn't end there. As Father Rios married us, my wifely duties were placed upon me. Cristiano hadn't hesitated to put his hands on me before, even knowing I was spoken for. That I was opposed to it. There was no question he would demand everything from me.

My trembling started anew, and he turned his head. I kept my gaze forward, even as the priest's speech slurred, or perhaps it was my mind that blended and muffled words to protect me from what I was hearing.

Father Rios went quiet, breaking me from my stupor.

After a moment, Cristiano said, "I do."

"Natalia," the priest said, "do you take Cristiano to be your wedded husband, to have and to hold from this day forward, for better, for worse, for richer, for poorer, in sickness and in health, to love, cherish, and obey till death do part you . . ."

Obey. I hadn't heard a word of Cristiano's vows, but somehow, I doubted he was under any obligation to obey *me*.

They both stared.

My chest was tight from holding my breath. I couldn't bring myself to say the words. I looked to the guards on each side of the priest. One had a face tattoo, a wrinkled dress shirt, and stood unevenly, but was dressed in the finest artillery. He gave me a close-lipped smile that made wrinkles around his eyes. The other wore a matching gun and restrained grin, with deep dimples and scars that peeked out from his collar.

I returned my eyes to Father Rios, who seemed to be whispering his own prayer while waiting for my answer.

Cristiano turned to me, laced our fingers together, and raised my hand between us. "He has asked if you'll take me as your husband, Natalia."

I can't. I can't say it.

After a moment, one of Cristiano's men said, "She does."

"I heard it too," the ugly guard said.

"*Por favor,*" the priest pleaded. "I can't proceed without her consent."

"Nor can I," said Cristiano. My palm perspired in his

rough one. He squeezed it gently. "Tell him, Natalia Lourdes."

Father Rios' fallen expression took my heart down with it. He was as trapped as I was. I straightened my shoulders and looked at Cristiano. His dark eyes danced. The sharp lines of his angular face almost softened with something like happiness. "I do," I said to him.

Cristiano stood and helped me up. He reached for my left hand. "I don't have your ring yet." From his pocket, he produced a considerable but simple diamond in a gold setting and slipped it on me. "For the sake of the ceremony, until we find one that suits you."

"I don't need one," I said.

He glanced at the priest, who nodded for him to continue.

"With this ring, I thee wed. With my body, I thee worship." Cristiano commanded my attention, and again, the others fell away. As his dark eyes drank me in, I only wondered how, if he'd not been to many weddings, he knew what to say. Or why he seemed to say it with such vehemence, as if he meant it.

It wasn't like he needed anyone in this church, not even the reverend, to believe it.

"With all my worldly goods," he continued, "I thee endow—*en el nombre del Padre, y del Hijo, y del Espíritu Santo. Prometo amarte y respetarte todos los días de mi vida. Amén.*"

He hesitated, as if he half-expected me to repeat the words back to him.

I promise to love and respect you for all the days of my life.

My new husband was turning out to be a riddle.

But I wouldn't mock the church and say what he asked of me.

We were mercifully interrupted. Out of nowhere, a man in cowboy boots and a matching hat appeared and clomped down the aisle to us. "*¡Felicidades!*" he said. "Congratulations to the happy couple."

"Remove your hat in the church," Cristiano said.

"Of course." The man did as he was told and held out a folder.

Cristiano opened it, looked over some paperwork, and rearranged the pages. Satisfied, he turned the file around for me. "Sign."

I glanced at the sheet on top. "What is it?"

"To legalize the marriage with a civil ceremony."

"Why all this trouble?" I asked, shaking my head. "You could take me to the Badlands and imprison me there whether we're legally married or not."

"I have my reasons." He nodded at the cowboy, who patted his pockets before producing a pen. "Sign."

I started to protest, but what could I say? And what did it matter? Signing on the devil's dotted line was no more permanent than the verbal agreement I'd already given. I had lost, and I feared I'd need my strength to fight bigger battles later.

The man started to put his hat back on, then seemed to remember Cristiano's order and held it to his chest. "I'll need those medical records, *compañero*. They're supposed to be done weeks in advance."

"I'm grateful for all the concessions you've made for my wife," Cristiano said, returning the folder to the man once I'd signed. "You have a friend in Calavera."

"*Gracias*, de la Rosa," the cowboy said, slipping the paperwork under his arm. He bowed to me, replaced his hat, and returned from wherever he'd come.

I found myself staring at Cristiano like everyone else in the church. He thought himself a god and expected the same of others.

He'd called me his *wife*. My fingers and toes curled. I

was what my mother had been to my father. In some ways, it was a stretch—the devotion between them had run deep, the love profound, and here I was marrying a man who I knew little better than I did a stranger. Yet that wasn't true. Cristiano had been a constant presence in my life, even after he'd left. There were similarities to our marriages too. My mother and father had trusted Cristiano with their lives and now, I was putting that same faith in him.

Trusting him with my eternal life as we descended into hell.

Promising him my love everlasting while my heart belonged to another.

Cristiano turned to the priest. "Finish it."

Father Rios nodded. "You may kiss the bride."

Cristiano gestured for my bouquet. For strength, I called upon a moment in which I hadn't feared Cristiano. A sunlit afternoon many years ago when he'd carried baskets of daisies and morning glory. I'd held Mamá's hand on our way back to the house, turned, and caught him smelling the flowers. He'd winked at me. I'd laughed, thinking it funny back then that it was more unusual to see him toting flowers than it would've been a gun.

I prayed, for my sake, that man still lived in him.

He took the bouquet from my nerveless fingers, unwrapping the rosary from its stems. "What do you think of it?" he asked.

"What?" I looked between us. "The rosary is from you? But how did you know?"

"It's not a replica. It was your mother's."

I could clearly remember her turning these beads through her slender fingers in this very church. The memory brought tears to my eyes. Now, I truly had a piece of her, but under such dire circumstances.

He pocketed it, then passed my bridal bouquet to a guard, who handled it with surprising care.

Cristiano cupped his hands around my jaw. He had to stoop a good deal to meet me, even as he lifted my face the rest of the way. He waited there, his unforgiving eyes boring into mine as if trying to read my mind. I had only one mounting thought, though.

Please, let this be another nightmare, for the darkness I've resisted welcomes me too easily.

Let Cristiano dematerialize into the black shadow that haunts my sleep.

Let him have mercy.

Let him release me.

He pressed his lips to mine, their yielding fullness a stark contrast to the firm hands that held me in place. He inhaled sharply, as if he'd surprised himself as well. My heart pounded. His mouth parted, and mine did the same, granting him access that he seized, plunging his tongue inside to find mine just as eager. I gripped his elbows as his fingertips dug into my cheeks, my knees threatening to give out. A kiss that promised lovemaking in one breath and fucking in the next.

He drew away, leaving me gasping. I kept my eyes closed as the silence grew weighty between us. Why did giving into his kiss feel like walking into darkness—a temptation I knew I *should* resist? I half-expected a soothing whisper from him, maybe even something sweet.

I eased my eyes open. He kept my face in his hands but had his head turned toward the back of the church. "Envision me taking her with the same fervor on this, our wedding night, brother," he said, then kissed me again.

I jerked away and slapped him. The sound of it echoed through the church—skin on skin, and Pilar's loud gasp—whereas my regret was immediate. Cristiano glared at me, working his jaw side to side, anger clearly building within him.

Even with the realization of what I'd done, rage burned in me. For the way he'd flaunted the kiss, something that should've been sacred no matter the circumstances. For how he'd used me to become even more powerful. For how he'd stolen my senses and tricked me into enjoying the kiss.

"You've ruined me," I said to him, and turned to look down the aisle at Diego. "And you let him."

I picked up my dress and strode down the aisle. If Cristiano didn't like it, let him shoot me in the back.

"Talia," Diego said, pressing his palms together in supplication. "Wait."

I pushed by him. "Go to hell."

Max blocked the door, stopping me with a curt shake of his head. There was nobody to help. Nobody but me.

I spun back and stood in front of Diego as my vision blurred with tears. "You were careless with my father's business and careless with me. Now I'll pay the price."

"You saved my life," he said. "I will forever be grateful to you."

I grabbed the lapels of his suit to push him away, but I couldn't. I didn't want him to go to hell. I wanted him to stay with me. Diego took my wrists. I fisted the fabric and buried my face in his chest. "You *know* what he has planned for me."

Without turning, I sensed Cristiano at my back before he spoke. "Take your hands off my wife, or I will add them to my collection."

I squeezed my eyes shut. I would soon see Cristiano's rumored museum of body parts with my own eyes.

"I'm sorry," Diego said, and we released each other.

"She is mine," Cristiano said. "Say it."

The tie of Diego's knot hung loose, defeated. I hated that he had put me in this position, but I hated how Cristiano rubbed it in our faces even more.

"She is yours in the eyes of God," Diego said, "but in every other way, she is mine. Saying otherwise won't change the fact."

I turned to Cristiano to plead with him not to react to Diego's baiting words, but he stood calm.

"As I told you before, brother," he said, each word slow and clipped, "once this was done, there'd be no turning back. She is mine. If you, or anyone, touches her again, I will rain down a fury the likes of which not even the Maldonados have seen."

Chills spread over every inch of my skin. He only said it to goad Diego, but his possessiveness gripped and thrilled me in ways that scared me.

Cristiano lowered his eyes and locked them on me. "Get out."

Instinctively, I knew he wasn't talking to me.

"Out!" Cristiano bellowed. He looked around, meeting eyes with each of his men and then Diego. "Everyone leave. You too, Max, and take the priest. I have business with my wife."

The church emptied quickly—too quickly. I couldn't even get a handle on my trepidation over being alone with him.

When it was just us, Cristiano walked forward until we were face to face. "Next time you slap me," he said, "save it for the bedroom."

I let out a shaky breath. My only comfort was being in the church. I had to believe he wouldn't punish me for my insolence in God's house.

He looked me up and down. "Hit me, rage against me, call me names. But I have two rules you won't break twice.

First, Diego will *never* touch you again. And second, you will not *ever* lie to me, even one more time."

I racked my brain for what he might be referring to. "I didn't lie," I said quickly.

"No?" he asked. "What did you think would happen when you came to my bed and didn't bleed?"

I swallowed my gasp and did my best to school my shock. He knew I wasn't a virgin—yet he'd gone through with the wedding anyway. "Not every woman bleeds," I said, careful to speak honestly.

"Not with Diego, I'm sure. He treats you like you're breakable. I won't. With me, you'd have bled, and perhaps you still will in other ways." He raised his chin. "Remove your dress."

What? My jaw went slack. He couldn't mean for me to strip down *here*? I ceased to breathe or function in any way but to stare at him—and shake all over with the force and speed of my hammering heart.

"Y-you can't," I said, my mouth completely dry. Even Hades would wait until he was back in the underground for this next part. "We're in a church."

"White doesn't suit you, my lovely wife." He circled me until he was at my back. I didn't even have the wherewithal to try to keep him in my sight. He wouldn't do this here. He *couldn't*.

He trailed a finger up my spine until he'd reached the top button of my dress, just under my hairline. He gripped the back of the collar with both hands, slipping his knuckles between the fabric and my skin. It was a warm caress that spurred panic in me as I realized what he was doing.

"Stop—"

He yanked the dress open, ripping my mother's lace.

I opened my mouth, and my chin trembled. I thought

I'd already known the worst of him, but he would prove me wrong. When his footsteps sounded again, I did my best to inhale back the urge to cry. My weakness would only spur him on.

Cristiano finished his circle and stood in front of me again with darkened eyes and lowered lids. "Now, take off your dress, Natalia—and let me see what my brother's freedom bought me."

ALSO BY JESSICA HAWKINS

LEARN MORE AT WWW.JESSICAHAWKINS.NET

White Monarch Trilogy

"Exciting and suspenseful and sexy and breathtaking." (*USA Today* Bestselling Author Lauren Rowe)

Violent Delights

Violent Ends

Violent Triumphs

Right Where I Want You

"An intelligently written, sexy, feel-good romance that packs an emotional punch…" (*USA Today*)

A witty workplace romance filled with heart, sexual tension, and smart enemies-to-lovers banter.

Something in the Way Series

"A tale of forbidden love in epic proportion… Brilliant" (New York Times bestselling author Corinne Michaels)

Lake Kaplan falls for a handsome older man — but then her sister sets her sights on him too.

Something in the Way

Somebody Else's Sky

Move the Stars

Lake + Manning

Slip of the Tongue Series

"Addictive. Painful. Captivating…an authentic, raw, and emotionally gripping must-read." (Angie's Dreamy Reads)

Her husband doesn't want her anymore. The man next door would give up everything to have her.

Slip of the Tongue

The First Taste

Yours to Bare

Explicitly Yours Series

"*Pretty Woman* meets *Indecent Proposal*…a seductive series." (*USA Today* Bestselling Author Louise Bay)

What if one night with her isn't enough? A red-hot collection.

Possession

Domination

Provocation

Obsession

The Cityscape Series

Olivia has the perfect life—but something is missing. Handsome playboy David Dylan awakens a passion that she thought she'd lost a long time ago. Can she keep their combustible lust from spilling over into love?

Come Undone

Come Alive

Come Together

ACKNOWLEDGMENTS

Many thanks to:
My editor, Elizabeth London Editing
My beta, Underline This Editing
My proofreader, Paige Maroney Smith
My sensitivity readers, Chayo Ramón and Maria D.
My release PA, Serena McDonald
Covers Designed by Najla Qamber Designs

ABOUT THE AUTHOR

Jessica Hawkins is a *USA Today* bestselling author known for her "emotionally gripping" and "off-the-charts hot" romance. Dubbed "queen of angst" by both peers and readers for her smart and provocative work, she's garnered a cult-like following of fans who love to be torn apart…and put back together.

She writes romance both at home in New York and around the world, a coffee shop traveler who bounces from café to café with just a laptop, headphones, and a coffee cup. She loves to keep in close touch with her readers, mostly via Facebook, Instagram, and her mailing list.

Stay updated:
www.jessicahawkins.net/mailing-list
www.amazon.com/author/jessicahawkins

CPSIA information can be obtained
at www.ICGtesting.com
Printed in the USA
LVHW041349110122
708163LV00002B/118